Praise for Jamie Fewery

'Will melt your heart'
Veronica Henry

'A beautifully told story of real love and real life. I loved it'
Miranda Dickinson

'Deals convincingly and movingly with issues around
mental health'
Mail on Sunday

'One of my favourite books of 2019 ... Astounding'
Nina Pottell, *Prima*

'Clever, moving, funny, insightful'
Zoë Folbigg

'Real and honest'
Heat

'I raced through it'
Daily Mail

Jamie Fewery is an author, columnist and copywriter. He has written for the *Daily Telegraph*, *Five Dials* and *Wired*, and works for a London-based marketing and creative agency. He lives in Berkhamsted, Hertfordshire, with his wife and son.

Also by Jamie Fewery

Our Life In A Day

The Way Back

JAMIE FEWERY

ORION

First published in Great Britain in 2020 by Orion Fiction,
an imprint of The Orion Publishing Group Ltd,
Carmelite House, 50 Victoria Embankment
London EC4Y 0DZ

An Hachette UK Company

1 3 5 7 9 10 8 6 4 2

A CIP catalogue record for this book is
available from the British Library.

ISBN (Paperback) 978 1 4091 7818 7
ISBN (eBook) 978 1 4091 7819 4

Typeset at The Spartan Press Ltd,
Lymington, Hants

Printed and bound in Great Britain by Clays Ltd,
Elcograf S.p.A.

www.orionbooks.co.uk

For the Fewerys (me excepted)

PROLOGUE

Ganton Villas – Hove, Sussex

He stuck a leg out the side of the duvet. The room was cold, or he was. These days he could quite easily catch a chill in Mediterranean heat. He coughed and whacked a clenched fist against his chest, trying to dislodge whatever had collected there overnight. The decades of fags and pints always affected him in the morning, when his ill health was felt most keenly. Gerry Cadogan hadn't woken up feeling comfortable in well over fifteen years.

Tina would be coming soon. She'd let herself in and start busy-bodying around the kitchen, making tea and refusing to put any sugar in it. Gerry couldn't understand this. At his age, cutting back would hardly make a difference to his long-term health prospects. But that was an argument he couldn't be bothered to have. A hill not worth dying on.

Gerry had to get it all done before she arrived. No doubt she would insist on his resting, which equated to sitting in front of the television for hour after hour, watching dull presenters force celebrities into flogging antiques, or some such. Occasionally he would ask to go for a walk, just down to the seafront where he could listen to the sounds of the gulls as they soared over the beach or hovered in the breeze over the coastal path, waiting for a dropped chip to dive for.

He missed Sandra. She was brash but she was always up for bending the rules. Gerry felt like more than just a cancer patient when she was around. Although, given that he'd not heard from her since she took a new job a couple of months ago, just a cancer patient was certainly how she saw him.

'Right then,' he said, climbing out of his bed and finding his slippers. They felt loose, as most of his clothing did now. The weight he'd lost since his health had gone south had made him almost half the man he was. Literally. He joked that liver cancer was a better way to lose weight than long walks and less beer. Very few people seemed to find that funny.

Gerry opened the pill case on his bedside table, where it sat beside a copy of *Tinker, Tailor, Solider, Spy,* and tipped that day's chemicals down his throat, chasing them with a mouthful of water. He stood up, pulled on the Watford F.C. hoodie Patrick had bought him for his last birthday, and gingerly stepped down the stairs.

Time was he would talk as he went about the house, making his morning tea and toast. Mostly to Sue, of course, with benign little bits of narration like 'I'll pop the kettle on, then' or 'marmalade this morning I think, love.' Just as he would have when she was around.

It was maybe six months ago that he'd stopped involving his wife in his day to day conversations, deciding that he sounded ridiculous, or like a golf commentator who'd lost his mind. People always said that they spoke to passed on partners – but really, how many of them actually did?

With his tea made, Gerry shuffled into his old office to set about his task for the morning. Around him, the walls were full of reminders of better times, a highlight reel of his life. In the centre of the room stood an old desk, topped with piles of unopened post and a lamp. There was also a laptop he barely knew how to use, hidden beneath a pad of paper and a Parker pen that he did.

Above the desk chair was a photo of his family – all six of them standing in front of the house he now lived in. It was taken on the day they got the keys, with him and Sue holding up a sign reading:

2

'CADOGAN FAMILY BUILDERS – THE MOST TRUSTED NAME IN HOVE!'

'Are you sure about this?' Sue had said when he pitched the idea of buying the place. It was big, much bigger than they thought they could possibly afford. But that meant it was also a wreck, with no central heating, holes in the roof and a mouse infestation so severe that the top floor wasn't fit to live in.

'It'll take three months. Tops,' he'd said, knowing full well it'd take at least nine (and in the end took two whole years to complete). He wanted the house to show what his nascent firm could do, something he could use to convince people that he was more than just a builder who'd started up on his own.

Recently, Gerry had been thinking how his life might have been different had he never started the firm and instead stayed on other people's jobs. The Cadogans might have had less money. But they'd probably be happier.

Behind his desk lamp sat the other photos that he looked at every day, always positioned so he could see them out of the corner of his eye during the late nights spent working on plans or settling the company's books. The photos were always a comfort when he had his late night whisky at his desk. They were all of his kids, mostly taken on various holidays and on special occasions like Christmas and birthdays. And from collections in the three albums on his desk.

'Christ,' he said, bending down to retrieve his big red metal fishing box from beneath the desk, where he'd been storing it since he had this idea. 'Weighs a bloody ton.'

Gerry set about emptying the box of reels, floats, hooks and weights. He dumped most of it in his bottom desk drawer – already so full of rubbish that he felt genuinely sorry for whoever'd be in charge of clearing it out when he finally popped it. The two beaten and battered books in the box (a good pub guide and a book of fishing tips) went on the shelf above his desk. And his hip and tea flasks went in a pile to be cleaned up later. He sprayed the box with a bit of disinfectant, hoping to get rid of the musty smell of river-soiled fishing kit and old bait.

First, he put the whisky inside, feeling a pang of regret that he'd never get to taste it. Over the years, the bottle had taken on almost human significance among the family. Always referred to as 'the Port Ellen' and looked at with either reverence by those who wanted some, or wonderment by those who couldn't believe he'd spent over a grand on it.

Gerry almost kissed the bottle. He had been saving it for his seventieth, which he knew he wouldn't reach now. And besides, the repercussions of a little dram were not worth it.

Next, he took the newspaper article and the brief, cursory letter. He remembered the day he received the battered, German post-marked envelope. It had set him on edge almost immediately. He didn't know anyone in Germany...

He had typed the contents of the article into Google Translate, one letter punched in with one index finger at a time. But he already knew what the story would bring.

Bad news.

Gerry put the envelope away into the most recent photo album, as he heard the door open.

'Bollocks,' he said. He could hear Tina in the hallway, taking off her great clodhopping boots and replacing them with slippers, unzipping her bag and fishing out the four tupperware boxes of healthy snacks she'd eat through the day. Tina was permanently on a diet that she couldn't stick to, which Gerry realised when he discovered that she'd been at his crisps.

'Where are you then?' she bellowed. 'Better not be in that garden of yours,' she said, referring to last week when she'd found him outside pruning and readying the perennials bed for winter. (Neither of them mentioned that he wouldn't be around the next spring to enjoy them in bloom again.)

The slap slap slap of her slippers against the ceramic kitchen floor. The opening and closing of the fridge. The click of the kettle's 'on' switch.

'It's still hot,' she called. 'So at least I know you're not dead.'

Tina laughed. Gerry shook his head and muttered, 'Christ almighty.'

This was her idea of a laugh. Sandra had made similar jokes, but hers landed better. Maybe it was her kind, jovial Geordie accent compared to Tina's estuary English.

Gerry quickly checked the photo albums to make sure that they were the right ones. Holidays in Cornwall and France, and New Year's Eve in 2009, each taken a decade apart. He put them in the fishing box next to the whisky, then tossed in the keys to his camper van and the copy of his will he'd been keeping on his desk.

But there was still one last thing to do before he was finished.

He had just picked up the pen Sue had given him for his sixtieth when Tina opened the door. She was wearing her pink nurse's uniform, with her greasy grey hair pulled into a bun behind her head, revealing numerous ear piercings.

'There he is,' she said. 'Working, would you believe?'

'Ish.'

'What's "ish" about it?'

'Well, I'm not really working. I'm making something for the kids.'

'And you should be resting up.'

Gerry resisted asking her what the fucking point of resting up would be. In a couple of months he'd be doing nothing but.

'Two minutes.'

'Have you had your break—'

'Tina, please,' he said, firmly. 'Two minutes. I need to get this done while I've got the energy.'

5

Affronted, she said, 'As you wish,' then left him to it. His office led off from the lounge, so he could hear her flop down on the big sofa and turn the television on to one of the morning programmes. A belligerent man was hectoring a guest about shopping in charity shops despite being wealthy.

Gerry shut the door and went back to his desk, where headed paper (**A Note from Gerry**) and a pen waited for him. He didn't know what he was going to write. He never did. Letters weren't his strong suit. When he and Sue first started seeing each other she used to send him long letters. He remembered how excited he felt seeing the Brighton postal mark. Gerry had rarely replied, and if he had, it was only ever a few lines scrawled on a postcard that would arrive smelling of whatever pub he'd written it in.

Before he started, he looked back down at the box. The albums, the whisky, the keys. *Just a sniff* he thought, taking the whisky out and pulling it open. Spying the empty miniature on top of his filing cabinet, he had a better idea, pouring a small measure into the tiny bottle. *Something for when the time comes. A way to raise a glass at the very end.*

He returned the bottle to the tackle box. Finally ready, he began to write.

28th September
Dear Jessica, Patrick and Kirsty,

PART 1

PART 1

CHAPTER ONE

Ballsbridge, Dublin

Patrick

Patrick felt his phone buzz away in his pocket. For a moment, he thought about ignoring the call, but knew it might be important. Without a look, he swiped his right thumb across the bottom of the screen.

'Y'hello,' he said.

'Patrick?' Kirsty replied. She sounded fragile.

Immediately he knew.

'Oh God.'

She said nothing.

'Has he?'

'The nurse called this morning,' she said, as he climbed down from the ladder and put his wallpaper roller on the windowsill. In a daze, Patrick almost walked into a carpet fitter going past with a roll of underlay hoisted on his shoulder.

'Dad's dead,' Kirsty said, as though to remind herself that it was true.

'Right.'

'Sorry.'

'I . . .' he said. 'Me too. When . . . ?'

'In the night they think.'

'Fuck.'

9

Silence.

Patrick found an empty room in the new block of flats he was working on and sat down in the corner. Bare cables and wires hung from the ceilings. The plaster walls were still an orangey pink, and the hardboard floor was covered in dust.

This was the first time he'd heard his sister's voice in about a year. The distance between them was a convenient excuse to conduct all essential correspondence by email. The last time they spoke was when Kirsty texted him with the results of a biopsy, and only because Gerry couldn't bring himself to deliver the news personally.

Her voice was both strange and familiar. Shaky with the shock, sadness and relief that all came with a long-anticipated death.

'When was the last time you saw him?'

'Saturday.'

'Right,' he said. 'Fuck.'

The only two responses he could muster.

Saturday was three days ago. Immediately Patrick's mind was filled with the image of his emaciated dad on his own in that big house. Such a friendly and sociable man spending his last days alone, with only a hospice nurse for company.

'I'm meeting a funeral director this afternoon,' she said, her sudden, business-like tone taking him by surprise. 'I don't expect you to do anything. But you are going to turn up?'

'Jesus Kirsty. Of course I'm going to turn up. He's my dad.'

'Well,' she said, somehow expressing every judgment and opinion she held about his lifestyle, choices, opinions and actions in one word.

'Well what?'

This time it was Kirsty who stalled. They had been here before – on the precipice of an argument that would put petty point scoring above the thing they should be talking about.

'Nothing,' she said. Patrick felt the tension disperse as they both backed down.

'So no one was there? When it happened, I mean.'

'No. He was alone.'

Patrick paused. 'Fuck.'

'I know. Tina found him when she went round this morning.'

He was about to ask who Tina was, before quickly remembering. In fairness, she'd only been in the job three months and he'd never met the woman. The previous one, Sandra, had left when her own husband suffered a stroke. She always referred to patients suffering from life threatening (or often ending) illnesses as being 'poorly', as though a body riven with tumours was the same as one fighting off a dicky tummy or a cold.

'Does Jess know?'

'I spoke to her earlier. I'd have called sooner. But you know,' she said.

He didn't.

'Anyway, Pat. I might have to ...'

'Oh. Sure,' he said. 'I'm sure there's loads to do.'

'Just a bit.'

'I'll look at flights. Hopefully get something ... soon,' he said. He was about to say *tomorrow*, but that would be impossible.

'No rush. I'll let you know when it is.'

'Thanks.'

'Okay ... so,' she said, clearly waiting for him to wrap up.

'Yep. Bye then,' he said, automatically slipping into the cheerful tone he always used to end a phone call, no matter how difficult the subject.

'Bye,' she said, quickly followed by three beeps.

Patrick looked down at the floor for a few seconds, before he was interrupted by a brusque Northern Irish man carrying a stack of laminate floorboards.

'You working here, pal?' he said, and Patrick got up.

'No, it's all yours,' he said, heading back to the room he'd been working in earlier.

'You okay?' His young site manager, Will, asked, actually meaning 'get back to work'.

'Fine,' Patrick said.

He worried that he looked strange. Ashen, pale, shocked. Upset, even. Though that *would* be perfectly normal for someone whose last living parent had just passed away.

'Cool, man,' Will said, putting his earbuds back in to where they spent at least six hours of every working day, and carrying on with whatever he wasn't doing.

Patrick looked at the wall he'd half papered, relieved to have something solid to focus on.

'Might just pop out for some air,' he said to no one in particular.

He staggered almost drunkenly through the flats and corridors towards the lift. Three floors down on Anglesea Road, he turned right and walked down the road to the cricket club. He sat on a bench away from the club house next to a young blonde woman staring at her phone as she rocked a pram back and forth.

Patrick leant forwards and pushed the heels of his hands against his eyes. They were wet. He let out one big, heaving sob, then drew a quick, deep breath and swallowed, pushing down whatever might come up. The woman next to him looked over. For a moment he thought she was going to ask if he was okay, and panicked. How could he answer that?

But she went back to her phone, on which Patrick could see a WhatsApp conversation playing out.

He took his own iPhone out from his paint splattered pocket. The lock screen was a picture of his daughter Maggie, wife Suzanne and himself on the beach in Cork.

Patrick looked like a better version of himself in that photo.

Slimmer, of course. His belly was only starting to push against his t-shirt then, instead of entirely breaching it like it did now. His side-parted, swept back hair was tidy and tight, unlike his current, almost chin length mop. Most of all, he looked *happy*. He was smiling in a way that had felt impossible of late.

Suddenly craving human contact, Patrick opened his recent call log and scrolled to Suzanne. He was about to dial, when he changed his mind. That would only make things worse. Instead, he went back into the phonebook, and picked out another number.

After two foreign-sounding British rings, someone picked up.

'Hey. It's me,' Patrick said. 'Look, I've got some news.'

Ganton Villas – Hove, Sussex

Jessica

She'd only cried once since Kirsty told her the news. Other than that, Jessica Lachlan had been stoic, insisting that she was 'putting a brave face on it for the kids' or that she'd 'had her moments'. The truth was that she had no idea why her father's death hadn't upset her more, reasoning that her numbness must have been down to one of two things:

Either her mum's death four years ago had prepared her for this moment.

Or she'd simply had long enough to mentally reconcile herself to her dad's impending death.

Almost a year had passed since the liver cancer diagnosis, and five months since the weekend in Hove where she learned that it was terminal.

Of course, in the back of her mind she thought that her lack of emotional response to her dad's death was down to something else.

13

Probably knowing that the funeral and the will would bring her into contact with her siblings. But she pushed that thought away. They didn't get on. Fine. Some people didn't. They were more like colleagues than family, interacting when they had to, out of necessity rather than choice. It was just the way things were.

Her husband, Dan, never understood it. As an only child, the idea of a large family was something he held in high regard.

'I want them to be close. Best mates,' he would say of their two, Max and Elspeth. And she would agree, worrying that they didn't have a good example to follow on either side of the family.

Jessica could hear Kirsty bustling around downstairs. She was in her element. Plenty to do, plenty to be needed for. As the only one of them to live locally, she had been first on the scene, and first to call and spread the news. Jessica remembered the blunt brutality of the phone call. How her sister had dispensed with pleasantries and got straight to the point.

'Bit route one,' Dan had said.

'There wasn't much else to say,' Jessica explained.

It was now four days since 'it happened', as Kirsty kept saying. Jessica didn't pull her up on this, although she was dubious as to whether a death could 'happen'. Wasn't it more a thing no longer happening?

Anyway. Four days.

On the first she had travelled down with Dan to meet Kirsty and her daughter Livvy at their old family home. They had sat together at the big oak kitchen table – the setting of so many childhood meals – drinking endless cups of tea, as the late September sun streamed through the window.

Every so often a friend of their dad's would come over to join them. They'd say something banal yet unequivocally true, like 'such a cruel disease', or 'such a lovely, kind man.' Statements that everyone could agree with and which didn't sugar coat the miserable years Gerry Cadogan had experienced since losing his wife.

The familiar beats her dad's weeks once danced to were no longer walks along the seafront (for years with their dog, and then without), lunches at one of three favourite restaurants, and the Wednesday matinee at the multiplex, where he and his wife would buy cups of coffee – taking their own biscuits wrapped in foil – and watch films Jessica never thought her parents would be interested in. (She once had a conversation with her mother about a Wes Anderson film they had both seen, in which Jessica mentioned his other work. This fell flat when she realised that Sue Cadogan had no idea who Wes Anderson was. She had just been to watch a film...)

Instead, Gerry spent his final years on solo walks, because he could not be convinced to either get a new dog or join one of Hove's seniors' rambling groups. Rather than the cinema, it was box sets. And the restaurant visits were now solitary trips to one of two pubs, where Jessica worried others wouldn't understand that, until recently, he'd been part of a big, close, mostly happy family. He wasn't just another hopeless regular.

Dan drove them home after that first evening. They had offered to stay for dinner, but her sister had declined with a somewhat martyred 'No, you go, Jess.' Jessica knew that Kirsty would use her larger role in the post-death clear out as a bargaining chip later down the line...

It was for this reason that Jessica booked a hotel in Brighton almost as soon as she could, and returned to join Kirsty in taking care of the house they grew up in.

'You really don't have to,' Kirsty had said when Jessica turned up back on the south coast without warning. 'Liv and I can do most of it.'

'I want to. Besides, it shouldn't be up to Liv to sort out her dead grandad's stuff, should it?'

'Why not?' Kirsty asked, permanently chippy and on edge over any comment that might suggest her daughter was treated differently to the other three grandchildren.

'Because she's four, Kirsty. That's too young.'

'What about your florist?' Kirsty said. Perhaps, Jessica thought, her sister didn't believe that the business she ran could possibly sustain more than one employee.

'I don't need to be there every day. The girls can run it,' she said, deliberately not expanding on the number of girls she employed (two).

Eventually, Kirsty relented and they planned what needed doing before Gerry's funeral in five days' time. Big decisions about coffin material (oak), music (Chas & Dave, The Faces, Elton John) and flowers (hydrangeas) were made together, with Patrick copied in emails in case he wanted to veto anything. Beyond that, it was a case of divvying up rooms to be decluttered before they hired a professional cleaner to remove whatever traces of Gerry might remain. They generally agreed that they were going to sell the house, although no one said it out loud except Dan. Not after what happened last time.

'We could put the money towards a holiday,' he'd said when Jessica called from her hotel room. 'You know, something to celebrate his memory. It's—'

'Don't you dare say "it's what he would've wanted", Daniel.'

'No,' he stuttered, trying to back track. He'd have to find a less obvious way to frame his desire to sell her family home and plug the money into a trip to Disney World . . .

Now, upstairs in Gerry's bedroom, Jessica consulted the list in her back pocket.

Lounge – Kirsty
Bedroom 1 – Jessica
Bedroom 2 – Kirsty

Bedroom 3 – Jessica
Bathroom – Prof cleaner
Toilet – PC
Kitchen – Jessica
Study – Kirsty
Loft – Patrick?

Five bin liners full of clothes for charity shops or clothes banks sat in the corner of the room. On the bed were two boxes full of books, trinkets, four framed photographs, three pairs of reading glasses and the contents of an emptied bedside drawer.

Admittedly, Jessica had expected to find this whole experience more heart wrenching. But her dad's bedroom had already more or less been removed of its character and familial touch when her mum died. Since then, Gerry had added very little of himself to the room, as if he knew that his time left in the house was limited and didn't want to bother doing it up. What had been her mother's bedside table still sat empty.

She did feel a pull on her heartstrings when she looked at the framed photos; windows to versions of her family that were long lost and forgotten. But she felt nothing more than that.

Still, clearing out Gerry's room made Jessica uneasy.

She was so worried that she might find something odd or tawdry that could alter her view of her dad, replacing his paternal nature with something more, well, male.

'Like what?' Kirsty had asked that morning, as they sat in the chilly garden, drinking cups of tea before the day's work began.

'You know. Magazines or something.'

'Oh Jess!'

'What?' she asked, laughing. 'You remember Uncle Derek,' she said, whose fondness for the top shelf was revealed when his puritanical daughter – their cousin, Clare – had cleaned out his flat after he died from a sudden heart attack.

Jessica sat down on the bed and looked in the mirror on top of the chest of drawers opposite. She looked tired, though she hated to acknowledge it. Recently she had wondered if her long, thin face – once all definition and structure – could now better be described as drawn, in the kind of way a pudgier face like Kirsty's could never be. She had also noticed some greys in her long, mousy hair, even picking one off the chambray shirt she wore to dinner last night.

None of this was helping, she thought. Stress. She had enough on her plate, what with the business and the kids and Dan. Perhaps it was a bad idea to throw herself into this as well.

Jessica pulled off one of her white Converse All Star trainers and massaged the sole of her archless foot, looking forward to getting back to the hotel. Waiting for her there was a book, a bath and a television, all of which she could enjoy uninterrupted – a rarity with a twelve (almost thirteen)-year-old and a six-year-old.

She had arranged to meet an old university friend in Brighton for dinner, but was thinking about cancelling. Sadie Darlington was now a well-known lifestyle writer for two newspapers and a magazine. Jessica had ended her subscription to the magazine when she saw Sadie's name and photograph emblazoned across the top.

'So what are you up to now, Jess?'

She dreaded the question. She'd last seen Sadie when she was leaving her job in children's book publishing to try and become an author herself. Sadie had given it the big 'you'll have to tell me when you've finished writing, I know *plenty* of literary agents'.

That was five years ago. Now all Jessica would have to say about it would be: 'Well I wrote around ten thousand words before I gave up. Two years ago I convinced my husband to invest our life savings into a floristry business. I only did that because I came terrifyingly close to having an affair and decided that if I wasn't going to end up shagging Chris Farbrace – remember him? – in a hotel room, then I needed something bigger going on in my life to distract me. Dan knows none of this, of course.'

With a deep sigh, Jessica pushed herself up off the bed, pulled the final drawer out and emptied it on the bed behind her.

'JEEEESS,' she heard Kirsty call, before she could start going through the contents. 'Come down here. There's something you should see.'

Kirsty

It didn't look like anything much really. A red metal fishing tackle box, maybe thirty inches wide, twenty across and twenty deep. Quite heavy though.

She could hear things moving around inside as she pulled it from the bottom drawer of her dad's old filing cabinet, the front of which was still decorated with a sticker saying CADOGAN FAMILY BUILDERS – THE MOST TRUSTED NAME IN HOVE!

On the top of the box was a handle and a key lock, with an envelope that Gerry had written *read me* on and taped to it.

'Do you want to . . . ?' Kirsty asked Jessica, offering her the envelope.

'No, you do it.'

Kirsty slid the envelope open, pulling out a piece of A5 lined paper on which their dad had scrawled in blue biro . . .

To whoever finds this,

This box contains a few items I'd like to pass onto my children.

Please do not unlock the box or take anything from it until after my funeral.

Gerry

Just below his name, he had taped a small key – the type to fit a cheap lock that would be quite easy to jimmy open with a paperclip and a bit of determination. Kirsty folded the paper with the key still attached and put it in her rucksack.

She sat with Jessica at the kitchen table, both now looking at the box as if it might explode at any moment.

'So. Just to be clear. You don't want to have a look?' Jessica said.

'No!'

'I wasn't saying we should.'

'Well why ask then?'

'You know. Just in case.'

'Just in case what? Just in case you want to betray a dying man's wish?'

'Oh don't be so melodramatic.' Jessica said, rolling her eyes.

'Well that's what it sounded like.'

'You want to know what's in there just as much as I do. Typical of him to get all mysterious after he's dead.'

'Jess,' Kirsty said, shocked but not disagreeing.

'Well it's not like him, is it? Fucking hell. Dad was the most honest man you could meet. He couldn't keep a secret. Now here he is playing sodding games with us from beyond the grave.'

'Don't speak ill of the dead, Jessica,' Kirsty said, recognising the pious note in her own voice.

'You know, sometimes—'

'I'm going,' Kirsty said, before her sister could finish her sentence, making for her old bedroom where she'd stored a change of clothes.

Regardless of how she sounded or what she said, she had no desire for conflict today. So far, the entire experience of emptying this home had been completely draining. Every opened drawer and emptied cupboard was an emotional assault. Her dad had kept things because they held sentimental value, and now here she was having to throw them away because they had no actual value to anyone else. Gifts she remembered her mother buying him. Souvenirs from holidays. None of it was worth a thing and she didn't really want any of it in her own house. If only, she thought, there was some sort of compromise between chucking stuff out and keeping it forever.

Of course, if her own home had been bigger, she would have been tempted to keep some things. But a two-bed top floor maisonette with no cupboard space worth recognising was no place for a hoarder.

Kirsty wanted nothing more than to get into her running gear and start back along the seafront towards home. Her daughter, Livvy, would be waiting for her there with her friend Clara (who was helping out by watching her after school), an oven pizza, and a bottle of red wine.

There was also work to catch up on. The school she worked for had been exceptionally lenient, allowing her time off to sort everything. 'I'm sort of the only one around,' Kirsty had explained, when her boss obliquely mentioned the siblings who might pitch in and alleviate the need for supply staff and shared lessons. She had made it sound as though Jessica and Patrick were utterly feckless and irresponsible, rather than the truth, which was that they simply lived a little further away than she did. But she was happy to let that image stand.

Even so, the marking was still largely hers. She had collected another stack of exercise books that morning, adding to the forty essays on *Of Mice and Men* from her GCSE group, the differences between each would be doubtless difficult to spot.

Tomorrow it was the weekend. It would maybe take one more morning before the house would be in a good enough state to call the cleaner – and, eventually, the estate agent – in. After that, it would be the countdown to the funeral next Tuesday. To Kirsty, it all felt impossibly fast and crucifyingly slow at once. She couldn't quite believe how recently her dad had died. Yet at the same time couldn't believe how long it felt until they could actually say that ceremonial goodbye.

Jessica had gone into the kitchen to wash up their mugs and plates they'd used for lunch.

'You alright in there?' Kirsty called, as she stepped out of her jeans and pulled off her t-shirt, replacing them with a pair of brightly patterned running leggings and a long-sleeved top. She kept her dark brown hair short and clipped neatly around the sides, but even so she used an Alice band to push her fringe up and off her forehead.

'Fine,' Jessica called back. 'I'll be off soon, too. You go.'

'I can wait,' she said, not trusting her sister to be in the same room as the box. Something about her suggested that she'd go looking. When they were children Jessica had always been the one to suggest rooting around in their parents' bedroom in search of Christmas presents. 'Got plans for the evening?'

'Yes. But I want to cancel them. Meeting Sadie Darlington,' Jess said, as though everyone should know exactly who Sadie Darlington was.

'Oh lovely,' Kirsty said as Jessica finished and went to the door, 'Shall we, then?'

Jess pulled her long, deliberately and fashionably oversized coat on and Kirsty slipped into her functional waterproof, clipping her running rucksack around her waist and chest. She warmed up by kicking her legs into the air, and watched Jess climb into her large, black 4x4. She locked the door to the house and began her run back home.

*

The route from Ganton Villas in Hove to Canning Street in Brighton was almost exactly three miles door to door. It would take her around half an hour, unless she decided to stop to catch her breath.

Kirsty was not a natural athlete. Her short legs and stocky frame didn't lend themselves to running and she'd have described herself as 'dumpy' once upon a time. However, in a fit of self-kindness after becoming both a mother and then a *single* mother in quick succession, she decided to do away with the deprecation and embrace some body positivity. She kept it up by reading affirming online articles and sharing them on Facebook every week.

Kirsty had run every day since Gerry's death. The time alone gave her space to think and come to terms with a few things. Like how she was now an orphan (although she didn't really agree with adults applying that loaded term to their loss of parents at a later age). Or that she had stayed on the south coast to be near her family homestead, rather than moving away, and was now the only Cadogan left there.

Today, she thought about the box and what it might contain.

Gerry was not a secretive or dramatic man. Rather, he was matter of fact and a stickler for the truth. The embodiment of the idea that hard work gets you somewhere. He was also kind. Kirsty never forgot kindness.

This was why it was particularly unlike him to do something like this. She had expected his will to be a standard split of assets, perhaps with a trinket or two left to each of them. Nothing dramatic.

'You'll each get something,' she remembered him saying a couple of months ago, when the cancer was getting worse. 'And there'll be some other stuff you'll have to divide up between you. With no squabbling.'

At the time, she was surprised. The relationship between the three of them had become so much more fractious since their mother died. Finance wasn't the problem. Rather, it was history, and how her death brought into relief the problems that had besieged the Cadogan family, and their respective roles in causing them.

Darkness was beginning to fall over Brighton. The lights lining the seafront walk had come on, casting an orange glow over the cyclists and walkers making their way home from work. Kirsty weaved in and out of them as she cut her path towards the pier, still busy with a few day trippers.

She stopped just past the pier, paused the true-crime podcast she was listening to – but hadn't really been concentrating on – and leaned on the blue-green painted railing to look out to sea.

Kirsty thought of Jessica meeting her old uni friend for dinner. And of Patrick out in Dublin.

She'd always thought she loved her own life, but it often seemed so lacking in excitement in comparison. Had it been a sacrifice to stay in Brighton for so many years? Or did she only think of it as such when she wanted to make her siblings feel bad for moving away and building lives that were so separate from her own?

'You say that you're happy with your life?' Nehra, her therapist, had said in their most recent appointment – the last one before her dad died. It was one of those questions that sounded more like a statement.

'I am,' Kirsty said, not even sure herself if she was putting on a front. Nehra was a slim, pretty Indian woman who Kirsty was both desperate to impress and slightly attracted to. Two things that meant she was probably an awful choice for a therapist. But they were two years in now and Kirsty couldn't bring herself to change. 'But every time I think about it I'm sure there's stuff I've missed out on because I stayed around here.'

'Such as?'

'I don't know really,' she had said. *Travel, work, people, sex . . .* 'I feel like I've sheltered myself, I suppose.'

'And you blame yourself for that?'

'Mmhmm,' Kirsty had said, which also wasn't strictly true.

She blamed Patrick for leaving the country when things between the Cadogans got tough. She blamed Jessica for her myopic focus on her business and the comfortable, magazine-like middle-class life she had built away from the rest of them. She blamed her parents for never telling her to do more or follow her dreams rather than staying put.

The trouble was that none of them were aware that they'd done anything wrong. They had lived their lives, and nobody had ever criticised them for it.

Kirsty pulled her mind away from the last time she was in Nehra's office, surrounded by books and pot plants and mid-century modern furniture. She thought about the box again and what might be inside it. And of her dad and when he might've put it together.

Then, keen to make the evening about something other than death and its aftermath, she put her headphones back in her ears, and started running.

Spire Hotel – Brighton, Sussex

Jessica

After she hit send on the text message cancelling dinner with Sadie, Jessica Googled the name of the takeaway pizza chain she only used when she was feeling bad about herself, and took a bottle of red wine from her tote bag. Really, it was too expensive and nice to down alongside a twelve inch meat feast and garlic bread. But she was in one of her 'fuck it' moods that usually came after a slow day at work, or when Dan was working away for the weekend and she worried about just who he might be away with...

She would normally cancel out the carbs, cheese and booze with some high intensity exercise the following day. But she only had one more morning with Kirsty in the house before she would drive back home to her kids, her business, and Dan. There would be no time for exercise. Besides, she needed to embrace this dreadful and unhealthy self-care if she was going to tolerate another day of piety and thickly laid on guilt from her sister.

Her phone buzzed.

Sadie: Oh shame! Don't worry love. Know how harsh grief can be. Wrote a piece about it last year. Next time xx

Then buzzed again. This time with the link to the article.

'Jesus,' Jessica said. 'Some people.'

She got up from the bed and went to sit in the uncomfortable, semi-circular pleather chair in the corner. Looking up at the bland painting of a rose above the bed, she navigated to her list of recent calls and hit the first one.

He answered within a few rings.

'I'm just getting the kids' dinner ready,' Dan said. 'Can I call you back?'

'I'll be in the bath.'

'Well after that.'

'Maybe,' she said. In the background she heard the ping of the microwave and Dan drop two plates down onto their kitchen counter. The sound of it placated her. He was doing exactly what he said he was. It would've been easy enough for him to get his mother to come over and do it, while he went out. Jessica was convinced that her parents-in-law would be happily complicit in covering up an affair for him should they need to...

'What is it?' he said, sounding exasperated. 'I've got two minutes.'

'Christ Dan. You do remember that my dad just died?' she said and felt instantly guilty for provoking him. Really, she just wanted to talk to him about her day.

'Sorry. It's just, well. This is hard work. Getting everything to-gether,' he said after a moment.

'I seem to manage every day.'

She could tell that Dan was about to retaliate but held back. 'I know,' he said, 'What is it?'

'We found something today. I wanted to tell you about it.'

'What? Not something dodgy?' he said, adding, 'or valuable?' with a note of hope in his voice.

'No. It was a box.'

'A box? Look, Jess, I'm really pushed here. If we could—'

'Dan. This is important.'

The line was silent for a moment, before Dan said, 'fine, look just give me two minutes.'

She heard him call, 'Max. Elspeth. Dinner. Now,' then the rustle of the cutlery drawer. After a minute, he picked up the phone again.

'Tell me about this box then.'

'It was just a metal box. Like a tool box or something. But he'd locked it.'

'And there was no key?'

'Kirsty took the key. There was a note to say not to open it until after the funeral.'

'Christ, Jess. It's probably some personal stuff he wants you to have. Some old crap.'

'Old crap?'

'You know what I mean.'

'Maybe,' she said slowly. 'It's odd though. That's not like Dad.'

'Well . . . Jess, people get strange,' he said, stopping himself. 'Not strange. What's the word? They get, like, sentimental. When they know it's . . . time.'

'Maybe,' she said again. 'I'm just curious about what's in it.'

27

'Well don't go opening it. You're like this with your birthday and you always end up regretting not having waited.'

'I think it's a bit more than that,' she said, deliberately not acknowledging that he was absolutely right.

'Look,' Dan said. 'I really have to go. The kids...' he said, letting the word trail off so it could mean anything: *are dismantling the furniture, have set fire to the lounge, can't eat a mouthful without fighting.*

'Don't worry. My dinner's here now,' she lied.

'Good. What are you having?'

'Caesar salad,' she said, lying again, with no idea why she was doing it.

They said goodbye and Jessica sat down on the end of the bed. Despite her husband and children less than two hours away and her sister in the same city, she felt impossibly lonely – hollowed out even. And the void she felt was being filled with regret and disappointment.

Her phone buzzed with a text message to say her food had arrived. She checked her eyes in the mirror and set off for the lobby.

Patrick

Maggie ran around the departure lounge, pretending to be a plane. It was almost half nine. Their flight was now delayed by another hour and ten minutes. Having gone from exhausted and slumped in his arms to running around with boundless energy, he knew his daughter was overtired and at risk of getting cranky.

He took out his phone and composed a text to Stu.

Patrick: Sorry mate. Still waiting. Will get an Uber if it's easier?

'Hey,' he called over to Maggie, who was clearly irritating a young and seemingly happy-to-be-childless couple. 'Hey, hey, hey.'

On the third shout, Maggie turned around and ambled back to her dad who hoisted her onto his knee.

Stu: No worries. Text when you're boarding. Will meet you at Stansted.

Patrick: Luton.

Stu: Yeah that.

'People are a bit tired, darling,' he told his daughter. 'Try not to annoy them.'

'Have you got any crisps?' she replied, blithely ignoring him.

'No. I've only got fruit. Blueberries?' he said, pulling a tupperware pot out of his rucksack and offering it to her.

He wondered if he should have crisps. And whether his not having any crisps was a sign of ill-preparedness. This was, after all, the first time he had travelled solo with Maggie. Usually Suzanne would be there too, and between the pair of them they'd remember more or less everything they needed to keep Maggie entertained through the flight, and fed and clothed at their destination.

This time, he was almost certain he had forgotten at least three key items of clothing, two essential comforting toys, and the only cup she would drink from, which he could picture now, still in the dishwasher.

Patrick wasn't sure if he was a bad single parent, or whether instead he could blame the circumstances. The purpose of the trip and what would happen when he arrived back in Hove – home as it once was – had been on his mind ever since Kirsty had given him the news.

That phone call was the first time they'd spoken in longer than he could recall, and it was horribly awkward and stilted. Their falling out years ago meant that any communication was strictly business-like and devoid of emotion and empathy. The same was true when she called again the next day to talk about the process of clearing out their old family home in Ganton Villas, a pretty road lined with whitewashed three-storey town houses.

At first, he was surprised at how quickly Kirsty wanted to begin the de-dadding operation. But anyone who knew the recent history of the Cadogan family would understand why she wanted the house empty and gone as soon as possible.

'Jessica's volunteered to come and help with the clear out,' she had said. 'Which is nice.'

'Yeah ... good. Y'know, I was going to offer to pay.'

'Pay?'

'Yeah. Get a removal firm or something. Or a couple of the lads might do it for a few quid.'

'Patrick.' She was both annoyed and shocked. Not for the first time, he knew. And probably because she was torn between wanting her siblings to turn up and help, and desperately wanting to avoid spending endless days stuck in a dead man's house with them.

'What?'

'I'm guessing this is your roundabout way of telling me that you're *not* coming?'

If he was honest, he'd considered hanging up right then. Running away would be a short-term solution. And if he put enough short-term solutions together, he would eventually get a long-term solution ...

'Well.'

'Christ, Patrick.'

For a second, he almost told the truth. Recent separation. Single parenthood.

30

'The thing is—'

But Kirsty made the decision for him when she spat, 'Dick.' And hung up.

It was probably better that way.

Still now, as the air steward finally announced the arrival of their long-delayed plane, Patrick's chief concern was if and how he would tell his sisters that his wife had left him months ago. It would inevitably be weird. They would wonder why he hadn't told them sooner, and the fact that he hadn't would say everything about the Cadogan children's relationships with one another. Then there would be follow-up questions, all difficult to answer and painful in their own way.

Yet for all that, he couldn't stay silent forever. The truth would eventually out. Besides, he wanted to move back to England. London probably, depending on how this stay with Stu went. Certainly not Brighton, whatever happened.

The plane ride went quickly. Maggie fell asleep, her head resting against his arm, her hands clutching his mobile phone. He didn't want to read and had found listening to music difficult recently, since every song lyric seemed to remind him of Suzanne. So instead, he sat with his head pressed against the cold plastic window, looking out at the black, starry night over the Irish Sea. Then down at the towns and cities below, marked by clusters and tentacles of light.

I could live in any of you, he thought to himself, enjoying the idea of anonymity and a fresh start. Before remembering that disappearing into a new life had huge consequences for people in the old one. Patrick knew that better than anyone.

They landed softly at Luton, as though the pilot was trying to make up for his tardiness by not waking anyone up. Maggie stirred as the brakes were applied and moaned, rubbing her eyes and brushing her curly brown hair off her forehead.

'Daddy,' she said, in that whining tone she always took when she wanted him to sit in her room until she fell asleep. He'd been doing a lot of that lately.

'Yes darling. We're there now.'

'At Stu's?' she said.

'Oh. No darling. On the plane still. Stu's waiting for us,' he said hopefully. Stu was the kind of person who might well just send Patrick some money and tell him to get a cab after all.

But no. When Patrick turned his phone on, a message was there waiting for him.

Stu: Here now. Fucking late.

Patrick: Sorry. Just landed.

Patrick was grateful that few people on the plane had anything more than hand luggage, so it took very little time until he and Maggie were through baggage collection and out through the arrivals gate. He noticed Stu as soon as they stepped into the busy hall, standing over near the doors with a sign that read MAGGIE CADOGAN. Patrick was sure his daughter would've enjoyed that were she not on the verge of walking while actually asleep.

He embraced his old friend, and together they went out into the cold night. Patrick felt strange to be back in England, and even stranger not knowing how long he was going to be here for.

'Welcome back,' Stu said, pushing their trolley of luggage while Patrick carried Maggie.

'Cheers.'

'And ... well. Sorry about your—'

'Yeah,' Patrick cut him off.

'And your—'

'Yeah.'

After a second or two, Stu adopted a noticeably brighter tone as he said, 'I'll get you home, shall I?'

'Please,' Patrick said, taking a deep breath and walking on.

CHAPTER TWO

Brighton, Sussex

Kirsty

The long, black Mercedes Kirsty, Jessica and Patrick were travelling in glided down Lewes Road, towards The Ring of Bells pub Kirsty had booked for Gerry's wake. It was strange how other drivers behaved around funeral cars, Kirsty thought. They were more courteous – slow, considered, mindful of who was around them and that something greater than quickly getting from A to B was at play.

Perhaps the government should put hearses and cars on the roads as a matter of course, she thought. To calm things down and make life safer for cyclists like her.

Next to her, Jessica was biting down on the knuckle of her forefinger and staring out of the window. She'd cried when the limousine had picked them up outside the house. And again in the crematorium. But both times had been measured and reserved. The occasional tear slipping down her thin face – all cheekbones and little flesh – before being being quickly swept away by a tissue from one of the two packets Kirsty had noticed in her handbag.

Patrick was far more demonstrative with his emotions. His came in short, almost violent bursts. Two or three great heaves and sobs, before he calmed down to look up once more at whoever was speaking about Gerry.

In grief as in life, she thought.

Afterwards, Kirsty noticed how crumpled Patrick's Order of Service was – the picture of their dad on the front with his dates all folded and scrunched. His frustration, sadness and anger was packed into the creases on the card. No matter, she thought. She had printed spares. He would want one as a keepsake.

'It was nice, wasn't it?' Kirsty said, breaking the silence as the driver slowed at some traffic lights.

Jessica managed a strained 'mmhmm' in response and Patrick nodded.

Kirsty felt she had conducted herself properly during the service. Gentle tears wiped away with a balsam tissue. And she had delivered the reading well. Gerry Cadogan wasn't much for poetry. But the Larkin struck the right tone, even if she didn't really agree with the author's worldview.

'It's strange, isn't it?' Kirsty continued. 'I know the man delivering the service had never met him, but I think he did well. It was almost as if he had met him. He didn't get anything wrong anyway, like at Uncle Mike's,' she said, thinking back to the doddery vicar who had spent Mike's entire funeral referring to their Aunt Sally as Sylvia.

She offered Jessica a tissue, who put up a hand to refuse it.

'Is Dan—?'

The hand again. Her sister apparently not in the mood for human interaction.

'As you wish,' Kirsty sniffed.

Patrick sat opposite them, legs stretched out across the black carpeted car floor. Next to him was a small, glass-fronted fridge, filled with bottles of Evian. Kirsty wondered if this same car was used for secondary school proms and hen dos – the only other occasions on which she'd had cause to use a limo. Maybe the driver would swap his smart top hat for a chauffeur's cap and ferry fortieth birthday celebrants and divorce parties into Brighton for the evening.

She proffered the same tissue Jessica had batted away to Patrick. 'I'm fine. Thanks,' he said.

'Good. It's a shame Suze couldn't make it,' she said, surprised not to have seen her sister-in-law at the funeral. Patrick had been non-committal about her attendance since he had arrived.

'Yes,' he said. 'She couldn't get the time off work.'

'Right.'

'Bastards. They really are. Totally unsympathetic,' he said.

'They couldn't cancel the trip?'

'No. Annual conference in America. She has to be there. You know how it is.'

'Of course,' Kirsty said, as the car came to a halt outside The Ring of Bells. She didn't know how it was. But this was not the time to push it.

A few black-suited smokers were outside. She faintly recognised most of them from dinners at their home years ago, or could picture them collecting payment from her dad for building jobs they had carried out for the family firm. Not quite friends, she thought, as she looked at them, laughing and sharing jokes. More well-wishers.

Nevertheless, it was succour to her that the funeral had been packed. Even if she did wonder where all these people were during his last couple of years. And why they thought they should show their faces at the send-off of the man who had given them so much work twenty-odd years ago, but not to turn up to say hello when he could barely stand.

'Ready?' the driver said.

'Could I just have a minute?' Jessica said. 'Need to sort out my eyes,'

'Nah,' the driver said dismissively. 'Don't worry about that. They'll be too busy dancing to notice.'

Her sister was visibly incredulous, but no one said anything. Besides, Kirsty did think it a little amusing, given the circumstances.

Patrick

He had no idea what he was thinking, really. Claiming that Suze's company had refused her leave and forced her to travel to America. Was he so desperate to cover the truth that he was willing to make himself look stupid in the process? It would all come out eventually, regardless of what he said.

In the meantime, he felt terrible about giving anyone this impression of Eoife, Suzanne's former boss. She would never have dreamed of making her work instead of attending a family funeral.

At least the America bit was true.

Three pints deep, Patrick scanned the pub looking for Maggie, who'd travelled over with Dan, Max, Elspeth and Livvy. He'd spent the entire journey in the limo terrified that his secret might have been revealed.

But no. Maggie had kept her counsel. *Mummy couldn't come because work wouldn't give her the time off.*

It was easier to demonise the technology company everyone thought Suze still worked for than Suze herself. And it was much easier than admitting that she'd left the two of them a month and a half ago and moved to San Francisco with the start-up millionaire she'd been having an affair with since the middle of last year.

Aside from Stu, the only person Patrick had voluntarily told so far was a builder who gave him a lot of work. He wanted to explain why his timekeeping might be a touch erratic as he struggled with getting Maggie to preschool and then himself to wherever they were working. Beyond that, there wasn't really anybody who *needed* to know. He knew very few people in Ireland, and those he did were mostly Suze's workmates who'd adopted them as a couple when she set up the office there. Unsurprisingly, these inherited acquaintances had been remarkably quick to drop him. An English painter and

37

decorator had little to offer the hipster end of the Dublin tech community, he knew that much.

'She's going to Skype to keep in touch, right?' Niall – Suze's former assistant's well-meaning husband – had asked when taking Patrick out for a beer a week after she left (the first and only time that had happened).

'Yep. She says advances in video technology mean that in a year's time it'll basically be like she and Maggie are in the same room. Trouble is I think she believes it.'

Suze had well and truly drunk the technology Kool Aid. It had started mid-way through last year. She would make statements about the end of cars and Artificial Intelligence meaning that humans wouldn't need to build things anymore. That sort of crap. When he found out about the affair, he realised her lover John had told her this stuff and she had swallowed it whole. John himself actually worked in a far less glamorous branch of technology – something to do with the cloud that Patrick didn't really understand. He had been in Dublin to an easier and cheaper alternative European base for his firm than London. He'd met Suze at a mixer for high-profile tech types and within months Patrick's marriage and the reason he himself had moved to Ireland were done for.

Patrick ambled from the bar over to the buffet the landlord had assembled.

'Some of Dad's favourites,' Jessica had requested. That meant chips, peanuts, doughy, soft sausage rolls – the cheap kind, with a clear and noticeable distance between where the sausage stops and the pastry begins – and a block of cheddar cheese. The only item to break up the beige food was a bowl of Wotsits, which Patrick grabbed a handful of, licking his fingers clean of the dusty, orange powder.

Kirsty joined him at the buffet. At the back of the table, behind the barely touched cheese brick, was a photo of their dad. It was probably taken five or six years ago if his lack of hair and the paunch stretching against his polo shirt were anything to go by. Gerry sat on a river bank, holding a fishing rod in one hand and a carp by its tail in the other, a broad smile painted across his face. He looked happy and kind, Patrick thought. His dad all over.

'Having fun?' Patrick asked.

'Oh terrific. What time does the karaoke start?'

She laughed a little.

'I've been thinking about the box you found.'

'Not now, though.'

'You don't think it's just his fishing stuff in there, do you?' Patrick continued, ignoring her. He was a little drunk.

'No.'

'I mean, it could be though couldn't it? Maybe he wants one of us to take it up. It's like that Elton John song isn't it? "My Father's Gun".'

'I've never heard that song.'

'"*From this day on, I own my father's gun*",' Patrick sang loudly. There was nothing wrong in singing at his dad's wake, surely.

'Stop,' Kirsty said, firmly. 'Anyway. It's not his bloody fishing stuff. That was all in the garage.'

'Was?'

'Yes, was. It went in the clear out. I donated it to a youth club.'

'And what if I wanted it? Or one of the kids?'

'If you had been *at* the clear out, you could've taken it.'

'You know I couldn't—'

'Besides,' she said, cutting him off. 'You live in Dublin. Unless you're going to fish in the Liffey, I doubt you'd get much use out of it.'

'Fine,' Patrick said, thinking it best not to push the conversation about his living in Dublin any further. Now wasn't the time to admit that he was presently living in Crouch End on his old friend Stu's couch, while Maggie slept in the spare room.

'Anyway, you'll find out later. We can open it back at home.'

'Yours?'

'No. *Home* home,' Kirsty said. 'Mum and Dad's.'

She took a chip, dipped it in ketchup and stuck in it her mouth, apparently with no joy or pleasure whatsoever.

'Aren't they stone cold?'

She nodded.

'Lovely,' he said, doing the same. 'Funny though, isn't it? We still think of it as home. Even though neither of them are . . . y'know?'

'Let's not get into it, shall we?' Kirsty said. 'We can go when it winds down here.'

Patrick returned to the bar and motioned at the young boy who had been assigned to serve them. Engrossed in whatever was happening on the screen of his iPhone, he didn't see Patrick's half polite, half irritated attempts for his attention. Instead, a woman he vaguely recognised looked over at him and smiled. As she came over, whacking the young boy's iPhone up and into his forehead, Patrick tried to place her.

Mary. Mara. Maisy. Meredith.

He was sure it started with an M. The names kept running through his head.

Moira. Martha. Maddie. Marianne. Melissa.

Maybe that, he thought. Melissa.

'Hello there,' she said. 'Long time, no see.'

'Hey!' Patrick said cheerfully. It was indeed a long time, he thought. If he was thirty-eight now, it would be getting on for something like eighteen years since he'd last seen her – most likely in a Brighton nightclub. He was certain that she went to his school, although was the year below him. His group would occasionally hang out with hers because Stu dated one of her friends – Tamara, or Tamsin . . .

40

Despite the years, she hadn't changed an awful lot. Still blonde. Still pretty, with prominent cheeks and an almost mischievous smile, as if she was always on the verge of telling a joke.

If only he could remember her fucking name.

'What's it been, eighteen years...?' he ventured.

'About that,' she said with a smile. 'You're struggling with my name, aren't you? Patrick Cadogan.'

'That obvious, is it?'

'You were basically chewing the side of your mouth...'

'Fine, yes. I was thinking Mel?'

'Mellll,' she said, elongating the sound of the 'L'.

'Issa?'

'Ooh. Not quite.'

'Mel-anie?' he said.

'Nope. Give up?'

'Yes.'

'Chloe,' she said, with a laugh.

'Fuck. Why'd you let me?'

'Bit of fun, I suppose.'

'You know it's my dad's funeral? Wake, I mean.'

'I do. Thought you could do with a bit of cheering up,' she shrugged. 'Anyway. What'll it be?'

'Guinness, please. And a whisky. What've you got?'

Chloe reeled off a list of names, looking up at the top shelf. Patrick barely listened, trying desperately to think of something else he could say to her to keep her from wandering off to serve one of the other punters.

'Oban,' he said, picking one at random and only because he could read the label OK.

'That a good one, is it?'

'Probably,' he said, as she flicked the tap back and Guinness began to pour into a pint glass. The whisky, he knew already, was probably a mistake. This would be pint four. And they still had that fishing box business to take care of later on.

'I am sorry, though,' Chloe said, putting the whisky down in front of him on the bar while the Guinness settled. This was the good thing about Guinness, he thought. Time. 'About your dad. He was a nice bloke. I met him when he did a few jobs around here. Never took any money for them.'

'Thanks. He was. How long've you been working here then?'

'This stint, two years. But I worked here during the summers when I was at uni.'

'Right. What made you . . .' he began, but trailed off, not sure whether asking why she returned to bar work might be seen as too personal a question.

'The big D,' Chloe said, with that smile again. 'I married Matty Hyde if you remember him?' Patrick nodded.

Matty Hyde was two years above him at school. Matty Hyde was very popular. Matty Hyde was a colossal dickhead.

'Then he fucked off with Sarah Barnes. If you remember her?'

'Shit.'

'Exactly. So I do three or four evenings here and I'm full time at the university.'

'Oh right. So are you a . . . ?'

'Senior Lecturer in Astrophysics.'

'Really?'

Chloe laughed with one big 'HA'.

'I work in marketing. Making student prospectus stuff and that.'

She put the fully settled Guinness in front of Patrick. Clearly to make her stay and talk to him, he would have to buy another drink. He downed the Oban and asked for another.

'You know they're nine quid a throw?'

'Really? Shit.'

'This one can be on the house,' Chloe said. 'Grieving son and all that.'

'You're very kind.'

'And you're very welcome. Now, you've got until I pour this and the time it takes to put it through the till to think up what you're going to tell me about yourself.'

'Right.'

'Unless you're going to down that Guinness and buy another one.'

Patrick looked at the pint and contemplated sinking the entire thing; all in the name of flirting with a barmaid he knew vaguely from years ago (but found very attractive nonetheless).

'I was living in Dublin,' he said quickly. 'But now I'm not. I've got a four-year-old daughter, nowhere to live, my wife's gone, and I have nothing in the way of work at the moment.'

'Jesus,' Chloe said, putting the whisky down. 'You've had a year of it.'

'Yep. Oh, and you can't breathe a word of any of that to my sisters. Them two over there,' he said, with a nod to the other room where Kirsty and Jessica sat at a small table, ignoring the darts match happening next to them.

'They don't know you've got a daughter?'

'Yeah. Sorry. They know that. Everything else – they haven't a clue.'

'Right,' Chloe said. 'Well there's a lot in there to talk about. You best buy another drink soon.'

She smiled and turned away, ready to serve one of the waiting darts players on the other side of the bar. As she went, she flicked the young boy's phone up at his forehead again.

Patrick, meanwhile, looked over at his sisters who both stared back, scowling at him. He thought he saw Jessica gently shake her head in disgust.

Jessica

Dan and the kids had left early. That much was fine. What was annoying was having to watch Patrick and three of Gerry's oldest friends go about ensuring that the float they'd put behind the bar sank. And what was even *more* annoying was knowing that her brother was only sat with those old duffers so he could flirt with that barmaid.

Patrick was drunk. Though she couldn't really tell *how* drunk because he had spent the last few hours perched atop a stool. He'd have to try to walk for Jessica to know how bad the damage was.

It was almost seven and the three men were on their third whiskies. They had raised their glasses to 'the man who liked a dram', in reference to Gerry's extensive and expensive collection of single malt Scotch. Which he'd kept it in a locked cabinet in his office, along with two thistle-shaped Edinburgh crystal glasses that he only brought out at Christmas.

'When can we go?' Jessica asked Kirsty. They were sitting at a table away from the bar, beneath a screen that had been showing Sky Sports News all day. 'They're basically the only ones left and I think the landlord wants us out.'

The pub was getting busy with regulars waiting for the quiz to start at half past. Bar staff had tidied away the remnants of the buffet and asked if 'there's anything else you need' four times now. 'Besides. I really cannot stand the way he's going on with that barmaid.'

'They knew each other at school for God's sake, Jess. He told me.'

'You can see what's going on there. I know Suzanne couldn't come, which is its own story. But really. That,' she said.

'We'll go soon,' Kirsty said, taking a sip of her coffee. 'Just let me finish this.'

'Look. I want to get back. I want to open that box. And I want to go to my hotel. Today has been—'

'Don't, Jess.'

'Don't what?'

'Moan.'

'I wasn't going to moan.'

'Complain, then.'

'I was going to say *exhausting*. Today has been exhausting. That okay with you?'

'Yes,' Kirsty said, taking another sip of coffee. 'Sorry.'

They waited a few moments more, until a fat bald man wearing a Brighton & Hove Albion away shirt took a seat at the end of the bar. He sipped from a pint of Coke and tapped a microphone three times.

'Lads and ladettes,' he boomed. 'The weekly Ring of Bells quiz will be getting underway shortly, taking us all the way up to last orders . . . when the bell ends.'

A loud, raucous cheer went up on the other side of the pub and Jessica stood up.

'Right. Enough of this.'

She marched over to Patrick, who was staring blankly into his whisky glass.

'Ready?' she demanded haughtily. 'Our Uber will be here in two minutes.'

That wasn't strictly true. In fact, she hadn't even ordered one yet, but Patrick wasn't to know. As he mumbled that he might stay for another, she opened the app on her phone and requested a car, relieved to find that one could be with them in four minutes.

'No. We're going *now*, Patrick,' she said, mentally adding *say goodbye to your friends*, as if she were talking to Max.

'Stay for one with us. We're talking about Dad's old cars.'

'Absolutely not. We're going back to the house to open this box. Then I'm going back to my hotel.'

'Well I might—'

'No,' she snapped, storming off towards the door. As she reached it, she turned back to see Patrick leaning over to talk to the barmaid again.

Part of her wanted to say something, to set him right. But another – much bigger – part of her knew that soon she would be back at home, he would be away in Dublin, and she wouldn't have to worry about it again.

'Ridiculous,' she rolled her eyes, stepping out into the cold night to wait for Karl and his black Audi A2.

Patrick

'C'mon,' Kirsty said with a tug at his suit jacket. 'Or she'll kill you.'

'Two minutes. I'll see you out there.'

Patrick held up his half-empty glass, hoping to convince her that he was staying to drink that rather than for ... well, other reasons.

'Fine. Thank everyone, will you?'

'I will.'

Patrick turned back to the bar and looked for Chloe. She was down the other end, next to the fat quizmaster. She was sitting on a high stool, eating Scampi Fries and idly swiping at her iPhone.

'Been summoned 'ave ya?' Jack, one of his dad's old plasterers, slurred between sips of San Miguel.

'Looks like it,' Patrick said, climbing off the stool onto unsteady legs. 'Better go say thank you.'

He sidled over to Chloe who looked up and smiled at him.

'You off?'

'I'm off. Came to say thanks. For ... well, this.'

'I'll pass that on to Dennis. He'll be touched, I'm sure.'

'Great. Aaaand ...' he swayed slightly on the spot.

'Aaaand,' Chloe repeated.

'Fuck. I don't know how to do this. Can I just give you my business card? Then if you want to . . . well, you can.'

'"If you want to, you can",' she laughed. 'That's almost poetic.'

'Very funny. Look, you don't have to . . . I just thought we—'

'Give me the card.'

Patrick fumbled around in the inside pocket of his suit for his wallet, from which he pulled a battered piece of white card that read *Patrick Cadogan. Painting. Decorating. Interior Renovations. Call for quotes.* His email address and phone number sat at the bottom, with a clip art picture of a paintbrush.

'Interior renovations,' she said.

'I didn't know what else to put. Suzanne said,' he began, but stopped short.

'Did she now. You're being given the hurry up, by the way,' she said, nodding towards the door of the pub, where Kirsty was motioning vigorously at him.

'Right. I'd better go,' he said. 'And you know. As I said. If—'

'I want to, I can,' she said. Patrick blushed, until she added, 'I might,' and he left.

Twenty minutes later, the three of them were outside their old family home in Ganton Villas, Hove. It was dark now, but the whitewashed front of the three-storey town house remained bright, partly lit by the yellowy glow of the streetlamp outside, which Jessica had driven into the day after she passed her driving test.

'Right. Shall we, then?' Jessica said, climbing out of the back door.

Inside, the house felt strange, cold and unwelcoming, which didn't fit with Patrick's childhood memories of the place. No one had been inside for the past few days. Even more bizarre, and almost uncanny, was the emptiness. The bare walls, rectangular outlines and hooks where pictures had hung. No furniture, save for the dining set and the couches in the living room. The curtains were still up, but there was no point in drawing them anymore.

'This way,' she said, leading Patrick to the kitchen while Kirsty disappeared to collect the box from Gerry's study. 'Tea?'

'Anything stronger?' Patrick asked as she bustled around what had been the scene of so many family dinners. Back then, the kitchen had been almost all oak-effect laminate cupboards and a faux-red-brick vinyl floor. Now it was a Nigella-inspired modern take on an old country kitchen – all the rage when it was installed back in 2005.

'You've had enough.'

'It's my dad's funeral, Jess,' he said.

'*Our* dad's. And another whisky isn't going to make it any better. You'll just end up sick and hungover. You're thirty-six. The hangovers are worse now.'

'I'm thirty-eight.'

'That's what I meant,' she said. 'Besides. The way you were going on in that pub. Sitting next to those old gits so you could chat up the barmaid.'

'I wasn—'

'It's disgusting,' she said, slopping milk into the mugs. 'Whatever's going on that's stopped Suzanne from being here . . . well, it doesn't excuse that. Carrying on like some twenty-year-old in a nightclub.'

He almost snapped and told her right then. That Suzanne had gone. That the reason she wasn't at the funeral was because she didn't even know it was happening. But the noise of the kitchen door opening distracted him.

'I hope that milk is alright,' Kirsty said. She was carrying the big red metal fishing box.

'It's all we have. I'm sure it'll be fine.'

'Happily top up mine with a tot of brandy,' Patrick said with a smile, and Jessica silenced him with a stare. He leaned back in the dining chair which had been missing one of its spindles for longer than he could remember. His white shirt was unbuttoned at the top, showing its dirty, yellowing neckline; evidence of its lack of recent outings.

'Well, here it is then,' Kirsty said. She heaved the box onto the table, in the middle of the three cups of hot tea and the remaining custard creams she and Jessica had been eating during the clear out. 'Ready?'

Kirsty

She fished the key from where it sat in the pocket of her slightly weathered handbag, nestled amongst a tube of Boots own-brand lip balm, three tampons and one Euro, thirty-eight cents in coins. She needn't have been so diligent about keeping it safe – the box could probably have quite easily been prised open with a bit of skill and a hairpin.

'Right, then,' she said, pushing the key into the lock. They were all nervous. None of them would admit it, but they were all worried that they were about to discover something they didn't know – that their absent dad was about to unearth the final Cadogan family secret. Their family had seemed so well-adjusted for so long – but that image had ended very suddenly and very painfully a decade ago . . .

She turned the lock, pulled open the lid and craned her neck to peer inside. Jessica did the same.

'What is it then?' Patrick said.

'It looks like a bottle of whisky,' Jessica said.

'Oh good. Crack it open.'

'Shut up, Patrick,' Jessica said.

'There's more,' Kirsty said. 'Mum and Dad's old photo albums, I think.'

She lifted three heavy, leather books out of the box and placed them down on the table. They had seen them before, but not for a while. One red, one blue, one black. All edged with gold leaf that was flaking away. They were part of a set of maybe ten albums beginning in 1978 – the year Jessica was born – and ending in the early noughties, when printing photos off became less and less the done thing.

Jessica took the whisky out, nestled in a box that read:

PORT ELLEN
Islay Single Malt Scotch Whisky
Bottled in 1984. Aged 10 Years.

Another envelope was attached to the box, reading *To my children* in Gerry's handwriting.

'Fucking hell,' Patrick said, grabbing the whisky.

'What?'

'It's the Port Ellen.'

'And?'

'Dad bought this in twenty-twelve. It cost him, like, two grand.'

'Two grand?!' Jessica exclaimed. 'For a whisky?'

'The distillery closed down in the eighties. It's a collector's item. He was planning to open this on his seventieth, but...'

Patrick trailed off. Gerry had never made it to seventy. He checked out at sixty-six, four years short and with his prized whisky still sealed and never tasted.

'Surely it's spoiled by now?' Jessica said. 'It's almost as old as me.'

'Whisky never spoils. It doesn't change from the moment it's bottled,' he said. Patrick was the only one to show any of their dad's interest in fine Scottish whiskies. He never went as far as accompanying his parents on their various trips north to small, obscure distilleries, though, where Gerry would go on tours and tasting sessions, while Sue sat in their camper van reading books with her feet up.

'Never mind the bloody whisky,' Kirsty cut in. 'Open the envelope.'

Patrick did as she told him, drawing out a letter scrawled in handwriting they all recognised from birthday cards, and to-do lists left around the house. It was written on the headed paper they all mocked him for. But before Patrick could begin to read, Jessica snatched it away.

A Note from Gerry

28th September
Dear Jessica, Patrick and Kirsty,

If you're reading this, then my funeral must have just finished. I hope it wasn't too morbid and that you remembered to play the Chas & Dave song!

I'm writing this because I've got something to ask of you.

You're all probably thinking that I want my ashes scattered on the beach, like your mum. But I want something different.

In this box you'll find the keys to my old camper. I want the three of you to take it and drive up to Islay where you can scatter my remains on the beach at Port Ellen. I've also put in a couple of photo albums and a bottle of whisky (a good one!) for the journey.

I know the three of you have had your differences. But I want you to do this for me. My last wish. Who knows, you might even enjoy it?

Happy travels.

> *I love you all very much*
> *Your Dad, Gerry*

Jessica

For a moment, no one spoke. Each waiting for someone else to react.

A trip across the entire country, stuck in Gerry's old camper van, with people they'd been nothing more than civil with for years. Just to scatter his ashes.

For Jessica, this was non-negotiable. Work, kids, Dan. They all needed her around. The others could go if they so chose. She could fly up and meet them for the ceremonial part – scattering his remains across the godforsaken beach that apparently meant so much to him. But spending days on end in a van? With Kirsty and Patrick? Absolutely not.

She looked out to the garden, lit by spotlights he had installed in the patio a few years ago. In the short period between Gerry's death and his cremation, it had become untidy. The hydrangea flowers were browning, the lawn needed a trim, and plants which Jessica knew should flower well into autumn had died. She felt bad for not tending to it. And she *had* thought about doing it with Kirsty while she was here. But to what end? They'd be selling the house soon to pay off the debt her parents had taken on years ago, after the financial crisis had necessitated the bail out of Cadogan Family Builders and the remortgaging of their family home.

She looked at herself in the glass of the patio door. The figure hugging black dress she wore for funerals and meetings with her bank manager was still pristine, the black heels she'd had on for the service recently replaced with flats. Her hair needed a trim, but it could wait.

'Jess,' Kirsty said. 'What do you—'

'Hang on.'

She realised she was prevaricating. In fact, she already had her excuse planned out. Commitments. And if that didn't work she'd use health. There was no way she'd be able to stand night after night on those cramped, uncomfortable camper van beds. In a *sleeping bag*, of all things.

No. Not with her neck.

Patrick took a sip of his tea and looked ready to say something, then drew back quickly, like a footballer throwing a dummy (as Dan and Max called it when they played together in the back garden). Kirsty folded up the letter and put it back in its envelope.

'You want me to say what I think we should do?' Jessica said. 'It's always left to the oldest.'

'Come off it,' Patrick said.

'Hardly,' Kirsty said.

'Well the answer's no, isn't it? Absolutely no way.'

'It's his final—'

'I don't care if it's his final . . . *whatever*, Kirsty,' she snapped. 'The idea that I can take . . . however long off for some . . . *jaunt*,' she said. 'It's absurd. It really is.'

'It'll have to be half term,' Kirsty said. 'I've taken too much time off school already.'

'It'll have to be *never*.'

'What? So you're saying yes?' Patrick asked Kirsty, ignoring Jessica's interjection.

'Of course,' she said, picking up a biscuit. Rather than taking a bite, she just held onto it, like it was some sort of edible stress ball. 'It's the last thing he wants us to do.'

'It's the last thing I want to do.'

'Hilarious, Jess.'

'Sorry. But it conveniently ignores my kids, my husband. I can't even *believe* he would think of this.'

'I think it's a nice idea,' Kirsty said.

'Nice? What's nice about spending days in that horrible old camper—'

'He bought a new one. A few years ago. It's not that grotty old thing.'

'It'll still be a camper van, Kirsty, still grotty.'

'It's a good way to travel. See the world and all that. Anyway, can your husband not take care of your kids?' Patrick said.

'He has work, Patrick. A very important job.'

'I'm sure he can take holiday, Jess. Even the fucking Prime Minister gets a holiday.'

'And my business?'

'You *own* your business. You can take holiday whenever you want.'

Jessica didn't answer this and wondered instead when to play the health card. That wouldn't be so easy to argue with. But it was getting cold in the kitchen and she wanted to head back to the hotel. After the funeral Dan had taken the kids to the arcades on the seafront and to have burgers; a joyful activity to compensate for their second family funeral in only a few years. He'd sent a photo earlier, oblivious to the fact that a selfie of the three of them drinking ice cream milkshakes from big metal cups might be insensitive just three hours after they'd sent her dad to the flames. Now, she wanted to get back to them.

'What about you?' Kirsty said, looking at Patrick.

'Well,' he said, slurring the word so it somehow sounded like it had an F in it. 'Pending childcare I suppose I'm in.'

'What do you mean "pending childcare"?' Kirsty said. 'Maggie will be back in Ireland with Suze. I was thinking more about whether you'd stay in England for a bit or come back for the trip.'

'Oh ... yeah ... right,' Patrick mumbled, not really looking at anyone. 'Well I suppose I can move a few jobs around,' he said. 'Exceptional circumstances and all that. I'll crash with Stu and Sarah for a bit. And Maggie ... yeah ... well, she'll go back won't she?'

'A four-year-old can't fly alone, Patrick.'

'No . . . yeah,' he stumbled again. 'Well, we can work something out.'

He took a sip of his tea and looked up at the ceiling.

'Jesus Christ, Patrick,' Jessica said. 'I wish you weren't so utterly pissed. It really is impossible to have a conversation with you. That barmaid—'

'So if we're both in,' Kirsty said, cutting her off. 'It's only—'

'No. Kirsty, the answer is no. You two can go if you want to but I'm not doing this. I know it's Dad's *dictat* or whatever you want to call it. But I'm too—'

'Selfish?' Kirsty interrupted.

Jessica stood up, grabbing her phone and her bag, and left the kitchen.

'Oh for Christ's sake, Jess. Where—'

'Toilet,' Jessica called back, as she stormed into the downstairs bathroom and slammed the creaky door behind her.

She ordered another Uber – this time to take her to the hotel – and sat down on the closed toilet seat.

Her thoughts immediately went to what the journey would be like; sitting contained in the van, everyone trying to be polite and non-confrontational until the inevitable first argument after a few hours. Of course it'd be about something trivial. Patrick would have left teabags on the draining board or Kirsty would have driven badly.

She couldn't imagine what she might do to upset the others. But there would doubtless be something. There always was.

After a minute more of staring blankly into space (as she quite often did in her own bathroom), Jessica's phone buzzed.

Your driver, Meral, is outside.

Quietly, she left the bathroom and snuck out of the front door. She looked back at the house from inside the car and could see the distant light of the kitchen through the lounge window. Otherwise the rest of it was in darkness. Her family home was shutting down, readying itself for when another group of people arrived, and brought with them their own politics and proclivities.

Jessica wondered if she'd ever see it again. Would it now be sold and her residing memory of Ganton Villas be a discarded husk she had fled from to avoid a squabble with her brother and sister?

'Seatbelt, please,' the driver – a brusque German woman – said.

Jessica did as she was told, still looking at the houses as the car pulled away.

CHAPTER THREE

Hove Caravan Park

Patrick

The caravan park felt like a graveyard for recreational vehicles. White shell after white shell parked next to each other as far as he could see, many of them filthy with dust, rain and months of neglect. Some had flat tyres and others had begun to grow moss – the signs of at least one summer spent alone in the park while its owners enjoyed other holidays.

'Where did it—'

'Row six, bay twelve,' Kirsty reminded him. She was being a little short with him today, clearly irritated at having to spend her Saturday (and the first day of half term) doing this, instead of going to the beach on what would probably be one of the last clement days of the year.

Once they had picked up and cleaned the camper van, they were due to collect their father's ashes in Hove, so they could accompany them on the trip to Scotland next Wednesday.

They had paid over the odds for a gold and black urn. Even though they knew from their mother's passing that the ashes themselves would be kept in a cheap plastic bag. Patrick remembered how he felt upon realising this, years ago. Death reduced to administrative and logistical ease and opportunities for undertakers to up-sell memorial paraphernalia to grieving families.

'I still can't believe we're doing this,' Patrick said.

'It's the right thing.'

'I know. But y'know, fucking big ask.'

'Don't, Patrick.'

'Also, we won't be doing it will we? Fulfilling his final wish. Not without *her*,' he said.

Neither of them had heard from Jessica since she walked out on them eight days ago, on that Tuesday evening after the funeral. They'd scoured the house calling 'Jessica', 'Jess', and a few times 'Jessie', knowing she hated the name and it might get a rise. When they knew that she had skipped out, they had rung her five times but received only one message in response.

Jessica: Back at the hotel. Stop calling. Not doing this stupid idea.

Patrick and Kirsty had spoken briefly after she'd left, and the understanding between them was clear: they were going to do it. Patrick knew he wouldn't be able to live with himself if he didn't. The guilt of denying Gerry's last request would pile up on the guilt he felt for not being there during his illness, and how he hated that Maggie was a stranger to her grandfather. Even if it'd be half an accomplishment without Jessica, it was one he wanted to do well.

Besides, staying in Crouch End was becoming unbearable. Stu and his wife were kind and attentive and loved Maggie. But he was all too aware that his new, unwelcome bachelorhood didn't fit their London lifestyle. They invited him to dinner parties, when he'd rather just be on the couch watching *Moana* with his daughter. Their evenings at yoga classes and high-intensity gym sessions shamed his infrequent three-mile jog around the park.

Recently he had taken to spending his lunchtimes wandering the streets, looking up at apartments and fondly remembering when he first moved to the city – the last time he and Stu had been flatmates between 2006 and 2011. Back then, they lived in Chalk Farm and spent their evenings in the Lock Tavern or watching whatever sport they could find on the telly. After a few years, Stu met Sarah, he met Suze and life found its way. Aside from having Maggie, he was fairly sure that was the happiest time of his life.

'Here,' Kirsty said, stopping at the plot – a patch of grass with a small concrete bollard someone had painted 12 on.

It was noticeably older than some of the others parked around it. And noticeably dirtier. A Ford Transit van, with a flimsy box fixed to the back, and a cabin above the driver's seat (that bit always reminded Patrick of a quiff). The windscreen was thick with grime, a wing mirror was held on with gaffer tape, and the wheel below the passenger's seat was flat, so the whole thing listed like a sinking boat. It looked sad, which belied the bright blue sticker down the side that read *THE ADVENTURER*.

'When was the last—'

'Around three years ago,' Kirsty said, pre-empting Patrick. 'A year after Mum died. He decided to go fishing in Norfolk. Near Kings Lynn.'

'And since then it's just sat here?'

'Mhmm.'

'Jesus. Shall we?' he asked, stepping towards the van, keys in hand. He wasn't sure what he might find when he opened the camper. Rats? A dead body? An entire family sheltering from the autumn rain?

Patrick unlocked the flimsy door (he'd always thought it would be so easy to just break in) and they were hit by a musty, damp smell as he opened it. He tried the lights, but the battery was flat and nothing worked. By the light of his phone torch, he and Kirsty climbed the three small steps onto the pine-effect vinyl floor inside, and started to poke around.

'Christ,' he said. 'Cosy.'

The Adventurer was smaller than he remembered. It took barely three steps to walk the aisle connecting the two bunks and bathroom at the back of the van with the driver's cab at the front. The little table didn't seem big enough to host a meal for four people – never mind the six the van claimed to cater for. And the bench seats either side of it were cramped and too upright. He couldn't imagine how they would fold down to form a double bed. On the other side of the aisle was the kitchen: a small fridge, a two-hob cooker and a gas-powered oven grill.

'It's cleaner than I thought it would be,' Kirsty said, hopefully, as she opened the lockable cupboards and picked through the family crockery that had migrated to the van. Old mugs with out of date chocolate bar logos sat alongside others bearing the former crest of Watford F.C. which Patrick recognised from decades ago. He was sure the plastic plates were the same ones they'd used on camping holidays in the early nineties.

'I wonder if it still runs?' he asked, climbing through to the driver's cab, while she looked at the little bathroom, which came with its own user's rulebook.

He put the key into the ignition and turned. The dashboard lit up to show a quarter of a tank of diesel. He turned it again, harder this time as though force might encourage the engine into life, and after a few sputters and coughs, the van started up. The light above the table immediately came on and promptly blew again, while the clock on the cooker beeped twice.

'Fucking hell.'

'Works then?' Kirsty said. She came up behind him.

'Yep,' he said.

They both sounded a little disappointed. Had the van been a write off, or at least required significant work, it might have given them an out. They could have flown up instead. But no. Their dad's fastidiousness when it came to vehicle maintenance had put an end to that. Even if it never went anywhere, he'd likely still have had it serviced yearly.

Against all odds, The Adventurer was alive.

Berkhamsted, Hertfordshire

Jessica

She checked her phone.

> Kirsty: I know you're ignoring us but thought you might like to know van works. P and I leaving Weds morning. In case you change your mind x

And she locked it again, putting the message out of her mind.

Jessica went back to the pot of ragu bubbling away atop her range cooker. She wanted to add more wine, as she might if they were having friends over or the kids were out. But some unknown voice nagged at her not to, like one of the vitriolic, moralising responses to a Mumsnet post about adding booze to food kids would eat.

Instead she filled her large, bowl-like red wine glass. It was part of the set Dan had bought to replace the wedding glassware he'd smashed intermittently over the years.

She surveyed the kitchen in an attempt to continue distracting herself from the message. They'd had it done last year. New stone floor, kitchen island with pans artfully hanging above it, everything chrome or dark blue. There were little things Dan had promised to change after the job, like swapping the taupe window blind for a wood-effect one, and the yellow light bulbs in the extractor hood for white ones. But they, or at least he, had learned to live with these imperfections now.

It was less than five minutes before Jessica caved and picked up her phone to read Kirsty's message again.

'Who's that?' Dan asked, appearing in the doorway, still in his work trousers but with his shirt untucked and grey slippers on.

'No one. Nothing.'

'Alright.'

'Well why ask if you don't care?'

'I was just . . . asking. I don't know.'

'It's no one,' she said again, returning to the ragu, then adding, 'Kirsty.'

'Oh right,' Dan said, brightly. 'What does she want?'

'Nothing,' Jessica, said, then barked 'DOWN! BOOTSY DOWN' at their cat, reminding herself of how much she regretted allowing a three-year-old Max to name their family pet years ago.

'Fine,' Dan said.

As he was about to leave the room again, Jessica relented. 'It's this stupid trip.'

He took a moment. 'What trip?' he asked.

'They're doing a trip. To spread Dad's ashes.'

'Oh,' he said, sounding surprised, which was entirely understandable given that it was the first he'd heard of it. 'Sorry. Had you mentioned—'

'No. I didn't . . . well I didn't think I needed to.'

'Are you going?'

'No,' she said, taking a big gulp of wine.

'Why? Have they not invited you? I swear to God. If those two—'

'They did. Well, he did. Dad, I mean,' she said, stirring the ragu so as not to make eye contact. 'I said no.'

Dan took a seat at the kitchen island.

'Sorry, Jess. I'm completely fucking lost here. Could you explain?'

So she did. She even read out Gerry's letter from a photo Kirsty had sent of it – Jessica did think it unfair of her sister to use emotional blackmail to make her do something she didn't want to.

By the end of it, Dan's face didn't tell her much. He'd laughed twice, though, at the memory of Patrick chatting up the barmaid, and at Jessica sneaking off that night. But he also seemed shocked that her dad would suggest a trip like this one. Perhaps because in the last few years Gerry had never so much as organised a meal out for the family.

'Well what do you think?' she asked.

'I think you should go. Clearly.'

'Really?'

'Jess. Do you honestly think you won't regret saying no in about five years' time?'

'Maybe,' she said, mouth half full of wine. 'It'll take ages though. Two days up. Two days down.'

'Four days, then?'

'Plus a day there. On the island. Probably.'

'Five.'

'We were going to book that holiday,' she said, referring to a last minute half term trip to Majorca she'd found.

'Yes. I was going to mention that. So you planned to book Majorca so you couldn't possibly go on this trip with Patrick and Kirsty?'

'Well . . .'

'It doesn't matter. I can still go with the kids. Maybe I can get Mum to come.'

'Dan,' she said, half pleading, half persuading.

'You should go.'

'The shop.'

'You were going to book a holiday!'

Jessica refilled her wine glass and took a beer from the fridge for Dan. They looked at each other for a moment, in the way they did if one had undermined the other's decision when disciplining Max and Elspeth. Then she broke away and pumped hand cream from the dispenser next to the sink into her palm, massaging it around her fingers.

'Which one's that?'

'Cardamom and bergamot.'

'Smells like a curry,' he said. She ignored him and flicked the kettle on. The loud, rolling boil made conversation momentarily impossible and Dan waited for the click before joining her by the hob, where she put a large handful of spaghetti on to cook. He took her in his arms.

'It's different for you,' Jessica said. 'You get on with your family.'

'And you used to get on with yours.'

'It's been years, Dan. I can't even remember the last time we had a normal conversation.'

'You got on well enough with Kirsty didn't you? When you were doing the clear out?'

'It was civil. We were more like workmates than friends.'

'Well there we go. Could be worse.'

'Yes but it's always there, isn't it? She'll always think we were trying to turf Dad out of his house. I'll always think she was naive about the whole thing.'

'And Patrick?'

'Says nothing. Of course. He never does until it's too late.'

'So that's the whole point, isn't it? Finally resolve all that shit.'

'But what if we're just not meant to get along? Some people don't. We fell out for a reason.'

'Jess,' Dan said seriously. 'Everyone knows that's not why you fell out. You—'

'No,' she said, pushing Dan away from her. 'Not now Dan. You can't just bring that up when—'

'I'm not. But you have to admit it had an impact,' he said, but Jessica was walking away from him, into the hallway.

'DINNER,' she called up the stairs. 'NOW.'

'Jess,' he said gently when she returned.

'No,' she said, noisily dumping cutlery onto the kitchen island and lifting a garlic tear n' share out of the oven.

'Just go,' he said.

Ganton Villas – Hove, Sussex

Kirsty

Kirsty snapped off a marigold and threw it into the sink. It was, of course, typical that she'd be the one to have to clean the sodding van. She'd brought Livvy with her to help out with smaller jobs like clearing the Tesco own-brand glacier mint wrappers scattered around the driver's seat, while she carried on with washing the floor, the crockery and cutlery, the cooker, bathroom and hoovering the beds.

Patrick, to his credit, had paid for it to be cleaned on the outside. Not that the outward appearance mattered too much. But the two of them felt it just needed doing (and there was the subtext that they'd almost certainly sell the thing the minute they got back). He had also bubble-wrapped the urn, remembering a childhood caravan trip on which a sharp bend in the Lake District resulted in three smashed bottles of beer.

'Thirty-seven, Mummy,' Livvy said, holding out two handfuls of sweet wrappers.

'Very good, darling. Put them in the bag,' she said, motioning to the bin liner on the passenger seat.

'Which one will be your bed?'

'I don't know darling. We'll see where Uncle Patrick wants to sleep.'

'I like this one,' she said, climbing up the ladder and into the bed above the cab. The quiff. Kirsty thought it looked cosy.

Seeing her daughter up there brought on a wave of guilt. She was going away in half-term week. There had always been an unspoken rule between the two of them that this wouldn't happen. The next few days were meant to be spent at aquariums and zoos, or at home doing arts and crafts, sometimes with her friends over.

But no. Livvy would stay the next few days at two different friend's houses (Kirsty didn't want to put the burden on just one of them).

'It looks nice, doesn't it? I wish you were coming with me,' she said, immediately regretting it.

Livvy looked sad as she said, 'me too,' and climbed carefully back down the ladder.

'Them people are leaving Grandad's,' Livvy said, looking out of the window at the juvenile, suited estate agent leading a youngish couple down the steps, away from the old family home. It had been on the market for three days and so far there had been five viewings but no offers.

Kirsty looked out and caught the eye of the estate agent, who gave her a thumbs up, but which the couple absolutely saw. She wondered how she must appear to them. Some mad old bat living in a camper van outside her dead dad's house. She wanted to go out and say 'I don't *actually* live here. I have a flat in Brighton.' But knew that would only make her seem madder.

'Come on, darling,' Kirsty said to Livvy, ushering her away from the window. 'I think we're almost done. Pick that up,' she said, pointing at a little Sainsbury's bag full of rubbish, while she took the bin liner. 'I think pizza tonight. As a reward.'

Livvy cheered and Kirsty's phone buzzed.

Jessica: What time are you leaving tomorrow? X

She read the message once, sent a screen shot of it to Patrick accompanied by an angry emoji and a shrug, then threw the phone back into her bag. She couldn't be bothered with her sister's guilt right now.

North Laine, Brighton

Patrick

He looked at the message from Kirsty and placed the phone face down on the table.

'You can get that, if you need to?' Chloe said. 'If it's about your trip.'

'It's not,' Patrick said. 'Carry on,' he added, urging her to continue with the gossipy stories about people they'd both been to school with. There was a particular focus on those who'd ended up in prison, divorced, or done some dreadful or stupid other thing worthy of unwanted attention.

They'd met half an hour ago, at a chicken wings and craft beer place that he was sure would be safe from Kirsty. Chloe had texted him two days after the funeral, asking how he was. From there on it had been almost constant flirting, until the easiest asking out of a girl Patrick had ever known. Perhaps having gone through marriage, kids and separation, the stakes of sending a message to suggest a drink were so low they were unworthy of any panic or over-analysis.

His main worry was still Suzanne. It had been a few months. Was that enough, he asked himself? Was he over her?

Well, clearly not. The over bit would take much longer. But something inside him said that he was okay to move on. Maybe if he'd been the one who had the affair and walked out on his spouse and child he might feel differently. As it was, he felt justified and happier than he'd been in a while.

'Come on,' Chloe said. 'I think there are more interesting things we can talk about than what happened to Donna Carter.'

'I don't think so. Stealing money from a bookie's of all places.'

'Patrick,' she said, a note of playful warning in her voice.

As with the other night at the wake, Chloe barely stopped joking and taking the piss, as well as smiling and laughing. She was fun company. He felt mildly guilty that she'd obviously made more effort than him, wearing tight dark-blue jeans, red high heels and a loose black shirt. Her hair was straightened too, falling either side of her pretty, happy face. Whereas he was in a pair of leather boots, jeans and a chunky lumberjack shirt with fur lining around the collar. At least he'd removed his beanie before she arrived and sorted his hair out in the toilet mirror.

'I want to know more about this trip. It sounds . . .'

'Mad?' he offered, as she searched for the right word.

'No. I mean, I've heard of people scattering ashes in special places. But it's usually a golf course or a beach or something.'

'I mean, we are doing it on a beach. Just not that local.'

'Why there? Why not Hove or something?'

'Fond memories apparently. Dad and Mum went there a few years ago for a whisky festival.'

'Sounds thrilling.'

'For him it was. Not so much for her. Anyway, the real reason he chose the Hebrides was because he wants us all stuck in a van together for days on end. I reckon that being so close would force us to make amends. Get back to being a family again and all that. A plan which is now firmly in the bin, thanks to Jessica,' he said, looking at his phone again.

'Do you think the two of them would?'

'What? Make up? Either that or they'd tear each other's head off,' he said. 'I don't know. They always got on, but there was usually a bit of tension. I suppose Mum dying just brought it all out.'

'And you? Do you get on with them?'

Patrick was reluctant to talk about this. To some people, his role in the falling out of the Cadogan children made him an innocent bystander. To others it made him complicit and worse than the other two.

'Ish,' he said. 'We don't really talk anymore. I mean, we're civil. But they both think I backed the other one. So I'm sort of playing both sides off against the middle. My own fault, really. I never speak out until it's too late.'

'Who did you back? And tell the truth.'

'Dunno. I sort of saw Jess's point. The mortgage on that house was ridiculous and Dad would just be rattling around on his own. But when Kirsty got upset I saw that, too. Family home and all. I didn't want to get rid of it either. But you never do, right?'

Chloe seemed to think for a moment. He worried she was judging him, thinking that with a little more gumption and honesty, he could have prevented the whole thing in the first place.

'There comes a time, Patrick,' she said, finally. 'When my dad died we had to sell the house we grew up in. Mum couldn't manage the garden by herself.'

'I know,' he said. 'We're dealing with it now though. There's been viewings this week.'

'Still. It's sad your other sister won't go. Even if they did end up killing each other it's your dad's last wish.'

'Bit of a devious one, don't you think? One of those when no one wants to do it but you can't say no.'

'Yeah. But he deserves it. You said yourself. Especially after what happened with—'

'Yep,' Patrick said, firmly. He was determined that tonight of all nights they would not open that box. Undoubtedly he and Kirsty would discuss it over the coming days, but until then, he was determined to keep a lid on it. 'Another?' he said, nodding to her now empty glass.

'Sure,' she said with a smile.

'Same again?'

'Please.'

Patrick picked up their glasses and got up from the table.

'Lovely,' he said. 'And when I get back, no family stuff. Deal?'

'Deal,' Chloe said.

Patrick went to the bar, relieved to have avoided talking about the one thing that people remembered his family for. The thing that was partly the reason he'd been so happy to spend the last few years living anywhere but Brighton or Hove. And why he was nervous about the prospect of returning when the trip was over.

CHAPTER FOUR

Brighton, Sussex

Patrick

The banging on the door woke him just before six in the morning. It was urgent and furious, as though someone was trying to warn them of a fire sweeping down the corridor. He checked his phone and waited for Kirsty to open up for whoever it was.

Really, he could do with another hour or two of sleep. He was due to do the first stint of driving that morning – three hours, if they'd planned it right, would take them as far as Nottingham, where they could have lunch at a service station and swap over.

He hadn't managed to drift off until past one; Kirsty's couch was uncomfortable and he couldn't stop worrying about leaving Maggie with Stu and Sarah for the next few days. She had only started sleeping well at home very recently, getting over the fact that whenever she called for 'Mum' Dad would appear. Patrick hoped that wouldn't all be set back again.

Besides, he hadn't left the bar with Chloe until midnight and was more than a little hungover.

More banging and no sign of Kirsty.

'Fucking hell,' he muttered groggily, in the same way he did when Maggie was a baby and woke up every thirty minutes with colic.

He dragged himself to the front door – flat feet slapping on the cold hardwood floor – making sure the front of his boxer shorts was closed, and his Gaslight Anthem t-shirt was covering his belly.

Just as he was about to open the door, the banging came again.

'I'm coming,' he said.

'Well hurry up about it,' the voice on the other side said.

'Jess?'

'Yes,' she said, as though it should be obvious. 'Now open the sodding door.'

Patrick took the chain lock off, pulled back the deadbolt Kirsty had installed after a break in down the hall, and opened the door to reveal his sister. She was standing there with a holdall and a handbag, wearing a beanie, puffer coat, skinny blue jeans and her customary Converse All Stars. He wasn't sure if it was cold enough for all that yet.

'At bloody last.'

Jessica hurried inside, dumping her bags on the couch where he had been sleeping.

'What are you doing here?'

'I've come to see you off, Patrick. What do you think?'

'I don't know. The last time I saw you was when you just "nipped to the loo".'

'Well if it's not obvious,' she said. 'I've changed my mind.'

It took a moment to register with Patrick. 'You're coming?' he said.

'Against my will.'

'What—'

'Dan made me. He said I'd regret not doing it and I couldn't get the idea out of my head. So,' she said, taking off her coat and throwing it over one of Kirsty's tatty, reclaimed kitchen chairs. 'Here I am.'

'Right.'

'And look, I've had to cancel going on a holiday for this. Elspeth is *furious*. So I don't want any crap.'

Just then, the bedroom door opened and Livvy ran through the open-plan living area shouting 'Auntie Jess!'

Patrick watched Jessica shake off her haughty exterior to greet her niece more cheerfully. The argument that was about to bubble up between the two of them quickly dissipated.

'So you changed your mind then?' Kirsty said, appearing in the living room, shrouded in a big, fluffy bathrobe.

'I was just telling Patrick—'

'After we've done all the hard work. Clearing out that horrible van and setting it up for this stupid trip. So you can turn up half an hour before we're leaving like a bloody rock star.'

'Listen. I—'

'You what?' Kirsty snapped. 'Liv go back to your room. Just for five minutes.'

The girl did as she was told and her mother rounded on Jessica.

'This is so *fucking* typical of you, Jessica. It really bloody is.'

'What? You wanted me to come? And let me tell you, describing the van as "horrible" is not helping.'

'I did,' Kirsty said, apparently choosing to ignore that last remark about the van. 'When we first spoke about it.'

'And now?'

'And now . . .' she said. Patrick wondered what would come next. *You can fuck off back home, you can forget about it, you can drive all the way?*

'Well, I suppose you'll just have to, won't you?'

'Kirsty, I'm sorry but I really don't know what you're getting at.'

'It's always like this isn't it?' Kirsty said, yanking a china cup from her mug tree and practically slamming a tea bag into it. 'You have to be different. You have to have it your way.'

'I decided *to come.*'

'At the last minute. And I guarantee it's not because you actually want to do this, it's because you don't want to feel guilty.'

'I've already told you Dan put me up to it. And so what if it is?'

'Exactly! It's always got to be on your terms, your way.'

'Right,' Jessica said, picking up her bag. 'Well I can see where you're going with this. And if the next three days are just going to be full of arguments, then I'm going back home.'

'Fine,' Kirsty said.

Jessica headed for the door, then Patrick called, 'Stop! For fuck's sake. It doesn't matter why she's here. It's more important that she is.'

Silence for a few seconds, disturbed only by the eerie whirr of the hamster in his wheel.

'Not like you to take—'

'Don't finish that sentence,' Patrick said to Kirsty. 'And Jess, don't be ridiculous. You're coming.'

The three of them looked at each other. Patrick could feel they were already close to talking, or rather arguing, about what happened after their mother died. And the trip hadn't even started yet. The veneer of relative politeness they'd maintained before and after the funeral had been scraped away, allowing the scratches and dents that had defined the last few years to show through.

But even though they needed to confront it, this wasn't the time. And Patrick knew it would be a layered argument.

There was the issue of what should have been done with the family home when their dad was left widowed and alone. Under that their generally recognised, but unacknowledged, roles in the family would come up.

And beneath *that* was the big one. The thing that defined the Cadogan children.

'Listen. At some point, we can all talk. But I suggest we don't do it now or we'll never fucking get on the road,' he said, taking his most measured, non-confrontational voice. 'And I'm not asking you to hug and make up or anything. But for the next three hours at least, let's either stay nice, or not talk at all.'

Jessica and Kirsty nodded. The latter went to put the kettle on.

It was another two hours before he and Kirsty were ready. She had to pack the last few things she needed for the trip, then said a long goodbye to Livvy, who repeated her plea to join them, and cried after being told no.

While all that was going on, Patrick snuck downstairs on the pretence of checking over the van but really to FaceTime Maggie. It was strange seeing her there, waving at him from Stu's iPad, as Sarah wandered in and out of shot, busying herself in the immaculate, designer kitchen only a childless couple could have. He promised to call her every day, and made a mental note to tell his sisters that he and Suzanne had the kitchen done, should either of them notice the plush backdrop when he was talking to his daughter.

Then, he texted Chloe.

Patrick: Thanks for last night. Had a blast xx

When he returned to the flat, he was almost relieved to see his sisters both sitting on the small couch tapping away at their smartphones. At least they weren't arguing again.

'This is it then,' Patrick said cheerfully, picking up his bag, encouraging them off the couch. He felt like a divorced dad trying to summon some enthusiasm from his kids, as he took them away for a weekend without friends and technology. Which was depressingly close to the truth.

Kirsty was the first up. She pulled up the handle of her wheeled suitcase and gave Livvy one last hug and a kiss on top of her head. Jessica finished whatever she was typing on her phone then did the same, citing 'work' as she put her coat on. A warning shot to remind them both that she was a busy, important small business owner, unable to rely on colleagues and out of office notifications like the two of them.

He wondered if they were feeling the same as he was: slightly sick at the idea of spending days together, and apprehensive of what they might rake over in the process.

But he kept it to himself and led the way out of Kirsty's flat, leaving her friend Trina who had just turned up and was playing with Livvy to distract her. They came out onto the busy suburban Brighton street, and crossed the road to where The Adventurer was parked.

'Here she is then,' he said, dropping his bag to open the door.

'She?' Jessica said.

'Yeah. Sturdy vessels are always female aren't they? Boats and that.'

'I think camper vans are the exception, Patrick. They are almost certainly male. I can't imagine Mum would've been too impressed with this . . . thing.'

'They bought it together.'

'You really think that?' Jessica said, pushing past him to throw her bag onto the lower of the two bunks at the back. Kirsty took the top one while Patrick bundled his stuff into the snug Elvis quiff above the cab, then sat down in the driver's seat.

'Who's joining—'

'I will,' Kirsty said, taking the passenger seat. 'We're really doing it then,' she said.

'Looks like it,' Patrick said. He glanced behind him at Jessica, who seemed slightly tearful.

Just as he was about to turn the ignition on, Patrick's phone buzzed and he pulled it out of his breast pocket.

'Suzanne?' Kirsty said, noticing him smiling.

'No,' he replied, instantly regretting it. 'Stu,' he lied, turning the key and revving the engine once. They pulled out onto the road.

Crawley

Kirsty

Two hours later they had barely passed Crawley. Patrick had struggled to navigate the van out of Brighton, persistently getting lost but refusing to acknowledge that he could be in the city he grew up in.

'I'm going the quick way,' he told Kirsty angrily when she'd offered directions from the passenger seat.

'There isn't a quick way. It's down Ditchling Road, then left onto the dual carriageway. Remember, I do live here.' She used the same tone she took when complaining to the two of them about how rarely they visited their parents, or that she was the only one with any remaining connection to their home town. But Patrick had ignored her and instead trundled uncertainly down a narrow street, now lined on either side with attractive little shops selling candles, home furnishings and coffee.

'I wish you'd settle on a direction,' Jessica called from the back. 'I don't want to get car sick. Or van sick, or whatever.'

Kirsty turned to see her staring at her mobile phone and sipping from the huge, milky coffee she had insisted on buying approximately five minutes after they set off. She decided to keep her counsel on how each of these might trigger any car sickness.

Finally, after almost half an hour, they were away and into the stop start traffic that had lasted all the way from Brighton to where they were now stationary on a motorway.

Either side of the road was thick with trees bearing autumnal colours. They would have been pretty almost anywhere else, but on the outer edge of this depressing strip of grey tarmac they were nothing – just a border between pleasant fields and torpid traffic.

'Auspicious start,' Jessica said from the back. 'With a fair wind we might be near my house by the evening. Could stop in for dinner.'

Kirsty looked over at Patrick who didn't rise to it. A minute or so later, she started up again.

'I wonder if this is what Dad had in mind? His three kids sat in a stationary van outside Crawley. With his ashes in a cupboard.'

'He probably thought it'd be more fun than this,' Patrick said. 'Check that fishing box to see if he left car bingo or something in there.'

'Oh God,' Kirsty said. 'Remember all those drives to France and Cornwall? Stuck in traffic while Mum made us play games.'

'Spot the Eddie Stobart truck,' Patrick said.

'Yes!' Jessica said, with a laugh. 'What was the other one?'

'Car quiz,' Kirsty said, remembering the pop trivia game they would play on their drive to wherever their summer holiday was.

'I remember seeing some cars with TVs in the back seats,' Jessica said.

'That was the dream,' Patrick said. 'I remember other kids who flew to their summer holiday. I always think Dad considered that cheating. There had to be an element of suffering before you got anywhere otherwise you wouldn't appreciate it.'

'The problem with those car games,' Kirsty said, 'was they were all fifteen years old. So none of the things we were meant to be looking for were on the road anymore.'

'Like that version of Trivial Pursuit he used to bring out at

Christmas. You had to remember that there would be out-of-date references to Yugoslavia and America had a different number of states.'

'He knew the answers by heart,' Patrick said, and they all fell into the kind of contented chuckling only nostalgia could bring.

Kirsty smiled at the recollection of their holidays together as kids. Evenings that would end with Gerry taking out a deck of cards or stack of dominoes from his bag (those and a few CDs were generally the only things he'd pack, leaving the rest up to his wife). The family gathering round a small table in a cottage, tent or caravan to play sevens, old maid or a game their mother called Nonsense, which in time they realised was known colloquially as Shithead.

'We should play some of his old games,' she suggested. 'While we're together. Like old times. I've got a deck of cards with me.'

'I'll never remember the rules,' Jessica said. 'Dan never plays cards on holiday. And the kids are always too engrossed in their sodding iPads.'

'I do,' she said. 'I played with Dad every so often. Mainly sevens or crib. Though he was too good at that for me. He used to play every week with a bloke called Bulldog Bill.'

'Bulldog Bill?' Jessica asked.

'One of his pub friends. He had a bulldog apparently which died years ago, but people still call him that. He was at the funeral, fat bloke with NHS glasses.'

'I can't say I remember him. I always thought that Dad didn't . . . you know . . . have friends.'

'One or two. Not close, mind. Just acquaintances he saw when he went in. Other men whose wives had died or left them, mostly. They actually called one of them Married Pete because he was still married.'

'Inventive nicknames.'

Kirsty heard Patrick laugh at this. Of the three of them, he was closest to the pub culture of jokes, nicknames and games Gerry was so familiar with.

'I'm glad, though. Just so you know,' Jessica said.

'What? About Bulldog Bill?' Kirsty said. 'I mean, he wasn't a great friend—'

'No. I mean that you still played cards with Dad. Grateful, I suppose, is more like it.'

Kirsty bristled at this. The notion that her relationship with her dad was in any way charitable, rather than happy, was almost offensive.

'You don't need to be grateful,' she said, resisting the argument that could break out. 'I actually enjoyed it.'

'Oh. I know. Sorry. You know what I meant though, don't you?'

Kirsty nodded, even though she really didn't. Better to avoid the conflict, she thought, as the van inched forward in the traffic. They were barely on their way yet.

Kirsty was desperate to get going properly, to feel this journey, however misguided and desperate, was actually underway. They were still close enough from home for a petty squabble to become an argument that could stop the entire trip. She wasn't sure which would be more likely to break first – the enforced friendliness between them, or the van.

She listened to Patrick recall one of Jessica's ex-boyfriends who used to live near where they were stuck.

'Remember when you told us he was into the occult and Dad called him Creepy Crawley?'

'Oh shit yes!' she said. 'Matt. Creepy Crawley! He looked like Robert Smith from The Cure, but if he'd put on two stone and had eczema.'

They laughed again, to Kirsty's relief. For now, she thought, it was okay.

Eventually, after another half an hour of inching forward and the occasional twenty metre lurch, The Adventurer rolled past the cause of the delay. It was another camper van, the front of which was blackened after what Kirsty assumed must have been an engine blow out and fire.

Warwick Motorway Services

Patrick

'Right, pit stop,' Patrick called from the driver's seat. He pulled off the motorway and followed the looping slip road in a wide circle, worrying this might cause the van to tip over. He parked at the back of the car park, where the van could take up almost three spaces.

Patrick had been in the driver's seat for almost four hours, most of which was spent alongside Kirsty who he'd forgotten had an annoying habit of pointing out potential risks as they went by. 'Watch him', 'careful there', 'God knows what he's up to'. He was never sure whether 'he' was referring to the driver, or the car as an entity.

He, meanwhile, had passed the last forty-five minutes wondering what he might get to eat. For whatever reason, all dietary awareness went out the window when he was on a long journey and he was content to snack and gorge as much as he could. He'd already been through two bags of Frazzles, half a bag of Percy Pigs and one of Kirsty's flapjacks, which he was dismayed to learn were sweetened with honey rather than golden syrup.

'How long do you reckon? Fifteen minutes?' he asked, as they trudged down to the glass-fronted service station, outside of which were four picnic benches. He wondered if anyone except smokers ever used the al fresco dining areas of service stations.

'Long enough for a coffee and a trip to the loo,' Kirsty said.

'Fine. I might call Dan. Check they're all okay.'

'Where'd you say they went again?'

'Majorca.'

'Nice,' Patrick said.

'Don't,' she said, stopping for a second to stretch out her legs. 'I still can't believe I'm ... wherever we are, instead of by a pool.'

'Warwick.'

'God,' she said dismissively, as the three of them went inside.

Since they had escaped the traffic near Brighton, the journey had been fine. Patrick had spent his time trying to spot football stadiums from the motorway, as he did as a child. While Kirsty took advantage of the newish Bluetooth radio their dad had installed to play a series of podcasts only she was interested in. Jessica slept, complained, applied hand cream and sent emails to her employees at the florist on a loop.

He had tried to keep the mood light, joking that he would 'treat' the two of them to the M6 toll road, and suggesting they listen to the mid-morning radio pop quiz and compare scores. But, in the manner of their old family trips, after a couple of hundred miles everyone was bored and he had lapsed into playing the role of Gerry Cadogan, trying to manufacture enthusiasm for a trip not everyone was into.

The journey so far had included two breaks – one in Surrey, which was depressingly close to home for a first stop and highlighted their lack of progress; and now this one, near Coventry. He had hoped to be further along by this point.

'How long before we call it a day?' he asked, as they made their way back to the van, carrying coffees, overpriced bags of sweets and, in Patrick's case, a prawn sandwich. He'd decided to discipline himself, although he was also eyeing up the Greggs concession next to the car park.

'There's a campsite just off the motorway in the Forest of Bowland,' Kirsty said. 'Probably another three or so hours.'

'I have literally never heard of the Forest of Bowland,' Jessica said.

'It's nice. I went hiking there with David,' replied Kirsty, refer-ring to the most serious boyfriend she'd had since Livvy was born. Although that seriousness may well have only been in her mind, as he broke it off to go travelling around South America after she suggested moving in together.

'Can we not just, sort of, park up in a services?' Patrick offered. Jessica looked like she'd been slapped. 'What?' he said.

'It's enough that we've got to sleep in a shitting van, Patrick. I am not doing so in a service station. Unless you're happy to pay for me to get a hotel room.'

'Just an idea,' he said, climbing into the passenger seat for Kirsty to take over the driving.

'A bad one,' Jessica said.

'Right. Ready are we?' Kirsty said, beginning her first stint of the trip.

Somewhere near Stoke

Kirsty

An hour's further driving on the M6 was enough to remind Kirsty how much she hated motorways. Everything was drab and boring. Even the shrubbery and fields that stretched off to the sides seemed to take on a strange greyness.

Evening was beginning to draw in, darkening the white, cloudy sky like black ink dropped into clear water. The luminous signs on bridges above the motorway warned her about closed junctions, and estimated times to destinations, taking into account distance and traffic. Behind her in the van Jessica was talking about her business, her family, her life. Every topic they got onto was always turned back to fit her experience or opinion.

'Well of course the great problem about living in New York...' she told Patrick at one point, as he sat there listening attentively. They'd been talking about his living in Dublin, but she had diverted the conversation to New York because her friend Sandra had just moved there. 'Is the space, isn't it? I mean, where do you go if you want to have more than one kid? Impossible. My friend Andrea did it for a year. She works in advertising and was on secondment. They left when she got pregnant for the second time. Said she simply couldn't live with another year of taking a buggy up and down in a lift just to get home.'

Patrick, for his part, nodded along, seemingly content to let her speak and never offer a viewpoint. Nonetheless the conversation danced and bounced around topics and issues. They spoke to each other like a client would to a hairdresser or taxi driver. There was no familiarity, understanding or knowing between them. No sense there was a history that united them, and a recent past that had divided them.

As the traffic slowed and the lit signs on a bridge displayed 40 in orange circles, Kirsty decided to break the pretence.

'Do you think we should talk about why we're here?' she called back into the van.

'Huh?' Patrick said, looking at his phone suddenly.

'I said, do you think we should talk. You know, about why we're doing this,' she said, louder this time, above the noise of the engine. 'About what Dad wanted.'

The silence that met her seemed to imply that Kirsty had suggested they abandon their children for a life on the road, rather than tackling why they were here in the first place.

'Well?' she prompted. 'We'll have to some time. Can't keep putting it off.'

'Why?' Jessica said. 'I mean, it's obvious isn't it? He said in that letter, he wants us to be friends again. And from where I'm standing we're doing just fine. Everyone is being polite.'

'Yes but that's just it. Polite. We're not actually talking about anything. It's all chit chat. It's all been chit chat since he died.'

'Well what do you want? If you want honesty, I'll give you honesty.'

'Jess—' she said, but it was no use.

'You took over at Dad's when we were clearing up. Made me feel like a spare part. And his only contribution,' she said, pointing to Patrick, 'was to flirt with the barmaid at Dad's funeral. Which, by the way, I think is disgusting. Just because your wife couldn't—'

'JESS!' Kirsty yelled. 'I don't want bloody honesty about the last week and a half. I want us to talk about what's happened to us.'

'So what. We have to go back over everything from when Mum died?' Jessica said, as Kirsty slowed the van down to a stop in the heavy traffic. A snake-like trail of red brake lights stretched out ahead of them. 'Because I don't think it'll do much good, will it? We disagreed then and, probably, will now.'

'You still think it was the right thing, then? To try and get Dad to sell?' Kirsty said. 'You know he was very happy there for years after Mum died.'

'I think it was the right thing at the time, yes. Anyway happy is stretching it a bit.'

'Not really. I saw a lot of him, remember?'

'Yes, Kirsty. We all know you saw Dad the most, you don't have to tell us. But if I can just remind you that I live two hours away and Patrick lives in another country.'

'Jess!' Kirsty said, firmly.

'What? By the way, the traffic's moving.'

Kirsty turned back to face the front, drove forward a hundred metres or so and came to a stop again.

'I want us to get past this. It's what Dad wanted.'

'Well I'm not stopping you,' Jessica said. 'But I don't know where this notion that things can just go back to how they were years ago comes from. Life changes, doesn't it?' she said. 'There's nothing to say we wouldn't have just ... drifted apart anyway. We used to be close, now we're less so. That happens in life. I have friends I barely even see these days.'

Kirsty said nothing to this. She had thought the same herself, barring the friends bit. Living in the same place she grew up meant that she found it hard to walk down the street without seeing someone she knew – whether she wanted to or not.

But she felt that it was only right they should at least *try* to do what Gerry had asked. Reconnect, rediscover and all that.

'I'm just sorry about the way it happened, I suppose. For Dad more than anything. He could never make sense of it.'

'Because he never accepted that what we went through made it hard for us to stay as we were. That little family unit.'

'You could just say that you're sorry too.'

Jessica waited a moment. Kirsty knew it was a wrench for her to admit fault, even when it was shared. But finally she muttered a quiet, 'Fine, yes. I am. You know I am.'

'Thank you.'

'But that doesn't mean everything just goes back, does it? Things are different now. You have your life. As I said, I've built mine somewhere new. And Patrick lives—'

'I don't,' he said. The traffic began to move but Kirsty didn't follow and instead turned to look at her brother. He'd been mostly silent so far, staring out of the window or nodding along to Jessica. Always keen to be one step removed from the family politics, non-intervention making for an easier life. 'I don't live there any more.'

Patrick

He wasn't at all sure why he said it. Perhaps it was because he could see where the conversation was going. And he really couldn't cope with an argument about their mother's death and what came after it while stuck in a van with nowhere to go. In truth, he'd hoped he might be able to get all the way up to Scotland and back without having to admit what was happening in his personal life.

'What do you mean? You've moved home?' Jessica said. 'Well, why on earth didn't you say, Patrick?'

'I said I don't live there any more.'

He watched his sister's face fall. 'Oh Jesus, Patrick. You've left? I knew there was something. I *knew* it. You can be so—'

'I didn't leave her, Jess. For fuck's sake. She left me.'

The change in Jessica's expression was small but telling. The disappointment she had felt in her brother's abandonment of his family was replaced not with anger, but a desire for detail and gossip. He'd rarely seen anyone so clearly desperate to know how things had gone pear-shaped for someone else.

'When were you going to tell us?'

'I don't know. Soon, I expect.'

'So you're what? Separated? Divorced?'

'Jess,' Kirsty said, mediating. 'Give him a minute.'

'No. It's fine,' Patrick said, although it was anything but. This was only the second time he'd had to explain the circumstances of his marriage break down, after telling Stu and Sarah, and he hadn't quite got the one-minute pitch down.

'I might just . . .' he said, unbuckling his belt to go to the small fridge and take out a beer. 'Anyone else?'

Jessica shook her head. Kirsty didn't respond.

'We're done. Suzanne and I,' he said, opening a bottle of Fullers ESB and taking a long drag. 'She left a month or so before Dad died. I would've come. For the clear out, y'know. But I didn't know what to say.'

'Jesus,' Jessica said, exasperated.

'*Jess.*' Kirsty said.

'It's fine.'

'It's not.'

'*Jessica!*'

Patrick took another swig, while the traffic moved forward again. It was getting dark outside. Light rain fell on the windscreen, droplets lit by the tail lamps ahead of them.

'She met someone new. Well, ish.'

'You know him?'

'Not really. He was a consultant at the company where she worked. Internet and websites and all that,' he said, not really understanding 'digital architecture' as Suzanne called it. 'He's some tit who calls himself a digital nomad. His name's John, but he calls himself Park.'

'Oh for God's sake,' Jessica scoffed, as Patrick knew she would. His sister thought herself the picture of liberalism and accepting of all lifestyles. But that often changed when she was presented with something she hadn't experienced – an infrequent occurrence where she lived. 'How does he even make any money?'

'He seems quite good at that bit. According to her he's a multi-millionaire. He invented some app, cloud thing. I don't know how it works. But someone bought it off him and he's set for life.'

'Well it doesn't sound like a real job.'

'I've heard of that,' Kirsty, much more benign and inviting, said. 'My friend Mabel was dating one. A nomad.'

'And what? He just nomaded off did he?'

'*She* moved on. Went to Liverpool or somewhere.'

'So that's it then?' Jessica said, now ignoring Kirsty. 'Your wife is to become a digital nomad?'

Patrick nodded. He still wasn't able to reconcile the idea of Suzanne abandoning their family in favour of moving from one short term let to another across America and beyond. While the whole thing would be bankrolled by a man who made his money in a way that was still baffling to Patrick.

'Poor Maggie. What a life. Surely you're going to fight it?'

'Well, that's the other thing,' he said, taking a sip of his beer. 'Maggie isn't going with her. She's staying with me. Full time, y'know?' he said, looking straight past Jessica, out the front of the van to the snaking red lights. 'So I'm a single parent.'

For a moment, it looked like Jessica was about to jump up and hug him – as though his wife relinquishing custody of his daughter was something to celebrate. He tempered the news.

'An unemployed single parent. Who sleeps on his friend Stu's couch. I'm on the scrapheap,' he said. 'Several scrapheaps.'

'So really, it's anything but fine,' Kirsty said.

'Hmm.'

Patrick sipped his beer again. Jessica, apparently now anxious about his predicament, went to the fridge and took one out for herself. Or maybe she was sympathy drinking.

'Well you can't stay living on Stu's couch, Patrick. It must be murder on your back.'

'It's not too bad,' he said, wondering why Jessica's first concern in all of this was his back. Then he realised it was probably related to something happening in her own life and so took on prime importance. 'They have a big couch. One of those corner ones.'

'Oh yes. Very nice. We were thinking of getting one of them,' she said. 'Anyway, you can come and live with us. We've got the room in the loft. And the kids would like it.'

Patrick almost spat his beer out.

'What?'

'You can't be serious, Jessica? Live in your house?'

'Just for a bit. Until you're right again.'

'Literally no chance. No offence Jessica, but we are just about holding it together on this trip. I'd give it maybe a week before one of us killed the other.'

'Well. The offer's there.'

'Excuse me,' Kirsty said from the front. 'What about Maggie seeing her mum? If she's all the way in . . . wherever it is. And you're here.'

'She will,' Patrick said.

He was hesitant about relaying what Suzanne had suggested. For some reason he worried they'd laugh at her or think she'd gone mad. Despite everything she had done – the affair, the move, the complete reframing of his life – he felt protective of her. Those last dregs of love, the silt at the bottom of the barrel, were still there.

If only love could die away at the very moment the relationship did, he thought. Why couldn't this tech genius she'd shacked up with invent something for that?

'How though? You can't just stick Maggie on a plane and hope she turns up where Suzanne is.'

'She has an idea,' he said quietly. 'She thinks she can keep in touch by video link, see her that way.'

'Oh come on now,' Jessica said, dialling her level of incredulity up a bit.

'Park or John or whatever has told her that parenting by video link is the next big thing. Apparently the technology is so good it'll be like she's in the room.'

'Sorry,' Kirsty said. 'She's basically going to FaceTime Maggie once a week and that's it?'

Patrick waited a second. There it was again – the instinct to protect the reputation and motherhood of his ex-wife. For a second he thought about reiterating the pitch she'd given him: the high quality video links she could get, the advent of hologram technology, the things Park was working on that she'd be able to use to speak to her daughter. And how everyone in Silicon Valley would soon be parenting this way, from the office rather than the nursery.

But really, that was nowhere near the truth. The reality was what he had told Suzanne over their kitchen table in Ballsbridge: *'You're abandoning your daughter to fuck some bloke in a load of Airbnbs. Don't fucking sugarcoat it, Suzanne. That's what's happening here.'*

'That's it,' he said, echoing Kirsty and remembering his rare show of temper that day when she announced her intention to leave. It was one of maybe three or four times in his life when he had allowed his true thoughts to override his innate fear of confrontation.

At first, he'd told her to take her time, willing to forgive the affair as a mistake. Patrick had also searched himself for blame. Perhaps he had been distracted with his dad's illness, and work and football, failing to pay her and Maggie sufficient attention. Maybe moving the two of them from London to Dublin was a mistake, despite Suzanne's enthusiasm for the job she'd been offered at a tech firm. She'd even talked about getting him an Irish passport, to bypass the Europe-wide passport queues the Brits might face after Brexit.

'What did I do?' he had asked her, his face puce with anger and beard growing damp with sweat and tears. 'If it's something I did you have to tell me.'

'It's nothing you did,' Suzanne kept reassuring him. From the moment he knew the full truth about her affair, she'd taken a half understanding, half irritated tone in response to his heartache. 'There doesn't have to be fault here, Patrick. It could just be that our journey has ended.'

This was the kind of thing she had started coming out with. Cod philosophy and buzzwords that littered blogs and vlogs from the people Park had told her about, who described themselves as Evangelists or Connectors. Patrick himself had met Park several times at drinks things and dinners. He was employed as a consultant, sallying in twice or three times a month to deliver a lunchtime lecture, describing himself as a Digital Visionary, rather than Snake Oil Salesman, as Patrick termed him. He did the same for three or four other companies, fully exploiting the emerging market for bullshit merchants the Dublin tech boom had created.

'Jesus Christ,' Patrick had said, stunned by the journey nonsense. 'You almost sound relieved that I've found out.'

'Maybe,' Suzanne said, placing her hand on top of his in a way that seemed patronising rather than apologetic. 'It's better this way. Now we can both continue with our lives.'

'And what would you have done had I never found out, huh? Just carried on screwing that tit?'

'There were plans in place. In a month or so we would have told you.'

'Plans?'

'We are going to California. Then maybe New Mexico and after that who knows. We don't like to schedule our lives too far ahead. And there are plenty of opportunities for Park around the world.'

'Fucking hell,' he said, still in disbelief.

'Patrick,' she said, locking eyes with him. As she did, he saw a woman he didn't know anymore. 'I want us both to be happy.'

'I *am* happy, Suzanne.'

'Well,' she said, looking away. 'That's unfortunate.'

At this, Patrick got up, left the house and went to the nearest pub – a place called Leary's that he had never been to before and quickly understood why. Two days later, Park picked Suzanne up in a taxi and she left for the airport.

*

'I'm just stunned, Patrick,' Jessica said. 'Stunned. Her ambivalence towards her daughter.'

'She might not be ambivalent,' Kirsty said, apparently keen to soften one of the worst things someone could say about a parent.

'That's the thing. She genuinely believes all this shit. You should hear some of these types.'

Patrick opened another beer. He had wanted to wait to tell them about all this. Firstly because he didn't really know how, but also because he hated the pity.

Sarah had lavished it on him ever since he turned up at hers and Stu's. The punch-jab combo of his marriage breaking down and his dad dying sparked her sympathies. Dinners had been sullied by tentative suggestions of therapy or counselling to help him accept or grieve or whatever it was a life coach might tell him to do. But Patrick was hesitant to admit that what he overwhelmingly felt was numbness. He had cried at both these recent, terrible life events. But now, in the midst of the aftershock, he had no clue how he would move on or what shape his life might take in the next year.

'And you had no idea?' Kirsty said. 'Until she told you?'

This, oddly, was the part of the story he was dreading telling the most. The part which made everyone involved look absurd and stupid.

'Sort of.'

'You didn't catch them, did you?' Jessica asked, clearly horrified and fascinated by the notion that he might have. 'I couldn't imagine.'

'Not as such. It was weird, really. The way it came about. Stupid, y'know?'

'You don't have to tell us,' Kirsty said, diplomatically.

'Unless it would help?' Jessica said.

'I'll tell you,' Patrick said. 'But you have to promise... *promise*, not to laugh.'

'Promise,' Jessica said.

'Fine,' Patrick said, casting his mind back a couple of months, to when he'd borrowed Suzanne's laptop to email a client back in England. 'Basically, I was using her laptop for some emails and stuff. And she'd left—'

'Emails?' Jessica interjected. 'So many times it's the emails. My friend Mary—'

'*Jessica*,' Kirsty hissed. The traffic had slowed to a halt again and she turned round to look at the two of them.

'No. Not emails,' Patrick said. This part was like the excruciating moment just before tearing off a plaster. 'Her FitBit.'

The two of them let the word settle. Jessica looked at her own wrist – at the ever-present rubberised band.

'No,' she said, shocked in a gossipy way. As though she'd been told that the husband of a friend she didn't like had been caught using an escort service.

Patrick nodded. 'She left the page with all her data open. Every Tuesday and Thursday at six-ish there was a massive spike in her heart rate. I knew she didn't run or go to the gym those days. So—'

'What? You just confronted her with it?'

'No,' he said, as if that was even close to the maddest thing about the absurd way his marriage broke down. 'She told me she had late meetings those days. Calls with people in the US and all that. So I went to her office at half five. Saw her come out and get into his car.'

'Did you follow them?'

'Didn't have to. She saw me,' he said, thinking back to the moment he was noticed, half hidden by a shrub in the courtyard of the building opposite her office. 'She admitted it right away.'

'She didn't deny it at all?'

Patrick shook his head. 'To be honest, she seemed kind of relieved. Like she was hoping to be found out but didn't want to have to tell me herself. That was pretty much the end, right there.'

He omitted little details. Such as how their fierce argument outside her lobby had been interrupted by a colleague of hers he vaguely knew coming out to say hello, and he had broken character to cheerfully return the greeting. And how Park had suggested they go for a coffee somewhere to find 'a resolution that worked for everyone'. This was as close as Patrick had ever come to punching someone.

But that was more or less the rub of it. He knew he could probably sell the story to the papers if he wanted to. The fool who discovers his marriage is over because of a fitness tracker. Fortunately money wasn't that tight yet.

'Oh Patrick,' Jessica said, as a long beep sounded behind them and Kirsty pulled away. 'I am sorry.'

He noticed the conflict in her face. Pity and laughter.

'You can laugh if you want to,' he said. 'I mean, it is genuinely ridiculous.'

And she did. A few chuckles at first, before Patrick joined in and the two of them spent the next few minutes laughing with each other, as if nothing between them had changed from what it was ten years ago.

The Forest of Bowland

Jessica

Three and a half hours later, they were approaching the campsite, set in The Forest of Bowland. The route off the motorway had taken them down a single-track road bordered by dry stone walls and hedges. The fields either side of them were busy with sheep, huddled together in tight clusters against the wind and weather. Kirsty had slammed on the brakes several times, having thought she'd seen rabbits, pheasants or deer about to lurch out under their wheels. Of the three of them, it would be typical that the only vegetarian killed an animal with the van.

Away in the distance Jessica could make out the silhouette of the hills, rolling away towards Yorkshire, set against the dark purple and blue of the night sky. This was deeper countryside than the National Trust parkland near where she lived. There were no signposted walks here, and certainly not a café selling nice hot chocolates and cakes to merry walkers. The rurality was only interrupted by the occasional farm house with a satellite dish strapped to the side of it and wheelie bins out the front.

Jessica fell forwards as Kirsty braked suddenly again.

'What the hell was that?' she said.

'Our turn, I think,' Kirsty said. 'I just missed it.'

'What's this place called again? Tea and Biscuits or something?'

'Something to do with cake,' Kirsty said, with all the patience of someone who'd been driving their family across the country all day.

She put the van into reverse, rolling backwards until they were level with a narrow, uphill road. It looked seldom used, with moss growing down the middle. Kirsty started driving up, the van struggling against the incline. Jessica looked out the window at the little brook which ran down beside the road, all rocks and crystalline water.

'Finally,' Patrick said, as they arrived at a large wooden gate, where a weathered sign read *Cakes and Ale: a family campsite*, as if it were a warning. Kirsty leaned out of the window and pushed a buzzer. An old man wearing a Barbour jacket and wellington boots appeared, accompanied by a sheepdog who looked almost the same age.

He whacked the bonnet of the van with a wooden stick, not seeming to care whether he might dent or scratch it. Jessica wondered how many other cars he'd done the same to, while their owners watched in confused shock. He then directed them to a patch of grass bordered by a hedgerow.

'Don't get many this time of year,' he said, through the driver's window, when Kirsty had parked the van.

'I suppose not.'

'Just you and that lot,' he said, pointing to three large tents in the middle of the field. 'Ramblers.'

The campsite was more or less just a field, interrupted by a few wooden poles which provided electricity for caravans, and the old man's cottage and garden. This was separated from the campsite by a privet fence no higher than two foot. Next to it was a small kiosk and a grim-looking shower block.

'Very good.'

'Anyway. Your electricity's here,' he said, whacking one of the wooden poles with his stick. 'It's free. But don't take the piss. There's a shop in the office. Not much there. So don't go looking for a hot meal.'

Kirsty politely thanked the man, who ignored her and walked away, throwing a muddied and bitten tennis ball for his dog to chase. Keen not to get into a conversation with a man she had absolutely nothing in common with, Jessica waited until he and the dog were long gone before climbing down the steps and out of the van.

'Lovely isn't it?' Kirsty said.

'I don't know yet. It's completely dark.'

'I mean the smell. Country air.'

'I get that quite a lot,' Jessica said. 'Very green where we are.'

Kirsty joined Patrick back in the van. Jessica could hear her pulling saucepans out of the cupboard above the sink, and putting the kettle on to boil. They were having stuffed pasta and pesto she'd bought from the services. Although Wednesdays were strictly speaking carb-free nights for the Lachlans, Jessica was willing to make an exception given the circumstances, and might not even mention it.

Jessica walked into the middle of the field, staring at her phone in the hope that she might see something other than 'No service' in the top left-hand corner. Her provider promised ninety-nine per cent coverage across the UK. Just her luck to find herself in the one per cent with bugger all. She put it away in her back pocket and looked up at the sky, as the cheerful chatter of the ramblers playing games drifted over.

Today had been okay. Ish.

There had been moments of nostalgia and remembrance. Before Patrick's big revelation. Since then he'd been quiet and reserved – the old 'do nothing, say nothing, make no fuss' boy re-emerging after a brief flash of honesty.

Privately, Jessica was pleased she was on the trip. Dan was right. She was sure everything that lay beneath their recent history would come up at some point. They were here to reconcile and recover, after all. But Jessica couldn't decide what position she'd take when it did. For all the hurt the aftermath of their mother's death had caused, she wasn't sure she would have done anything differently.

Jessica still had the email Kirsty had sent her, back when her sister found out that she and Dan were making plans to sell their family home.

They had convinced Gerry it was the right thing to do and even found him a nice little flat to move into. Ganton Villas was too big for an old man on his own, and too stuffed full of bad memories to see out his remaining years. Besides, there was a large mortgage on the place, after the bank had helped bail out his business in 2009.

The whole argument was so fresh in her mind, as though it had happened last week rather than three years ago; one of those things that never fades no matter how many years pass.

Kirsty had been seething with anger when they met later in the kitchen of Ganton Villas. An emergency family meeting had been called – odd because they had never had a normal family meeting before, and also because it took five days for the emergency to be acted upon.

'How fucking dare you, Jessica?' Kirsty had screamed. 'It's so fucking manipulative. While he's still *grieving*.'

'The place is mortgaged up to the hilt!'

'Yes. And we know why. Do not bring that into it, Jessica. Do not.'

'We're the guarantors,' she said, drawing Kirsty's attention to the fact she and Dan had agreed to back the remortgaging of the house after Cadogan Family Builders almost went bust. The bank had been unwilling to lend a couple of her parents' age a significant amount of money without backing from people who'd be in work for the next twenty years at least. 'And I think that gives us some say in what should happen.'

'More say than me? More say than Patrick?' Kirsty had asked, verging on the hysterical. 'More say than Dad?'

Jessica had paused for a moment, looked at Dan, then said, 'Yes. If you must know.'

That was probably the moment which did it. For a second, she'd thought Kirsty was going to hurl a mug of hot tea at her.

From there came the accusations that she and Dan were trying to force through the sale of the house so they could use a chunk of the money to pay off their own mortgage. Which wasn't strictly untrue, though did slightly misrepresent their intentions.

Patrick, who'd joined the emergency family conference by Skype, mostly stayed out of it, as usual. Although he found himself on the sharp end of Kirsty's anger when she discovered he'd known about Jessica's plan and thought it 'more or less a good idea.' (He later fell out with Jessica too, when he finally spoke up to say he felt he'd been used as a patsy.)

'I'm not sure why you think this is so calculated,' Jessica had said. 'It's just common sense. Why would he want to rattle around in this big old house?'

'Expensive old house,' Kirsty intervened.

'That's not really the point.'

'It's our family home, Jessica. What we do with it should be a family decision.'

'And I'm asking why he would want to live here still?'

'Because it's my house,' Gerry had intervened from where he was sitting – mostly ignored – in the corner. 'I bloody built half of it. It was a wreck before your mum and I got here,' he said. 'I didn't raise you lot to think of property and money. I raised you to value hard work. Graft.'

He stood up, a little uncertain on legs that had spent the better part of the last month lazing in front of the television.

'Now, I don't know what I want. But if it's causing this kind of grief, you can all forget it. All of you.'

With that, Gerry left for the pub. Patrick made an excuse about his wife needing help with the baby and hung up. Jessica and Dan walked out without much of a goodbye and Kirsty stayed to clear up the kitchen.

No member of the Cadogan family spoke to one another for at least a week after that argument. Each of them felt betrayed in their own way: Kirsty for being kept out of a big decision; Patrick for thinking that Jessica had used him to get a majority over Kirsty; Jessica herself for realising that her family were holding onto the house for sentimental rather than practical reasons. There were few things she hated more than needless sentimentality.

That evening was the root cause of them being here today. A falling out that was never repaired. But it was a split built on years of deeper pain engendered by a member of their family who left without explanation or trace.

*

Just then Jessica felt the buzz of her phone. She pulled it out to check it, hoping for a message from Dan or one of the kids. But it was only a notification about her florist having a new Instagram follower.

She went back to the van, where Kirsty was sitting by the table in her fleece top, legs covered by a blanket, sipping from a plastic cup full of red wine. Patrick had gone to the bathroom block to shower, not wanting to venture out in what would inevitably be a freezing cold morning tomorrow.

'Pour me one, would you?' Jessica said.

For a moment, they both drank in silence, looking out of the window at the black night. Stars had appeared – far more than she was used to seeing at home. There the light pollution of nearby urbanity served as a reminder that they were not wholly in the countryside, but set between comfortable little market towns filled with good restaurants, cafés and branches of Waitrose. Out here it was very different. The sky was lit with so many beads of white that it was impossible to decipher the constellations she liked to show Max and Elspeth sometimes.

'Poor Patrick,' Kirsty said, finally.

'I know. I was just thinking the same,' Jessica said, which was a lie. She was thinking about home, her kids, her business, her husband, her cancelled holiday, the crappy phone reception that stopped her from getting through to them. 'I still can't believe it took him so long to admit it. It's not as if we're going to judge *him*, is it?'

'Can't you?' Kirsty said. She seemed surprised. 'Jess, that's the whole reason we're here. Ten years ago we might have been the first people he told about it. Not now. The fact that he literally couldn't bring himself to say anything until we were stuck together in a confined space says a lot.'

Jessica sighed with frustration.

'What?'

'Well we can say ten years ago this and ten years ago that all we want. I just think it's odd. He always bottles things up.'

'And I'm saying this is why Dad requested we do this together. He wanted us to go back to what we were before... all that.'

'And you know that, do you? I mean, his note wasn't exactly specific.'

'Fine. I'm inferring it,' Kirsty said, testily. 'It's a fair assumption though, isn't it?'

Jessica waited a moment before she spoke, wondering if the thing she wanted to say might spark something.

'And do you think it's actually possible?'

Before Kirsty could answer, the door opened and Patrick climbed back into the van, wearing jogging bottoms, Adidas sliders and a yellow Watford Football Club shirt. His hair was wet and messy, his face pallid.

'Fuck me it's cold out there.' He shuddered like a dog trying to dry itself. 'What?' he said, aware that both of them were staring at him.

'Nothing,' Kirsty said. 'Drink?'

'Please. I'll cook, shall I?' he said, taking the two packets of stuffed pasta and a jar of pesto out of the fridge.

'Sorry. I was going to.'

'It's fine,' he said.

'I was thinking,' Kirsty said, handing over the wine. 'We should open the box after dinner. Go through the first photo album. Like Dad said.'

'And the whisky,' Patrick added.

'Sure,' Jessica said, quietly. She went back to what Kirsty was going on about earlier. This obsession with making everything like it was years ago. As if that was right and this wrong; the past was the natural order of their relationship, the present an aberration that had lasted too long.

'Everything alright?' Kirsty asked, looking at her.

'Just missing the kids. No phone signal so no texts. If they sent any.'

'I'm sure they did,' Kirsty said, kindly.

Jessica got up and paced down the van.

'Does this thing have proper heating?' she asked.

'Sort of,' Patrick said.

'How can it sort of have heating?'

'Well, no radiators. That thing down there can blow out hot air,' he said, pointing to a little circular vent down by the door. 'But I can't guarantee it won't give you carbon monoxide poisoning.'

'Think we might have to take the risk,' she said.

Patrick soon laid a huge bowl of pasta, three plates, three forks and another bottle of wine down on the table, then took the red metal fishing box out from underneath the table.

'For later,' he said, joining the two of them.

Kirsty

Kirsty was unsurprised that it was left to her to do the honours. *Just like everything else*, she thought to herself, knowing better than to comment on this to the others.

Once they had eaten, going through two bottles of red wine and any number of anecdotes about old family holidays in the process, she picked up the red box from where Patrick had left it. She turned the key that had stayed in the lock since the evening of their dad's funeral, and opened the lid.

There it all was again. As if nothing had been touched for a fortnight. The letter, the whisky, the albums.

'Here you go,' she said, handing the Port Ellen to Patrick, whose face suggested she'd just lifted the Holy Grail itself out of Gerry Cadogan's old fishing box. He unpacked it, then laughed to himself.

'What?' Kirsty said. 'There's nothing wrong with it is there?'

'No. Not at all. It looks like the old man had a bit though,' he said, pulling the cork out. 'Seal's broken.'

'He was told not to drink,' Kirsty said, disbelieving.

'I suppose when you've got a death sentence a little dram doesn't matter,' he said, going to pour them each a measure.

'Not for—'

'Just a tot,' he said, cutting Jessica's protestation short and pouring three large shots. He added a drop or two of water to each, following their dad's oft repeated advice about how to drink good whisky.

'Right,' Kirsty said. 'This one first, I suppose.'

She lifted the album out of the box. It was about the length and width of a vinyl record and made of blue leather, with a little gold trim around the edges that was flaking away in parts. She put it down in the middle of the table between the three of them – Patrick and Jessica facing one another, her on the end. Kirsty caught sight of herself in the plastic window opposite. She looked nervous.

'Here we go,' she said, turning the cover over to reveal the first page.

On it was the date and place in the top left corner, written in biro by her mother's hand.

July 1990. Coverack, Cornwall.

And below that were three photographs.

The first was Jessica, wearing a pink shell suit and perched atop a purple Raleigh bicycle with sparkling purple fronds sticking out of the handlebars.

The second was of their parents, sat at a bench table outside a pub, raising glasses of beer and wine towards the camera, smiling and red eyed.

And the last one was the four Cadogan children together, sat on a sea wall.

Jessica, Patrick, Kirsty and there, on the end, with a gap-toothed smile, Andrew.

Kirsty took a breath and dived back into a trip that had happened when she was just over a year old. She couldn't remember it. But maybe the others could, she thought, as all three of them went in.

July 1990 – Coverack, Cornwall

'Three, two, one,' Sue shouted, and the four of them smiled at the camera. 'Cheese.'

They all shouted back at her. Two high-pitched echoes, an excited squeak from the baby, and Patrick shouting, 'sausages', as he always did.

They were in a small Cornish fishing village, perched on a wall opposite the chip shop, where Gerry was putting in an order for more food than his family of six could feasibly consume. The man behind the counter recognised him, as he did all of his regular annual tourists. It was agreed among most of the town businesses that they would be friendly to visitors, as a sort of collaborative marketing effort. All except for one tackle shop, whose owner sold nets, buckets and spades for kids during July and August, but seemed to resent anyone who had the temerity to buy them.

Coverack was their family place, the way some people had a particular resort in Spain, a favoured holiday home on the east coast, or a campsite in France. This was it for the Cadogans. Every year they would spend the second week of July in a cottage just off the coast road. The rear of it looked onto fields that seemed to stretch out forever, while the front faced a small, rocky, sandy beach. Every evening this would disappear under water and appear again wet in the morning, decorated with bright green, glistening seaweed.

The house belonged to a Cadogan Family Builders client – an old woman named Jayne who owned six properties along the English coast. They had first gone down there when it was only Gerry, Sue and Jessica, back in 1979. Jayne had needed a new wall building in front of the driveway after a drunk driver had ploughed into it. Knowing that Gerry had a young daughter and little money, she offered him use of the house in exchange for the work. They'd returned almost every year since – the first few visits paid by way of odd jobs and repairs, then later by cash, as Gerry Cadogan formed his own business and began to earn a little more money.

It rained a lot during their week there in 1990. The Cadogans spent the majority of their time under yellow, plastic ponchos walking across farmland and up and down coast roads.

Earlier that day they had been at Tintagel, where Jessica got carried away and spent the full twenty quid they were each allotted for holiday money on Arthurian tat. This included a rune stone tied to a piece of black string and a 'true history' of the sword in the stone, written by some local author-cum fraudster.

'Right,' Gerry said, emerging from the chippy with five boxes. 'That bench over there.'

'What about the seagulls?' Jessica said, in the slightly whining voice she had developed as she approached adolescence.

'Bugger the seagulls.'

'Gerry,' his wife said.

'Not a swearword, Susan,' he said, his gruff voice softened by a touch of a laugh. 'Anglo-Saxon for dig.'

The children took their places on the bench and Sue handed each of them their box of food, as well as a wooden fork. Patrick immediately stabbed his into Andrew's arm and received a hot chip to the face in response.

'Oi,' Jessica said.

'You're not Mum.'

'Yes, but I am,' Sue said. 'So you don't stab your brother, and you don't throw food.'

Gerry and Sue perched on either end of the bench, picking at chips and trying to cut away portions of fish with wooden cutlery that wasn't up to the job.

'Two more days left then,' Gerry announced, throwing a chip down to Gray, their Labrador, who he'd named after the Watford manager, Graham Taylor. 'What are we up to tomorrow?'

'Beach,' Andrew said, through a mouthful of chips.

'Are there any more places like today?' Jessica asked.

'Not really,' Sue said, refusing to consider another day marshalling four children around a castle, particularly when three of them got bored after fifteen minutes. 'I think we should go to the beach if it's sunny. Board games and a walk if it's not.'

This seemed to please all of them. Or rather not displease any of them.

When they had finished eating, Sue and Gerry packed up the rucksack with spare clothes, uneaten snacks and their camera. She stuck the wooden swords they had bought the boys at Tintagel in the top, the hilts and handles poking out. Then they began the walk back to the family people carrier, with its perpetual smell of wet dog.

The next morning, the sun broke through the windows of the cottage. It was warm. As if summer had finally decided to make an appearance. Andrew took this as a sign that the beach would be the plan for the day, and immediately dressed in his Superman swimming trunks and Italia 90 t-shirt. Gerry had bought it for him in a fit of excitement, as England got through the competition (Gerry himself had thrown his England shirt to the bottom of his wardrobe when they went out in the semi-final, where it would remain for years to come).

Andrew took the camera from where it had been left on the kitchen work surface. It was a Kodak Hobby – a flat black bulky thing, almost the size and shape of a cassette tape, with a flash that popped out of the top when activated.

He went into the garden alone and started shooting, taking pictures of landscapes dotted with sheep, the little beach opposite the house, and two close-ups of bees nestled in the flowers.

'One. And two. And three,' he said to himself as he took the photos, mindful of how much his dad complained if photos were wasted and they had to buy yet more film. 'Four. And five.'

Going back inside, he took photos of Patrick asleep in their shared bedroom. He was an untidy sleeper, looking as though he'd been dropped onto the mattress from twenty feet in the air, rather than tucked carefully into bed by his parents the previous evening. He did the same for Jessica, before placing the camera back where he'd found it, hoping that his mum wouldn't notice that the winder number was significantly lower than it was last night.

An hour and a half later, they were all collecting up their things and heading out from the house to the busy beach.

'Mum,' Andrew said, walking slightly behind Sue. 'Can I do the photos today?'

'What do you mean, "do the photos"?'

'Take them.'

'Maybe one or two. I'll show you how to use the camera.'

'Okay,' Andrew said, almost revealing that he was actually quite familiar with it already.

They arrived and set up their stuff as far away from one family as it was possible to get before they'd be intruding on another. Kirsty was carried down to the sea by her mother, who stood patiently as her daughter waddled uncertainly into the water and back again, almost in tears at the cold. It was a dance they did almost every weekend on the seafront at Hove. Jessica, meanwhile, sat reading a *Sweet Valley High* novel that had done the rounds of her friendship group. She lounged in one of the cheap outdoor chairs they carried with them, all chipped white paint, rusting metal and a faded floral motif. Nearby Patrick and Gerry kicked a light, flyaway ball to each other, father testing his son's ability to head and volley, still wondering if there might be a future player among his kids.

'On your head, Andy,' Patrick shouted, and kicked the ball towards his brother. He aimed a speculative kick at it and missed, allowing the ball to bounce towards an old couple, both of whom were either asleep or dead. He was never one for football, occasionally playing in the garden with his brother, but refusing to join the local Sunday league team, as his dad had once suggested.

Most of the boys at his school had only one goal in life and that was to be a footballer. Andrew was different. He wanted to join the army, and listened with interest to his grandad's stories of life in the RAF. The first step, he was told, was the Cubs. Then the Scouts. These places would give him things like a spirit for adventure and camaraderie. He was never sure how much his dad approved of his plans though.

Andrew retrieved the ball and kicked it back, shouting, 'Mum! Camera.'

'It's in the bag,' Gerry called back. 'By the sandwiches. And don't waste all the bloody film.'

Patrick kneed the ball into the air twice and struck a half volley that was caught by the wind and looped towards the sea. Gerry set off on a gentle run to get it, his belly bouncing inside his yellow polo shirt, wispy short hair caught by the breeze.

That was when Andrew started taking pictures again – one of his brother and father, one of his mother and little sister, one of Jessica reading. He liked to be equitable, always worried that someone might lose out; the middle child who could see what those older than him had, and what those younger didn't.

Kirsty noticed him holding the camera up and smiled.

'Can't see you,' Andrew called.

'Use the zoom,' Gerry said, jogging over to him and leaving Patrick with the ball under his foot, posed like Roy of the Rovers on the cover of a comic book.

'What's a zoom?'

'Here. You use this little thing. Push it that way to get closer, that way to come back. Now you can take a photo of your little sister.'

Andrew did as he was told, zooming in on Kirsty who was now wriggling in her mother's arms.

'Proper little David Bailey, you are,' Gerry said.

'Is he a footballer?'

'Not quite.'

'How many're left on there?' Sue said, marshalling Kirsty back from the sea and instructing her to sit on a towel.

'Four,' Andrew said, looking down at the little dial.

'Oh right. Well just one more,' she said, directing a glance at Gerry who was clearly about to start complaining about the cost of film and the amount of it they seemed to get through. 'How about one of all of us? You take it, Andy.'

Sue collected her children together and arranged them on their picnic blanket, with her and Gerry stood behind.

'More?' he said, under his breath.

'He needs hobbies. Don't discourage him,' she said. 'Tell us where to stand Andy. And make sure we're all in.'

Andrew, set apart from the rest of them, zoomed in and out, as much for the novelty of it as the practicality.

'Dad and Mum, get shorter,' he said and both his parents crouched slightly. 'Patrick and Jess stand closer together.'

They did as he told them.

'We're ready,' Sue said.

'Okay. Three, two, one.'

The family smiled and Andrew pushed the button, feeling the satisfying click that came with committing what was in front of him to memory.

Patrick

He was still looking down at the photo album, lying open between the three of them as though it was a board game. He refilled each of their cups with the special whisky, also mindful that it had to last more than an evening.

'Do you remember that holiday?' Jessica said.

'Sort of. But not really. I remember Coverack. When did we stop going?'

'Mid-nineties. When Dad got the place in Portugal,' she said.

Patrick remembered the villa in the Algarve. Gerry had bought it off plan, following a few good years for Cadogan Family Builders. Not a man for flashy cars, the usual symbols of the working-class boy done good, Gerry was more interested in foreign property and a box at a football ground. He nearly achieved the latter when he sponsored a pitch-side advertising hoarding at Brighton & Hove Albion for a season, part of which included a dinner with the chairman. Patrick had gone with him, as the only member of the family who took an interest in football. He remembered the game as a one–nil win for Watford, played out on a cold September evening.

'I barely remember it,' Kirsty said. 'How old was I then? Five? There was one year we went without you,' she said to Jessica. 'You'd gone away with some girl from school. And you,' now talking to Patrick, 'spent the whole week off with your mate Steve, trying to chat up girls and buy fags and cider. It was just me and Andrew for the whole week.'

And there it was. The first mention of his name since the trip began. Each of them had been so careful not to bring it up throughout the post-death cleaning up and funeral planning. Summoning the memory of him rarely did any good and their lost brother generally created more questions than answers. They were almost certain he wouldn't turn up at the crematorium – he hadn't done for their mother.

Patrick looked again at the final photos in the album. Kirsty on the sand. He and his dad playing football with the flyaway balls they used to buy in the nineties. One of the entire family in the rain on their last day. And another taken on the sunny beach, with only Andrew missing.

'Funny how he's not in that one.'

'He took it,' Jessica said, quickly. The memory of that holiday no doubt fresher in her mind than anyone else's. 'Mum gave him that old flat camera that looked like a video tape.'

'I remember that thing. Dad used to go mad about using up the film.'

The three of them went quiet again. Patrick was thinking about Andrew at that age. How he tried endlessly to make him play football or cricket or tennis, or whatever his sport of choice was that month. But never with any luck. His brother was more interested in photography, or books or a board game. An insular, quieter child, unlike his boisterous older brother. Andrew was particularly fascinated by their grandfather's stories of life in the RAF, although none of them really believed that he'd ever fit in with the army himself.

It wasn't a shock when Andrew, aged seventeen, decided to join up as a trainee paratrooper. But it was also no surprise when Patrick later found out that he had left early under difficult circumstances, after little more than two tours and four years in the service.

Unavoidably, Patrick's mind drifted back to the day he discovered Andrew wasn't where they thought he was – in the barracks, between tours of Afghanistan. The email had been sent by a man named Kev, apparently one of the few friends Andrew had made in the service.

He'd found Patrick's contact details online where he was listed as a tradesman. Patrick didn't have the email anymore, having lost access to that particular address, but he could still recall the message. Almost word for word.

Hi Patrick

Sorry for the message out of the blue. I left it a while before I decided to get in touch.

Your brother Andy left the regiment six months ago and I've heard nothing from him since. Have you? Or your family? Couple of the lads bit worried here. Said he was going up London or something but we dont know. Just thought you should know. No one knows why he left.

Let me know if you hear from him.

Kev

At the time, Patrick had kept the email to himself.

He'd travelled to London in a panic almost immediately, heading straight for Camden because it was one of the few areas he knew well enough to walk around without an A to Z. He hadn't been there long before he accepted that simply turning up in London to search aimlessly for a missing serviceman was beyond futile.

He began to call shelters and drop-in centres over the city, describing his brother in the vague hope that a social worker, volunteer or carer might be able to pick out a young man with dark hair and an attractive, angular face from the thousands of have-nots who came into their places every night. The only feature that potentially marked Andrew out was the bump half way up his nose – the result of a high and mistimed tackle in a school rugby game he'd been a reluctant participant in.

Despite his persistent failure to find Andrew, Patrick kept trying. He cancelled jobs he'd been booked on, much to the consternation of clients who'd been expecting to have their living rooms wallpapered or painted. He went back into the capital with photographs to show the shelter volunteers and outreach workers this time.

'Fuck's wrong with you?' he remembered his dad saying on the phone one day when Patrick deferred the work Cadogan Family Builders had recommended him for. 'Old Simkins has been on at me this morning saying you didn't turn up.'

'I called her. Can't get out of bed, Dad. Been chucking up all night.'

'Fuck's sake. Make sure you're there tomorrow. Most trusted name in Hove, remember? Can't have you bollocksing that up when I'm planning to retire.'

In truth, Patrick was in a service station on the way to London again. He had organised the city by areas in which he could focus the search, rather than tackling the enormity of it all at once.

He knew it would have been easier with Kirsty's or Jessica's help, or even one of his parents. But he didn't want to put them through the uncertainty and worry. Or the possibility of finding the boy they believed was in the military instead sitting outside a cash machine, asking for small change. Patrick knew there was a fair chance he'd fallen into drugs or addiction of some kind. That the Andrew who left for Catterick and a life in the services could now be in a grotty underpass with a needle in his arm.

The breakthrough didn't come until his fifth trip up.

'I know him,' a worker at a shelter in Lambeth said, when Patrick showed him the photo. It had taken half an hour to get through to this place on the phone, and another fifteen minutes to convince someone to meet him. 'Paul isn't it?'

'His name's Andrew. His real name anyway.'

'Fine. Well he calls himself Paul when he comes here.'

'How often? I mean, how often does he come here?'

'Most days. Doesn't always stay though. A lot of these guys save up the money they have for nights when it's raining or cold. Been alright out recently.'

'Do you know where he goes? Like, when he's not here?'

'Haven't a clue, mate.'

'I'm his brother,' Patrick said, desperately, which seemed to soften the man's heart.

'Look. There's a chance one of the counsellors will know. But they won't tell you. Some of 'em have debts and that. Dealers mostly. You don't seem the type, but if we told you where to find him then . . . Well, you know.'

Patrick was frustrated, but he understood.

'Can I wait here?' he asked. 'Just in case.'

'Not in here. But there's nothing to stop you hanging about outside.'

'Right,' he said, a little disappointed.

'Tea?'

'Sorry?'

'Tea mate? Keep you going while you're waiting,' the man said with a kind smile.

'Thanks,' he said.

Patrick took his polystyrene cup of weak tea out onto the street and sat down on the kerb opposite the shelter. He tried to pass the time with the crime novel he was reading, but got distracted every other paragraph by people passing. Any one of them could be his brother.

The man from the shelter brought him out two more cups of

tea and a digestive biscuit. They were small acts of kindness, but ones that demonstrated to Patrick the spirit of people who worked in these places.

Around six in the evening a small group began to assemble outside the shelter's doors. Destitute, dirty, unhappy-looking men, some of them sipping from cans of strong cider. One guarding a McDonald's cheeseburger. He studied each face intently, wondering if he could be Andrew. But none of them fit the profile.

Until at half past, Patrick noticed a man turn the corner at the end of the street. He was wearing combat trousers and a large, black puffer jacket. He had stubble and scruffy dark hair sticking out from below his baseball cap, and was carrying a Sainsbury's bag for life stuffed with a sleeping bag, as well as a backpack equally full.

It was unmistakably Andrew, although he looked older than his twenty-one years. As he approached the other men, he kept his head down – apparently not interested in making friends or allies.

There was no can of beer in his hand, but he did have a metal water bottle clipped to his bag. A touch of his life in the services still evident. He didn't see Patrick watching him from across the road and turned to face the wall, waiting with the others for the shelter to open.

Unsure how to approach him, or what to say, Patrick stood up and stepped tentatively into the road.

'Hey!' he called, and a few of the men looked up. But not Andrew. He called again, this time adding, 'Andrew Cadogan.'

Patrick thought he noticed his brother's shoulders drop. Disappointment at being discovered? Surely not, he thought. His voice would be familiar and kind, suggestive of home and salvation.

Or maybe not.

Slowly, Andrew turned around to face his brother.

Patrick crossed the road and approached him carefully, worried that Andrew might try running. While he'd been training in the military Patrick had been busy developing a beer belly – there would only be one winner in a race between them.

'Andrew,' he said again. 'What—'

'Why'd you come?' he said. 'Why did you fucking come here?'

Flecks of spittle hit Patrick's face. His breath smelled stale – as if the last thing he'd drunk had been a coffee, hours ago.

'Because—'

'I wanted to get away.'

'You're living rough, mate,' he said, pleadingly.

'That's my choice.'

'Andrew. Come on. What happened?'

'It's none of your fucking business,' he said, angrily. 'You didn't care when I went away. Why care now?'

A few of the others started looking round, anticipating a fight.

'Look. Just give me ten minutes. We'll get a tea or something,' Patrick said. Andrew looked as though he might refuse, and Patrick wondered again if he'd go. But something within him also clearly understood that the jig was up. He'd been found and would have to explain himself.

'Fuck's sake,' he said.

'Please.'

Andrew didn't quite nod, but gave his assent. They walked to a Pret a Manger around the corner and Patrick bought them drinks. He knew he must've looked like a Good Samaritan, not just giving this bloke a hot drink but his time too. *If only you knew*, he thought to himself as he paid the cashier, one eye trained on his brother to ensure he didn't disappear.

Patrick felt guilty. It was true that he hadn't been overly enthusiastic when Andrew decided to join the forces. And since he'd been away in barracks, he had been bad at keeping in touch. Patrick had his own life and friends. Family was family – he'd taken it for granted, like everyone did.

But what had he done that was so bad Andrew didn't feel he could be honest with him, going so far as to choose this life instead? Or what had they, the family, done?

'Cheers,' Andrew said as Patrick handed him the tea and two sachets of sugar.

'Do you need something...' he began, not sure how to pose a question like this. 'I mean, do you want something to eat?'

'I'm fine.'

'Right.'

'I ate earlier. Sausage roll,' he said. Patrick could see how he might accrue enough in a day to buy himself something warm.

'So,' Patrick said. 'I ... I don't know what to ask really.'

'Then why are we here?'

'Fuck. Have a guess, Andrew.'

Neither of them said anything for a second. They took sips of tea that was still too hot to drink.

'I'm not on drugs. Just in case you're wondering,' Andrew said, bluntly. 'Been offered them enough fucking times. But I'm not.'

'Good ... That's good.'

'Don't be patronising.'

'Fine,' Patrick snapped. 'Well then tell me what happened. Tell me why one minute you're in the army, and the next you're sleeping rough. Without telling a single person about it. Eh? It's not as if there's no money to help you out. Or a fucking bedroom for you to stay in.'

Andrew looked ready to snap back and Patrick was aware of the other people in the café looking at them, perhaps worried this vagrant was going to kick off.

'I left,' he said finally, having calmed down. 'I had enough and I left.'

'You don't just leave the paras, Andrew.'

'Well I did.'

Patrick knew that wasn't it. This was half a story, but he decided not to pursue it.

It would take him another week to learn that his brother had been taken off active duty for an extended period of time, due to the results of some psychological evaluations following his return from his most recent tour. When he was told, Andrew had trashed the office of the general who'd given him the bad news, and had then done the same to his room. He was discharged six months before completing his service.

'Fuck Andrew. Why didn't you just come home?'

'Because I wasn't ready. I didn't want to turn up and tell you all I'd failed before I got any sort of rank. The army was my plan for life. And I fucked it.'

'So what?' Patrick said. 'You thought you'd sleep out for a bit? See what else came your way?'

'I've never slept out,' he snapped back. 'I get hostels, shelters. There's usually a bed.'

'And when there isn't?'

'There is,' he said. Patrick knew this was also a lie, but again didn't want to push it.

The two brothers remained still for a couple of minutes. They both looked out the window, onto the busy street.

It was Patrick who broke the silence.

'So what now?'

'Well, in an ideal world, you'd leave me be for a couple of months. Until I'm ready,' he said.

Patrick found this unnecessarily cruel. He had done nothing wrong. 'But I can tell that's not going to happen.'

'I've got the van,' he said, almost pleadingly. 'I'll give you a lift back south. You can stay with me for a bit. Or I'll get you a room somewhere. No one has to know what's happened.'

'How—'

'We'll tell them you failed a medical or something. You called me to come and pick you up and you don't want to talk about it. Fuck, they'll probably be relieved that you're out of the forces.'

'Nice to know.'

'You know what I mean, Andrew. Having a son on tour is terrifying. Anyway, beyond that you tell them as much or as little as you want. If you need money you can do some jobs with me. I'm behind on everything anyway.'

Patrick said this with a glance that told Andrew it was his fault; that the time he'd spent looking for his brother had impacted on his work.

Andrew seemed to consider it for a moment before he said, 'Fine. But I'll find my own place soon, okay? Then we can tell them I'm back.'

'Whatever you want,' Patrick said. He thought he noticed a smile, maybe a little note of gratitude, creep across Andrew's face. Then again it could have been nothing. 'I'm parked round the corner,' he said, and together they left the café, walked to his van, and drove back to Brighton.

'Do you think about him much?' Kirsty said.

Patrick was staring out of the van window, into the now impenetrably black night with nothing but the lights in the ramblers' tents visible. He was wondering where his brother might be now, after his second, and much more successful, disappearing act. It felt like everyone Andrew Cadogan knew became lost in the mysteries and questions he left behind.

'I see him sometimes,' Jessica said. 'You know, when I'm in London. I mean there are people who look a bit like him. They have the same colour hair or way of walking. There's always that moment when you wonder if it could be him, but then realise it's just your brain playing tricks.'

'I know what you mean,' Kirsty said. 'For the first few years I used to look out for homeless men who were around his age. Just in case.'

'Did you ever ask? If people knew him?'

'Once or twice.'

'That's why you volunteered at the shelters for Christmas?'

Kirsty nodded, looking a little ashamed that her charity work was less altruistic than people might've assumed. Patrick, meanwhile, shuddered at the secrets he was holding.

They still didn't know the half of what happened when Andrew left the army. To the best of the family's knowledge, Andrew failed a medical because of his asthma and couldn't continue in the job he'd always wanted. They knew nothing of the violent outbursts, the homelessness, the search around London until he was finally found.

Patrick wondered if he would ever tell them the whole truth. The things that might explain a little more about the brother they still loved, despite not knowing where he might be, who with, or even if he was still alive.

'What about you?' Jessica asked Patrick, shaking him out of his reverie.

'Every day,' he said, reaching into his backpack by the door for his wallet. 'I keep this,' he said, pulling out a crumpled photograph. He placed it on the table.

The picture showed a young man in his early twenties. His light brown hair was styled and messy. He wore a Libertines t-shirt, a chunky wrist watch on a leather strap and dark-blue jeans. A broad smile was drawn across his face, surrounded by a little stubble. In his hand was a half-full bottle of Corona, with a lime wedge stuck in the top. He remembered where it was taken – The Hope and Ruin in Brighton. They were there to watch some up and coming band that never up and came. Andrew's girlfriend, Mel, had taken the photo.

'When was this?'

'March, two thousand and nine.'

'Two months before,' Jessica said and Patrick nodded.

The three of them looked at the photo for a little while longer. For Patrick, this was like booting up the memory of his brother, reminding him of the face he looked for in every desperate thirty-something man on the street.

Patrick could go weeks, months sometimes without looking at the photo. During these times Andrew drifted back into an earlier version of himself: the quiet boy who didn't have a clear place in the world; the teen who became obsessed with fitness, but who had no interest in sport; the man who tried to become his father's son, and failed. And who one day, back in 2009, announced his decision to leave their family and never come back.

'Are you surprised he didn't come? To Dad's, I mean,' Kirsty said.

'He didn't come to Mum's,' Jessica said. 'He probably doesn't even know he's dead. If he isn't . . .'

'Don't,' Patrick said.

'I just wonder sometimes,' she said. 'Does he ever think about us?'

'I said don't. It doesn't do anyone any good. Speculating like this.'

Jessica took a final sip of whisky and said, 'You're right. And it's late. We can talk about it more tomorrow, with clear heads.'

At that, she climbed off her seat and got up from the table, then headed to the small bathroom in the back of the van.

It was freezing now. Patrick remembered the feeling from holidays years ago. Bone-aching cold. The damp that was impossible to avoid, and the feeling you could never be dry and comfortable while you were spending the night in the van.

He took a sip of the whisky, the heat of it all the more noticeable against the cold.

'Is it nice? As they go,' Kirsty asked. 'I don't know a lot about whisky, apart from what Dad told me. It all just tastes like fire to me.'

'It is, yeah. Y'know, if you're into that sort of thing.'

They heard Jessica spit into the sink, open the bathroom door and slam it shut again. Patrick looked around to see her climb into the lower bunk and pull the curtain across to separate herself from the two of them.

He and Kirsty looked at one another, as if to say *if she wasn't here now we'd talk about her*.

'I'm going to do the same,' she said, with a smile. 'Night.'

'Night,' he said.

As she was getting ready for bed, Patrick put the whisky back in its case and placed it, along with the photo album, in the fishing box again. Then he picked up his photo of Andrew, took one last look, and slipped it back inside his wallet.

PART 2

PART 2

CHAPTER FIVE

The Forest of Bowland

Jessica

The pounding rain woke her earlier than she'd hoped. Jessica's strategy was the more she could spend of this trip asleep, the less of it she would have to experience. But here she was at six in the morning, curled up in a sleeping bag, listening to the drumming on the van roof.

She was a light sleeper. Always prone to being woken up by a creak on the stairs, a cough from her husband or the hoot of an owl. The therapist she'd seen a couple of years ago told her this was because of all the things she had running around in her head at any one time.

'Small business, family. All those bits you do for the school. It's no wonder, really.'

She liked to believe this because it made her feel important and busy. But she didn't admit to the therapist she was actually the type who would create something to worry about whatever the circumstances. That was her way.

Jessica checked her phone. No messages. No signal. She opened the clock and timer app, scrolled through alarms set for 6:43, 6:48, 6:56 and 7:08 and turned off the one she had set for 7:12.

She was also a bit hungover. Four glasses of fairly average red wine and two whiskies was more than she'd usually drink in the course of a week, let alone a single evening. Particularly the whisky, which she didn't touch unless it was an unavoidable element of a cocktail. Dan liked it – it was one of the few things he had been able to bond with her dad over, given that he was more into rugby than football, and had absolutely no understanding of the building trade, other than the fact that the people who did work on his own house seemed to dislike him. Jessica herself preferred a decent, cold vodka with a bit of tonic.

As she reached for her water bottle to dull the furry taste in her mouth, Jessica heard the creak of the ladder in the living area. Patrick was clearly up, but she wasn't sure she wanted to go and speak to him yet. Last night had ended strangely, as things always did when the mystery of Andrew re-entered their lives.

Though not one to make such comparisons, Jessica generally believed that she had had the hardest time dealing with his disappearance. Max was three at the time – just about able to understand who made up the circle of important people in his life, and notice when one of them left.

The year that followed was pockmarked with questions like 'is Uncle Andrew coming?', 'will Uncle Andrew come over?' or 'where's Uncle Andrew?' before or during family occasions. If her mother was there these would invariably lead to her breaking down and leaving the room, after which Max would ask 'what's wrong with Nanny?'

The little boy had had little interaction with Andrew. But when it came to family get togethers, he was quick to point out any deviation from the normal cohort of aunts and uncles, free of the filter which would have stopped an older child bringing it up.

Eventually, Jessica had to explain.

'Uncle Andrew won't be visiting anymore. He's decided to go away,' she had said, almost adding *for a bit*, but deciding not to – as much to avoid raising her own hopes as much as Max's.

'Where's he gone? London like Daddy?'

'We don't know sweetheart. But he has gone. We just have to hope that he's okay.'

That was a typical interaction. The kind she had upwards of two dozen times. Once when Max was even sharper in his questioning.

'Is Uncle Andrew dead?' he had asked, having recently learned about death when the grandmother of his friend in reception passed away. Said friend had treated everyone in the class to his parents' quasi-religious explanation of death and the afterlife. The classic tale of grandparent in the sky, looking down, accompanied by the habitually terrified guinea pig that had snuffed it last year.

'No,' Jessica had said, shocked and tearful.

'Just gone away?'

'Yes,' she said. She was convinced her brother was alive, but equally sure that if he died she would never know about it.

'But not to London.'

'No darling.'

'Somewhere else then.'

'Yes.'

By this point, Max happily lost interest and sat down on the floor to push a wooden car around a wooden track.

'We'll see him soon then.'

Jessica didn't correct him, knowing that to do so would inevitably involve going back to where they'd started a few minutes ago. Instead, she had hurried to the upstairs bathroom, where she sat down on the closed toilet seat and cried.

Eventually the young boy learned not to ask, or stopped caring. Nonetheless, the constant need to explain in basic terms that a member of their family had just decided to leave them weakened Jessica. It compounded the relentless inner voice that asked what she could have done differently, or how she could have prevented it altogether.

None of the others had to deal with that. They could never know what it was like.

*

Jessica pulled back the little drape next to her and looked out. The view was obscured by raindrops on the plastic windowpane, as well as condensation on the inside which she wiped away.

It was starting to get light outside, but the sky was dull and grey. In what was ostensibly a divvied-up field, rather than an organised campsite, a few early risers milled around their small group of tents, drinking from tin mugs. All of them were wearing garishly coloured walking gear. Birds flitted in and out of the hedgerows that bordered the site, and beyond that the bare green hills rolled into the distance.

She thought about being at home. Waking up on her memory foam mattress to a sunrise-simulating alarm clock, then going downstairs for a decent coffee and making porridge for the kids. She'd take them to school and carry on to work afterwards, sitting in the back office doing paperwork and listening to the radio while the girls out front created bouquets and sold bunches to the customers. The florist seemed to enjoy a steady stream of business, regardless of what day it was. She thought about running home after work, having a glass of wine and cooking dinner, waiting for Dan.

She liked her life, and still resented this trip for interrupting it.

'The right thing to do isn't always the easy thing to do,' Dan had told her. She always imagined this would be the kind of thing he'd say if he ever left her.

'I know. It's the awkwardness I won't be able to stand. Everyone tiptoeing around like things are fine again.'

'Don't be awkward then. Say what you think.'

She checked her phone again. Still nothing. Still no possibility of anything unless some signal caught a breeze in the nearest town and came their way.

Jessica quickly unzipped her sleeping bag and climbed out of bed. There were Patrick and Kirsty up and about already. Patrick handed her a mug of tea as he sipped at his own.

These people really don't know me at all, she thought.

Patrick

'Sleep well?' he asked Jessica, who mussed her hair. It really didn't look any different to how she wore it during the day – deliberate messy versus accidental messy.

'Average,' she said, putting down the tea he'd given her and assembling a filter coffee. This, he imagined, was one of her compromises. Roughing it. Had it been up to her, she probably would've brought an entire Nespresso machine, complete with four different choices of coffee. 'The rain woke me up.'

'I find it quite soothing. It's like white noise or something,' Kirsty said.

'Urgh.'

'How long have you been awake for then?'

'Half an hour maybe,' she said, pouring water into a little paper triangle full of coffee grounds.

'You should've come out. I was doing a bit of yoga outside,' Kirsty said.

'Isn't it a bit cold for al fresco yoga?'

'Nippy. But it's so relaxing out there. So quiet, except for the birds. There's that lovely smell of grass, fresh air, and woodsmoke from the cottage over there.' She pointed to where the farmer lived.

'Oh I forget,' Jessica said. 'You're one of the autumn people, aren't you?'

'What do you mean "one of the autumn people"?'

'You know. Love the colours of the leaves and scarves and all that stuff. I remember it from years ago. You were always there with a bobble hat and a Starbucks red cup on the first of October. Regardless of how warm it still was.'

'It's nice, I suppose,' Kirsty said, apparently a little taken aback at this morning character assassination.

'Anyway, I can't do yoga,' Jessica said, firmly. She made it sound as though it was a physical impossibility rather than a life choice.

'What do you mean? It's just stretching and relaxation.'

'I tried it once with Tam and couldn't concentrate on anything. When we were supposed to be doing deep breathing I was thinking about a meal plan for the week,' she said, taking a sip of her coffee. 'I have far too much going on to be present in the moment.'

'Well—'

'I was just thinking,' Patrick interrupted, noticing the simmer before the boil. Jessica and Kirsty would take these little shots at each other, critiquing lifestyle and choices: Jessica eager to make everyone aware how busy and important she was; Kirsty equally keen to emphasise her holistically 'good' life – all vegetarianism, yoga, mindfulness and positive affirmation and empowerment. It would get progressively more pointed and nasty until one of them snapped, then Patrick would take a side and they were into a three-way argument. All of which could happen in as little as fifteen minutes.

'What?' Jessica said.

'Why Islay?' Patrick said. 'And how did he know we would actually come on the trip?'

'Sadism,' Jessica said. 'What kind of man makes the people he loves spend days on end in a freezing sardine tin, looking at photos of themselves as they used to be?'

'Jess,' Kirsty said.

Patrick faked a laugh. His sister's tone made him uncertain about bringing this up. But he'd been pondering it for a restless hour before he drifted off to sleep last night.

At first, Islay had seemed a strange place to send them. Nothing bar a few holidays and his love of whisky bound Gerry Cadogan to the Hebridean island they were heading for. So why would he insist his ashes get scattered there instead of Cardigan Bay or Derwent Water or any of the other places he and their mum used to love visiting? Or even on the beach half a mile from their own house, on whose shingle stones they walked every day for decades?

He couldn't escape the thought that maybe this island was something to do with Andrew.

They'd all known Gerry had occasionally looked into private investigators to track him down. These were mostly ex-police officers or servicemen trying to turn a few quid by helping suspicious men confirm their fears about a cheating wife; or indeed helping suspicious wives confirm what they had always known deep down about the shits they married. Usually he was talked out of it by their mother, who would tell Jessica, Kirsty and Patrick what their dad was thinking of doing.

'If he mentions it, just tell him it's a bad idea. I can't see how any good might come of it,' she would usually say, convinced that if they found Andrew by such underhand means it would only push him further away. If he was ever going to return to their fold it would have to be on his own terms and perhaps not for decades.

But after he lost his wife, and with his own time running out, maybe Gerry had gone for it? He finally paid one of those grumpy PIs to search out the son who'd deserted him, breaking his heart in a way he could never have imagined.

'What do you think?' Patrick asked Kirsty. 'You've been closest to him these past few years. Did he never mention it?'

'No. But it's not hard to figure it out. Islay's far enough that we'll have to talk. He hated the fact that we fell out. Every so often he'd ask if I'd spoken to one of you and when I'd say no he'd always tell me what a shame it was and how we should sort things out. "You only get one go round. Might as well be nice to people",' she said, taking her voice down an octave to imitate their dad. 'He'd say the same thing every time.'

'We are nice to each other,' Jessica said.

'There's a difference between nice and civil. Nice is being a family. Civil is how you speak to someone in a call centre.'

'Right. I get all that,' Patrick said. 'But why Islay of all places?'

'He liked it there. He had that whisky. I don't know.'

'As I said. Sadist,' Jessica said. This time she was smiling.

'Or there's an ulterior motive,' Patrick said.

Kirsty

'Don't,' she said, firmly. 'I know where you're going with it. I went there myself before we left. But there's no chance, so you shouldn't get your hopes up.'

Patrick looked crestfallen. Ever the optimist, ever the one most likely to follow their dad's advice about looking on the bright side, being kind, staying happy. He always searched for the good in situations that were otherwise irredeemably bleak. It was no surprise to her that Patrick kept a photo of their brother in his wallet – a permanent reference point should he need to identify him. Of all of them, he was the one who never gave up hope that he might come back.

Kirsty had no idea why that was. And while she felt almost cruel for crushing Patrick's hopes, it was better that way.

She had thought about it herself, the day after they first went through the fishing box and letter. Kirsty had done some Google searches she hadn't attempted for a while: Andrew Cadogan; Andrew Cadogan name change; Andrew Cadogan missing person. The same websites she'd visited years ago were still there, looking a bit dated now. She clicked on his dormant Facebook page, updated with the rest of the site, but still stuck in 2009 – the last post was from six weeks before his disappearance:

134

CADOGAN FAMILY BUILDERS AVAILABLE FOR HIRE.
EXTENSIONS. REPAIRS. BUILDS. GARDENS. NO JOB
TO SMALL. GIVE US A RING FOR A QUOTE.

Below this was his phone number and the company's logo which
Andrew had spent too much money having designed when he took
over the running of the firm.

After that, Kirsty had tried typing in 'Andrew Cadogan Islay',
'photographers Islay' (in the hope that his new life might have given
him the chance to work on one of his hobbies), as well as 'new people
Islay', wondering if the island community was so tight knit that the
arrival of a new person might make the local headlines – which it
didn't.

Gradually, reality replaced hope and she stopped. Apparently
Patrick hadn't done the same.

'I know,' he said, after a minute. 'I do. It's just that Dad used to
talk about hiring—'

'And he never did. Patrick, you've got to trust me. He never
did. Dad died not knowing where Andrew is. We'll probably do
the same.'

'How do you know, though?' Jessica said.

Kirsty had been watching Patrick so intently that she'd almost
forgotten her sister was there.

'Because he would've told me, Jess. I saw him every other day
for years. If he'd hired someone, I'd know. If he'd found him, I'd
know. If he'd made contact, I'd know. We've got to get rid of this . . .
thing,' she said, searching for a word – an entity – into which they
could bundle all the remorse and guilt and shame they felt about
what happened.

'And how do you propose we do that?'

'I don't know, Jess. I really don't. But hoping that he's going to be waiting for us on some bloody beach in the Hebrides is not going to help any of us come to terms with why he left.'

Kirsty tossed her mug into the sink. The handle broke off as it hit the hard metal basin.

'Shit,' she said, picking it up and putting it into the bin. 'Look, we've got to get on the road in a minute. Jess, it's your shift. Let's just go, shall we?'

CHAPTER SIX

The Scottish Borders

Patrick

It was just before midday when Jessica drove past a huge sign depicting a Saltire and a message welcoming them to Scotland, in both English and Gaelic. Patrick waited for one of the others to comment. Had it been him driving he would've cued up 'Flower of Scotland' to play as they crossed the border.

But no one said a thing, or even acknowledged it at all. Surely, Patrick thought, it was some kind of moment – crossing into the country where their dad's remains would be scattered, to be picked off by seagulls or whatever?

Perhaps the knowledge they still had hours of driving left was a dampener. They had to get through the Trossachs, Loch Lomond, and lots of deep countryside before they'd arrive at the boat which crossed over to the island.

They had steadily progressed north, with the dramatic hills of the Lake District to one side and the outer edges of the Yorkshire Dales on the other, in silence. Occasionally they'd crest an incline and a vista would open out of the most stunning landscape England had to offer. At one point during a shift to relieve Jess, Patrick had even shocked himself by driving a little too fast down hill and coming close to tipping the van over and into the central reservation. But it all passed without a word. Except for, 'Tebay services, that,' from him, as he pointed out the service station which was famed for having an artisan butcher and an independent café.

He knew why, of course. If they were anything like him, his sisters were lost in thoughts and memories of their brother. How just over ten years ago he had changed the shape of the Cadogan family forever by choosing to no longer be a part of it.

Kirsty and Jessica were probably going over the things they could've done differently before he left, the ways they came to terms with it when he did, and how they sought him afterwards. Just as he was.

After Andrew's disappearance the family had ploughed on gamely, intent on holding the diminished unit together. It was as if one of them had died younger than they should have, and in doing so had given the rest cause to understand the value of what they had.

But, in truth, something had fundamentally altered. Even though Andrew was rarely the most vocal or active member of the Cadogan family, his place within it was crucial to the whole edifice. It was sad that it took his absence for anyone to truly realise that, Patrick thought, as he opened the email app in his phone and typed into the search bar *andrew.cadogan33@g—.com*.

Patrick had saved the email in its own folder, titled A. He also had a printed version in the Nike Air Max 1 shoe box where he kept old memorabilia, like gig tickets, souvenirs and particularly meaningful greetings cards.

Andrew's email was short and perfunctory – written with no reply sought and no questions encouraged. It was completely unlike Andrew in its tone, to the extent that Patrick wondered if his brother had had help in writing it. But then again, in the weeks and months that preceded him sending it, Andrew Cadogan had probably read enough letters from lawyers and banks to be able to imitate that kind of over-formality.

From: andrew.cadogan33@g—.com
Sent: 18 May 2009 10:20
To: patrick@patrickcadoganhomeimprovements.co.uk
Subject: Me

Patrick

I want to tell you that I've decided to leave our family.

By the time you read this I'll have gone. I'm not telling you where I'm going, and I'm asking you not to try to find me. I've thought long and hard about this. I don't feel like a Cadogan. Maybe I never have. But this is not a passing mood. You will never see me again and I'm asking you to respect that.

Andrew

Patrick remembered reading it for the first time and feeling a kind of deep shock – a nervous sickness that was entirely new to him. He was on a renovation job in Worthing, working with a building contractor he had befriended a couple of months previously. He put down the tea he was drinking, and went to another room, away from the loud radio one of the guys on the job had set up.

He read the email twice more before he typed out his reply.

From: patrick@patrickcadoganhomeimprovements.co.uk
Sent: 18 May 2009 10:26
To: andrew.cadogan33@g—.com
Subject: Re: Me

Mate. Can we talk? Please don't do this. Give me 5 mins.

And the automatic reply came immediately.

From: andrew.cadogan33@g—.com

Sent: 18 May 2009 10:26

To: patrick@patrickcadoganhomeimprovements.co.uk

Subject: Re: Me

This email address is no longer in use and is not being checked.

His permanent out of office had already been set up.

'Y'alright there?' a voice he didn't know said. He hadn't noticed the man in the corner of the room fitting a radiator.

'Fine.'

'Y'sure? You look a fright.'

'I'm sure. Back in a bit.'

Patrick had walked through the half-deconstructed house, ignoring the workmen carrying on around him and narrowly avoiding tripping on a bucket, until he was out onto the coast road, looking at the sea. He didn't know whether to call anyone or not. It was half ten, so the email from Andrew had only arrived ten minutes ago. If he had sent it to everyone, then there was a fair chance neither of his parents had read it yet. Kirsty certainly wouldn't have unless she was surreptitiously checking her computer during a lesson. Jessica was the only one of them who, like him, had a smartphone, and so was never more than a click away from her emails.

He didn't want to have to break it to them. But then, knowing what he did about the last time Andrew went AWOL, could he really do nothing?

Whatever the answer, Patrick realised that Andrew would have set off already on whatever he had planned for his new life, to no longer be a Cadogan.

Patrick left it a moment longer, wondering what he should do as he paced up the road, past the Victorian hangover that was the

Burlington Hotel and the old town houses of the seaside town. Until the phone rang in his hand.

Mum.

'Hello?' he said.

'Have you heard from Andrew?' she said, without a greeting. Her voice was panicked.

'Yes. Well, an email.'

'Jessica got it as well. She just called,' she said, making Patrick feel bad for prevaricating and not contacting his parents as soon as he saw it. Jessica was always so much more sure of herself and what she should do any situation.

'He sent it to you, then? The email?'

'We got a letter. It was waiting here for me when I got back from zumba. It didn't come in the post.'

'So he must've—'

'I know, he can't be far. Dad was at work but he's now gone looking for him. He's told me to stay here, just in case he comes by. Oh but Patrick,' she said, her voicing cracking a little. 'I feel so useless just doing nothing.'

Patrick didn't reply. He didn't know what he could say. She was probably right, but then so was his dad. In either case, he very much doubted that Andrew would go back for one last look at the house, as though he was moving out rather than leaving forever.

'What did it say?' he asked, after a moment. He almost flinched, wondering if the note Andrew had sent to his parents contained worse than what was in the email. 'Was it—'

'He said he was leaving and by the time we read it he'd be gone,' she said, and Patrick realised then that they must have all received the exact same form of words. 'I just can't believe he would do this. I know he was upset, but why couldn't he talk?'

'I don't know,' Patrick said, again thinking back to the time around the family kitchen table. Andrew had made his final plea for help and they had all basically ignored it.

The line went silent again for a few seconds and Patrick guessed that his mum was probably thinking about the same thing.

'Look. I'd better go and keep the line clear,' she said, never understanding the capacity of mobile phones to field more than one call at the same time. 'You'll call me, won't you? If he gets in touch,' she said. Patrick agreed and they both hung up.

He worked well over time that day, unsure what else he could do that would be either more useful or distracting, and he was the last man on site. The hours were interspersed with phone calls from Kirsty, Jessica and his mum, all of whom had congregated at their family home in Hove. There was just one from his dad, whose voice sounded unlike Patrick had ever heard it before – sad, resigned and scared.

The last time they spoke was at nine in the evening, when they had all stopped searching. Although none of them said it, they realised he was gone.

'What now then?' Patrick had asked Jessica, who called him while Kirsty worked on getting their parents to try and eat something.

'I don't know what we can do. I suppose for the time being no news could be good news. It would mean he's still...' she trailed off, coming as close as any of them had to admitting that Andrew's notes also hinted at something far more terrifying.

'Can we not report him as a missing person? You don't have to wait you know?'

'Mum said that. But I don't know Patrick, I really don't. If he wants to go then maybe reporting him as missing would push him further. Make him feel like we don't respect his decision.'

'Jesus, Jessica. Surely we have to report it.'

'Maybe,' she said, soberly. 'But as I say, I don't know if it's a good idea.'

That week was the start of months of searching. Checking every article they could find about the death of a young man. Calling homeless shelters to see if anyone fitting the description of Andrew Cadogan had arrived recently. They never went as far as reporting him officially missing, but there were moments when Sue in particular almost cracked.

Until gradually, as the months passed, the family began to come to terms with his decision. Learning to live off the hope that he might one day choose to reverse it. And a large part of all of them was still waiting for that to happen.

Thinking back to that time, Patrick now understood that Andrew going removed the cornerstone from their family. After that, it was only ever a matter of time before everything else collapsed. And they could never be the same again.

The final blow came later, just under four years ago, when Sue Cadogan was hit by a stolen car in Brighton and died at the scene. Their varying responses to that event – Jessica trying to get Gerry to sell the house, Kirsty pushing for one of them to move back closer to what would always be home, Patrick remaining non-committal – became the catalyst for the falling out they had never recovered from.

The avoidable loss of one family member was compounded by the unavoidable loss of another. At the time it felt like theft, Patrick remembered. The closest thing he could pin it to was when he was eleven and the house in Ganton Villas was broken into and ransacked. That feeling of intrusion, of an alien presence defiling what was theirs.

They all became like veterans of a war which would define the remainder of their lives in some way.

Patrick knew that argument, still unresolved, couldn't remain buried under the other purpose of this trip. Scattering the ashes was a ruse. Talking and coming to terms with things was the real point of what their dad had asked of them. He just couldn't do it in life. That was Patrick's reading of his letter anyway.

'I have a question,' he said. Kirsty, next to Jessica in the passenger seat, turned around. She looked mildly shocked, as if her brother were a monk who'd just broken a thirty year vow of silence by asking someone if they'd like a drink.

'Do you think,' he continued. 'We'd be like this, y'know, estranged, I mean. If Mum hadn't . . .'

The question seemed to hang there a while, before Jessica said, 'Well I think estranged is a bit strong.'

'You know what I mean though. Things are different between us. After that night . . . well we basically didn't speak a word to each other for a year.'

'I'm not sure it was as long as that. A few months maybe.'

'Come on, Jess. You know as well as I do that we, like, properly fell out.'

'I know things were a bit difficult. But don't you think you're being a touch melodramatic?'

'Not really, no. None of us has had a proper, meaningful conversation with each other for nigh on four years. We don't write. We don't talk. Unless it's fucking admin, we'd never send a text,' he said. 'We became that family who don't speak to each other. Neither of you ever came to Ireland when I was living there.'

'You didn't invite us!'

'Exactly. That's exactly my point. Before . . . all that, I would've. We went from people who met up every few weeks to barely exchanging Christmas cards. And I'm asking if that would've happened if—'

'I did go to Ireland, actually,' Jessica said. 'If you must know. Dan had a trade trip there.'

'Right. So that's even worse isn't it? You actually visited the country I was living in and it didn't even occur to you to get in touch.'

'We were very busy, Patrick. These trips are—'

'Fine,' he snapped. 'Fine. Fine. Just pretend I didn't even ask the question. Nothing's changed. Everything's fine,' he said.

'I just don't know what you want from this, Patrick? A weekly lunch? Family meet ups? One of those tedious sodding family WhatsApp groups everyone has these days? What?' she said. 'We're here to spread Dad's ashes.'

'We're not though, are we? We're here to reconnect. It's in his letter.'

'His letter said nothing of the sort.'

'It's what he meant.'

'He said he hopes we enjoy it. It's hardly a plea to put the family back together.'

'So why did he do it then?'

'I don't know, Patrick. His reasons went with him, didn't they? And maybe you two are here to "reconnect" and be all nicey nicey. But I'm here to do what he asked. That's it.'

'Oh for Christ's sake! The two of you. Shut the hell up,' Kirsty yelled. 'I'm sick of it. Absolutely sick of it. Stop thinking of *nothing* but yourselves. And you can stop piping up with what you really think four years after it bloody matters.' She said to Patrick. 'In case you hadn't noticed, I was the one who was there for Dad after it all happened. After he lost his son. Lost his wife. And you two tried to sell his house from under him.'

'I didn't,' Patrick said. He could feel this was it, the tensions that had arisen in previous conversations and petty squabbles over the last day were ramping up now.

'As good as damn it, Patrick.'

'You agreed with me,' Jessica said.

'Who cares? Neither of you have any idea what happened the last four years. You turn up at Christmas on separate days. Call once a fucking month when the guilt gets the better of you.'

'And there it is. The poor me act. You chose to stay in Brighton,' Jessica said. 'You can't blame us for that. I have my life to live.'

'Fuck Jessica,' Kirsty yelled. 'No one cares about your pointless fucking life.'

At this a loud, shocking bang silenced them and the van lurched left across the motorway. Jessica, stunned, let go of the steering wheel for a second as car horns sounded behind them and they rocked from side to side. Patrick was sure they were going to tip over, and even in this moment of panic he had the clarity of thought to realise he wasn't wearing his seatbelt. Kirsty screamed, then the van suddenly righted itself and limped onto the hard shoulder, where it gently came to a halt. Jessica, breathing deeply, slowly began to sob.

CHAPTER SEVEN

Gretna

Kirsty

'You know,' Jessica said. It was a few minutes after the van had come to a stop. Some deep breathing, guided by Kirsty, and a few sips of Kirsty's water with mint leaves had calmed her enough to talk. 'You'd feel terrible if that was the last thing you said to me before I died.'

Kirsty looked at her with a mix of anger and incredulity, marvelling once again at her sister's innate ability to make any situation about herself. She tried to muster a reply, but found nothing. Instead, she turned to Patrick, who was holding his forehead.

'Are you okay?'

'Yes,' he said, through clenched teeth.

'What happened?'

'Hit my fucking head. Smacked it on the window when the van lurched.'

He was talking as he might if he'd stubbed a toe and was blaming the door he'd walked into.

'Oh God. There's no blood is there? Can you see straight?'

'I'm fine, it just hurts.'

'Patrick,' Jessica called from the front. 'What's your name? Tell us who you are.'

He shot a look at Kirsty.

'You might be concussed,' she called again.

'I'm not concussed, it just hurts. What the fucking hell happened anyway?'

'I don't know,' Jessica said. 'I just felt it go, I suppose. It lurched.'

Kirsty got out of the van. They had stopped on the hard shoulder about a mile past Gretna services. To one side of them was a steep, littered bank and a few trees. To the other ran two lanes of speeding traffic heading north. A light rain was falling and it was cold. Kirsty wrapped her grey cardigan tighter as she walked around the front of the van to assess the damage.

'It's the tyre,' she called back. 'Left front. It's blown.'

Looking back down the road, she could see a strip of rubber and a couple of long, black wavy lines in the road where Jessica had slammed on the brakes as she lost control of the van.

'Right. Well, it's not my fault,' Jessica called out of the window. 'It just... well. It just went, didn't it?'

'No one's saying it's your fault. It's not anyone's fault. It's probably because the bloody thing hasn't been driven for years.'

'What, so more of them could go?'

'I suppose we just have to hope not.'

'Well I'm really not sure about driving—'

'Don't then,' Kirsty said, walking away and getting back in the van. 'There's a spare on the back,' she said, stopping short when Patrick looked up at her.

'What? I suppose that's me then is it?' he said grumpily.

'No. Sorry, I...'

'What is it?'

'Your,' she said, but didn't know what to say. A huge red lump had formed on his head, just above his right eyebrow. 'Well... you...'

'What is it?' he said, picking up his phone, opening the camera and turning it to the selfie mode. 'Oh for fuck's sake,' he said, touching the lump and flinching. 'I look ridiculous. It's the size of a fucking golf ball.'

Kirsty began to laugh a little.

'Oh good. Funny is it?' he said, grumpily. 'I look a proper dickhead with this.'

'Sorry.'

'Ridiculous,' he said, slamming his phone down on the table.

'Well it's not as if you're going to be meeting anyone on a bloody Hebridean island are you? It'll just be Jessica and me.' Then she said, with a smile, 'Maybe you could send that barmaid a photo of your battle scar?'

'Oh so we're alright to joke about it now, are we?'

'Patrick,' she said, trying to mollify and calm him a little. 'It's just a bump on the head.'

'Whatever,' he said, seeming to snap out of his mood. 'Hadn't we better start changing this tyre? Otherwise we're never making that ferry today.'

Patrick got up, grabbed his waterproof and stepped out into the rain, while Kirsty sat in his vacated seat and took out her phone. There were three messages. Two from Trina, though typed by Livvy, including selfies of the two of them. Plus a WhatsApp message from Trina herself.

Trina: Hows it going? Killed anyone yet? Xx

Kirsty replied.

Kirsty: Was OK. Now stuck on side of road in Scotland with flat tyre. J on thin ice. P fine xx

Trina: Oh no! What happened? Xx Ps where in Scotland? Big place x

Kirsty: Just burst. Near Gretna xx

Trina: Shit. Thats quite far south. Aren't you meant to be getting the ferry later? Xx

Kirsty: Thanks for the reminder

Trina: Sorry. Didn't meant to upset you. Livvy misses you xx

Kirsty: Sorry too. Just grumpy xx

Trina replied with three emojis that said it all – one sad face, one van and one explosion. Kirsty slumped back into the chair, leaning against the window where Patrick had just bumped his head.

They had come to a halt in an inordinately depressing place. To Kirsty's mind, they should now be on the way to the Trossachs, to drive around the lakes and hills of Scotland. Instead, here they were, on a road side in a place only famous for hasty weddings. Everything seemed grey when she looked out of the window. Even the trees, which were turning from summer green to autumnal golds and reds.

'Not going to apologise then?' came the prodding, pointed voice from the front seat.

'For what?'

'"No one cares about your pointless life," wasn't it?' she said. 'No. Sorry. "Pointless *fucking* life".'

Kirsty sighed. Both at the tedium of her sister trying to coax an apology from her, like a mother determinedly pushing a splinter out of a child's thumb. And at the fact that she knew Jessica deserved one.

'It's a figure of speech.'

'Not one I've ever heard before. And if that's the best—'

'Fine. Sorry,' Kirsty said firmly, as the left front of the van raised up a little and the water in her glass tilted with it. 'I was out of order. Your life isn't pointless.'

'Depends on your view, I suppose,' Jessica said, getting up from the driver's seat and joining her sister at the table. Kirsty was about to suggest they step off the van, which they were probably meant to. But it was raining harder now and the thought of standing out on the hard shoulder, watching Patrick change the tyre, was more than she could stand.

'What do you mean? Your life isn't pointless.'

'I don't think so. But I can understand some people might see it that way. It's not exactly high stakes, is it? Running a suburban florist. Spending time with Dan and the kids. I'm not changing the world.'

'Well who is?'

'At least your job has some impact.'

'I teach secondary school English, Jessica. It's not *Dead Poet's Society*. Last week I marked thirty-five essays about *Of Mice and Men*, thirty-four of which were pretty much identical.'

'And the last one?'

'He'd read the wrong book.'

Jessica laughed. Outside they heard Patrick growl as he tried to wrench the tyre off.

'You know Dan's thinking about going into politics again?'

'Oh God. Not the council?' Kirsty said, remembering the two years Dan was a Conservative councillor for their little market town, quitting after someone painted TWAT on their driveway in the dead of night – he attributed it to a protest against the rise in tuition fees.

'No. One up, I'm afraid.'

'Not...'

'Sadly,' Jessica said. 'There've been meetings and dinners with people. They're all awful, of course. And I get stuck with their awful wives.'

'Always wives, is it?' Kirsty said, with a knowing, slightly judgmental, tone.

'Usually. I know you live in Brighton, but in the rest of the world barely anything's changed. Once in a while I'll be sat next to a husband at one of these things. They always look uncomfortable and barely speak. Like Dads at a baby group. Anyway, my point is, that kind of life can be seen as a bit futile. It's all front, isn't it? When I went to university I was going to write books. You know I never met up with that journalist friend of mine in Brighton. Couldn't face it.'

'I'm sure you still could—'

'We've talked about it. Dan and I. We could get a nanny, or I could do three days a week or something. Let someone else manage the shop.'

'Why don't you?'

'Too much faff. The party would worry what the constituents might think. They like things to be traditional. It's dreadful, I know. But it is what it is.'

'I don't mean to be rude, but they sound fucking hideous. The people who'd vote for him, I mean.'

'Oh Christ they are. The most judgmental, curtain-twitching arseholes. You know, once, when he was on the council, I thought about not voting for him. No one would have known, would they? Except me.'

'You should have! A tiny act of defiance and all that. Besides, think of what Dad would say.'

'I know. He never quite got used to the fact that Dan was one of them. He called us to say congratulations when he got elected, but you could tell that he was also sort of furious about the whole thing,' Jessica said. 'I never told you did I? Before we got married Dad had a talk with me. Said that he'd raised us with what he called "proper values". And even though we had more money than he did when we were growing up I wasn't to forget what he'd taught us. I think it was when he realised who Dan's dad was.'

Kirsty laughed. She could picture it. Her dad worried about what the corrupting influence of upper-middle-class money and status might do to his firstborn. The notion that hard work and honesty might be replaced by favours and nepotism. And the compassion, empathy and kindness he had worked to instil in her could be eliminated by a more egoistic worldview.

Arguably, they'd all let that happen. Perhaps if they'd stayed more true to Gerry Cadogan's maxims and aphorisms they wouldn't be here, trying to reconnect.

'Funny that we've stopped here isn't it?' Jessica said.

'Why?'

'Gretna. Of all places.'

'I've never been here before. What happened in Gretna?'

Jessica

She had thought about it as soon as she saw the sign on the left side of the road. Shortly before she felt a sudden loss of control and the van's terrifying lurch, surely only narrowly avoiding a collision with another vehicle. But she hadn't commented on it at the time because they were arguing and Kirsty was being dreadful.

'The wedding,' Jessica said.

'What wedding?'

'You can't seriously not know?'

'Jess,' Kirsty said, firmly.

Now, she was surprised to hear her sister genuinely ignorant of the relevance Gretna had for their family.

'Did Mum and Dad never tell you about it?'

'What?' Kirsty said.

'Their wedding. This is where they got married, back in the day. They eloped. That's what people did back then when their parents wouldn't allow the marriage.'

'Mum and Dad eloped? You're joking aren't you? I always thought they got married at St Philip's,' Kirsty said, sounding like she was trying to convince Jessica this was actually the case. 'There's the photo on the telly,' she said, referring to the gold-edged photo frame, depicting Gerry Cadogan in a grey suit and Sue in a white dress. They were stood smiling outside the church ten minutes from their house. The photo used to sit on top of their parents' television cabinet, alongside two of each of their four children. They had all been taken down a couple of weeks ago, during the big clear out.

'I can't believe you don't know,' Jessica said.

'Jessica,' Kirsty said firmly again.

'That photo was a set up. Mum's parents insisted they have the marriage blessed by the local vicar. But the wedding actually happened up here.'

'Seriously? Why the bloody hell did they elope?'

'Nan and grandpa didn't approve. Of Dad, I mean. He wasn't the right fit for their family.'

'I thought they loved Dad.'

'They grew to, when the business started to do okay. Back then, he was a builder from Watford who'd met their daughter on a night out after a football match. Mum's family were all about the services and they'd planned for her to marry some captain or colonel,' she said, thinking back to her last memory of her grandfather; the distant, surly man who spent most of his time complaining from behind a copy of the *Telegraph*. 'Not Dad, basically.'

'So what? They just ran off?'

'Yep.'

'When was that?'

'Seventy-eight,' Jessica said, hesitantly, waiting for her sister to catch up.

'So that was when . . .'

'Mum was five months gone. That's why they did it. Dad proposed as soon as he found out. But they kept the pregnancy from their parents. They were still pretty young, Mum had just turned nineteen. Dad asked grandpa if he could marry her and he refused, so they did a runner up here.'

'And the photo? Mum doesn't have a belly in it.'

'The one on the telly?' Jessica asked and Kirsty nodded. 'That was taken when I was three months old. Nan and grandpa refused to see Mum and Dad when they found out she was married. It was only when I was born that they started to talk again. On the proviso that the vicar could bless them. There was some silly reception at a bowls club and that was that. It's why there are no photos except for that one.'

'Jesus.'

As Kirsty processed it, Jessica thought back to her earliest memories.

Of the flat they lived in near the Lanes – now it would cost a fortune, but back then it was a draughty, damp and cold place, only made liveable by Gerry's skill as a tradesman. She remembered the herringbone floor, eventually carpeted, the walls covered in pine cladding rather than paper, and the formica kitchen that smelled of Dettol and dust.

They'd lived there for three years, with Gerry doing jobs on the other properties the landlord owned in exchange for cheap or zero rent. He and Sue put that money away to eventually buy their own place. Her dad often spoke of moving back to Watford, if only to get away from the judgmental, disapproving eyes of his parents-in-law and their friends. But by the time Sue became pregnant with Patrick, roots had been set down on the south coast. Gerry determinedly retained his Watford accent – some mix of Estuary English and mockney – and his fervent love for the football team he grew up supporting. Yet his true home was now on the coast.

The Cadogans moved to the house on Ganton Villas two months before Patrick was born, and there they stayed. It was more or less a wreck when it was bought, with running water the only amenity on offer. Over the course of the next few years, Gerry set about renovating the house into a home. And by the time Kirsty was born, it was complete. For a few years at least.

'I can't believe they never said anything.'

'I always thought you just knew.'

'Mum used to say she couldn't remember much about their wedding. That weddings weren't a big deal back in those days.'

'I suppose that's true. Maybe they only told me because I was there, they felt like I had a right to know.'

Just then, Patrick got back onto the van. He was soaked and his hands were black with dirt and grease from the wheel. Jessica could see that Kirsty was upset, perhaps feeling betrayed by people she had spent the better part of her adulthood worrying about and caring for.

'Are we good to go, then?' Jessica asked.

'No fucking chance,' he said angrily, turning the tap on and rinsing the worst of the dirt from his hands.

'What?'

'Call the RAC or someone. It's completely stuck. The wheel's bent to fuck after swerving across that road. And my fucking hands are raw trying to sort it out,' he said, turning to show them his palms, red and slightly bloodied in places.

'Right,' Kirsty said calmly. 'Well we'll just have to give someone a ring and get this sorted then won't we? Get them to change it.'

'It's more than changing it, Kirsty. It's fucked. The wheel is buggered and not coming off that axle.'

As Patrick spoke, Jessica started to panic. More time spent here meant less chance of catching the ferry. Another day on the road, another away from her family and her life. She simply couldn't countenance any more time on this silly trip.

'No,' she said, as Patrick took it upon himself to telephone for help.

'What do you mean no? Jess, if Patrick couldn't get the wheel off, I don't fancy your—'

'I mean no to waiting hours here. Absolutely not. If we miss the ferry this evening then I'm afraid that's it for me.'

'We can just catch the morning one. It's not ideal, but we can spend the evening at the port. I'm sure there'll be a pub or something.'

'No!' she snapped. 'Kirsty, I'm saying no. If we don't make it you can drop me off at . . . Edinburgh airport or something.'

'Across the other side of the country,' Patrick said.

'Fine. Sodding Glasgow or Dundee or Aber-fucking-deen. I don't care where. I'm telling you that I'm not having this trip last longer than planned. Either that or we just find the sea and scatter the ashes there.'

'Jess!' Kirsty said. 'Dad said Port Ellen beach. You can't just chuck them any old place. Or doesn't it matter to you? We'll claim we did it and throw another lie on the Cadogan pile.'

'I mean that it's the same sea, Kirsty. It's all connected.'

'Oh of course. So why not just scatter them in the Pacific or the Indian Ocean? Christ, you could've gone on your Mediterranean holiday and thrown them in the sea there. It's all the same water isn't it?'

'Don't be facetious, Kirsty.'

'Well don't be a selfish twat, Jessica.'

'Enough!' Patrick yelled.

Patrick

He had been listening to them through the open passenger window as he tried to change the wheel. Snippets of their conversation caught his attention, between his full-bodied efforts to loosen just one of the bolts holding the wheel to its axle.

Even as they talked about the truth of their parents' marriage, he had anticipated how things might easily tip into an argument.

'This is ridiculous,' he said, directing his irritation at both of them.

'Tell her,' Kirsty said.

'You're just as bad,' Jessica goaded.

'Both of you! When does it end, huh? You're nice for about two minutes. Then it's a row again.'

'She—'

'Just shut up. And grow up,' he yelled.

Patrick was talking about the present. But really, he could've been describing any time in their lives over the last twenty years.

There had always been tension between Jessica and Kirsty. The wisdom of the oldest sibling pitted against the privilege of the youngest. For the most part, they kept it beneath the surface. But it was made worse when Kirsty emphasised how much closer she was to their parents, remaining in Brighton as she did, being a more loyal member of the family than those who'd left to live their own lives. Or when Jessica was overly selfish and sensitive.

Patrick couldn't stand how these little aggressions and battles for status became more important than the facts themselves; how they obscured the thing that really mattered.

When their mother died, Kirsty laid the guilt on thick, as she inevitably spent more time caring for the grieving widower, who struggled to so much as boil an egg. Then their dad dying became a competition between who could do more work around the house.

This trip itself was evolving into an attritional battle to fulfil what he'd asked.

'Ridiculous,' Jessica said, to herself as much as anyone else. She got up from the table and went to her bunk.

Years ago, they had both learned to climb down from any approaching conflict with some time away from each other, venting to their partners. Or just as often to Patrick, who'd agree with whoever was talking to him, if only to avoid more conflict. Afterwards, they would usually go back to being amicable and even friendly. But now, with the veneer of friendship rubbed away, there was only family to bind them.

Kirsty was at the table, flicking through her iPhone, blanking the world around her. He had never felt more like a parent, cajoling two rowing teens. That his only child was not even at school and the rift he was trying to bridge was between his two adult sisters made the feeling all the more strange.

He sat down at the table and picked up the red fishing box. Kirsty looked alarmed as he flipped open the lid.

'Not now,' she said. 'Just because we're stuck—'

Ignoring her, he pulled the first album out – the one they had been through the night before. He opened it onto a page depicting the four of them together, sitting on a sea wall.

On the far left was Kirsty, dressed in a green floral skirt, trainers and a pink t-shirt. Next was Patrick in his customary bright yellow Watford shirt and a pair of denim shorts. Then Jessica, her long hair obscuring much of her face. Finally, on the end was Andrew.

'We are going to talk. About him. For once, we're going to actually say what we think about it.'

At this, Jessica stuck her head out of her bunk.

'What do you mean? We talked about nothing else for years after he left.'

'We talked about where he might be. We talked about what he was thinking. But we never actually spoke about why we thought it happened. Why *he left us*. What we might have done. And,' he continued, before Kirsty could butt in again. 'We've never talked about how we feel about it today.'

'What are you? A counsellor now?' Jessica said from the back, sounding bitter.

'No, Jessica. But if you're going to fuck off before we finish this trip we should probably try and get something out of it.'

He waited for Jessica to get out of her bunk and rejoin them at the table, then peeled back the cellophane which covered the photos. He picked up the one of the four of them and put it down on the table.

'I feel the same as I did then,' Kirsty said.

'Which is?'

'Sad, I suppose. Worried for him.'

'No guilt?' he said. 'You never think there might have been something we could've done to stop him leaving?'

'Patrick. He gambled away half the business. He had a problem. *We* can't feel guilty for it.'

'He asked us for help.'

'Dad gave him a job, let him run the business. Less than a year later, he's bankrupted himself, almost run the business into the ground, and Mum and Dad are remortgaging their house to save it. If Dad hadn't gone back full time maybe—'

'Don't say maybe he wouldn't have gotten ill, Kirsty. Fuck, he had liver cancer.'

'I'm saying I doubt the stress did anything to help.'

'And I'm saying that I don't think the two are connected. Yes, it was bad for Dad to have to run the business again. Especially while . . . all that was going on. But we could've done more.'

She seemed to consider this for a moment. Or perhaps she was going back to that time at Ganton Villas. A few months before he disappeared, when Andrew brought the family together to ask them for help to save the business.

Gambling wasn't quite the word for it. Andrew had loaded money into various investments and funds, taking advice from an old army friend who had left shortly after he did and was now working in the City. It wasn't just that the advice Andrew was given was bad, it was that he acted on it while the financial crisis was crippling the country's economy. And when one investment failed, Andrew would simply reinvest elsewhere, like a desperate man trying to make a living at a dog track.

Patrick still remembered the conversation as though it had happened that very morning.

'Why?' a heartbroken Gerry Cadogan had asked. 'After last time, why?'

Andrew had hesitated a moment. Gerry was referring to two years previously when Andrew had gone to his parents, remorseful and broken, to ask for help with money. He hadn't been able to stay in a job for more than three months after leaving the army, and spent long periods unemployed. That had been the prompt for Gerry and Sue to offer him a job.

Unlike his brother, he'd shown little to no interest in the family trade. But the suggestion was that he'd spend a year under his Dad's wing to understand the business side of Cadogan Family Builders, and a few months with his mum to learn about accounting, payroll and the limited amount of marketing they did. Then he would take over the commercial side of the operation. He lasted barely more than a year.

'I'm not earning, Dad,' he said, pitiful and sobbing in front of a whisky poured for him by Gerry, who looked at his son with huge disappointment and just as much love. 'Business is bad. I was taking my basic but nothing else. So I just thought—'

'Jesus, Andrew,' Gerry scoffed.

'I've tried. I've really tried.'

'You gambled the bloody company money,' Sue chimed in. 'Thousands, Andrew. There are people who work for us that want paying. And we're not going to be able to because of this.'

'We'll find a way,' Gerry said, as an aside to his wife.

'It wasn't gambling, Mum,' Andrew said. 'It was risky. But—'

'Fuck's sake, Andrew. It was as good as,' Patrick said. Kirsty and Jessica were also both there, but neither spoke. 'Fucking high-risk investments with company funds. No fucking wonder.'

'Everyone's struggling,' Andrew said, imploringly. 'Graham said—'

'Forget Graham,' Gerry said. 'And if I ever meet him I'll rip his fucking head off.'

'What do you need?' Jessica asked, calmer than her dad.

After a second or two, Andrew spoke again.

'Twenty,' he said, sheepishly. 'Maybe a bit more. We're quoting for a job now. If that comes in . . . just twenty.'

To Patrick the silence seemed to last for ages. As though Andrew's request for money were a suggestion that the family business should pivot to sell drugs instead of conservatories to boost its coffers. It was Kirsty who eventually broke it.

'You're not serious? Tell me, Andrew. You can't be fucking serious.'

Another silence.

'Who the hell has twenty grand sitting around? Thirty, I should imagine. When it actually comes to it.'

'I didn't think one of you . . .'

'Oh. So it's a whip round you're after? Everyone chuck in their life savings to bail you out.'

'The business. This isn't for me, I'll find a way for myself. This is just for the business.'

'I'm just about to go to uni, Andrew. Patrick's got his own work on. Jess has two small kids. Who do you think has that kind of money?'

'I didn't mean you.'

'Well why am I here then?'

'Because I wanted us all to talk about this. Just because you're young doesn't mean you don't have a say.'

'Patronising much?' she said, almost patronisingly herself. The comment started off an indecipherable hubbub of bickering, accusation and argument. Patrick struggled to make anything out, except for the occasional word: irresponsible, stupid, bankrupt. The only voice he couldn't hear was Andrew's, who halfway through looked right at his brother, full of regret and resignation. Then Gerry yelled 'stop' and ordered them all home.

Was that the moment? Patrick wondered now. Was it right then that he made the decision to leave; that he decided he was no longer part of this family.

Sure enough, Gerry had thought about giving him the money. And a few days later told his son that he would remortgage his house and use the money to bail out the business. But he also said that Andrew could no longer be a part of it, and would receive nothing to address his own situation. But had Andrew's decision to go already been made by the time Gerry Cadogan delivered the bad news?

Patrick had revisited that look, that moment, so many times during the intervening decade that he was unsure how accurate his memory of it actually was. Did Andrew smile? Was he tearful? Did he offer a shake of the head to indicate that their family as they knew it was over?

Or did he simply sit there, in silence, listening to his family argue over the mess he had made, each of them taking their usual role in difficult situations: Gerry patriarchal and authoritative; Sue determined that everyone have an equal say; Jessica applying whatever she could to herself and her life; Kirsty defensive and argumentative.

There was only one true version of what happened. Yet Patrick carried several with him, as though it was an actor's showreel. And no matter what he did, he could not escape the notion that he knew something bad was going to happen, but did nothing to avert it. After all, he understood more about Andrew than the others ever did. Or would.

'What then?' Kirsty said. 'What could we have done? I was nineteen years old.'

'Maybe not you,' he said. 'I don't know. I could've spoken to him. I might've been able to help.'

'You couldn't afford—'

'It's not just about the money, Kirsty,' Patrick snapped. 'He wanted some compassion from one of us. No one gave it to him. Everyone blamed him, shouted at him, told him it was his fault.'

'It was,' Jessica said, slowly and carefully. 'His fault. He lied. If he'd asked for help before we could've—'

'"This is your own stupid mess.",' Patrick said. 'That's right isn't it? What you said to him.'

'Don't, Patrick. Don't level that at me now.'

'But that's what you said.'

'And I regret it! Things are . . . different today. You have to accept that Andrew could be very destructive. Just because he's gone doesn't change who he was.'

Patrick was going to argue this, yet he knew he couldn't. Not with any conviction or validity anyway. After Andrew left the army his life had been fraught with problems. Growing pains that became embedded. The drink driving conviction at twenty-one, the fights in town on nights out, the arrests, mornings Patrick had collected him from drunk tank cells. All self-inflicted. And all belied the relatively quiet, kind man they knew their brother to be deep down.

Then there was something even bigger. A secret only Patrick knew, after Andrew had confided in him.

'Mel's pregnant,' he had said, over two pints of Guinness in the King's Arms pub in Brighton. 'She's getting rid of it on Friday. I just wanted someone else to know.'

The revelation ended with Andrew taking a sip of his beer and so closing the topic down. Patrick tried to prod and get more out of him. How he felt about it, when it happened, did he support the decision? But 'fine', 'not sure' and 'yeah' showed him that Andrew wouldn't be drawn further on the matter. Mel had been the one steadying force in Andrew's life. A nice, northern girl who'd been down in Brighton for university and met him there.

Two months after the termination, they split up.

'I know,' Patrick said, looking up at Jessica. He was on the verge of telling them everything. But was now the right time? When things were so volatile?

'I just still think one of us could've done something. Before he went.'

Jessica

She watched her disconsolate brother get up from the chair and open the fridge. He took a can of beer out and pulled back the ring, quickly catching the overflowing suds in his mouth.

'Aren't you driving later?' Kirsty asked, disapprovingly. 'When we get to the Trossachs? You said you wanted to.'

'Bugger the Trossachs,' he said. 'Anyway, I can have one.'

Jessica wondered if she should say what was on the tip of her tongue. It felt like now was the time for honesty. The very least she could do was make a gesture towards their father's desire for them to make amends and begin to let the waters close over their past.

'I really think whoever does that bit should be compos mentis. It's quite twisty turny according to the map.'

'Well you do it then. I'll swap shifts.'

'Patrick. That's not how this is supposed to—'

His insistence on talking about Andrew had succeeded only in bringing back consequences without any answers. None of them knew anything for certain about why he had left. They knew even less about where he might be now.

Jessica reached down into the fishing box and took out the second album. The red one, the colour of a passport, if a little dusty and dented.

'We said not yet,' Kirsty said.

'I know we did. But it looks like we've got a while here before anyone turns up. Besides, by the time we get to a campsite we'll be too tired to pay it proper attention.'

'Jess.'

'She's right,' Patrick said. 'They said he'd be two hours. Maybe more. We might as well, what else are we going to talk about?'

'That means you're actually going to stay then?' Kirsty said. 'Not just dump his ashes in any old bit of water?'

'Kirsty,' Patrick warned.

She relented. Jessica placed the album between the three of them and put the kettle on again. She turned the cover over to reveal the first page, where there were two photographs. The first showed their whole family, lined up against a low brick wall. The second was Patrick and Andrew, both holding fishing rods.

June 2000 – Bazouges Sur-le-Loir, Loire Valley, France

The trip had been arranged as a way to celebrate Jessica finishing university. She was twenty-two, and had been studying English literature for three years at UCL, with a further year spent on an exchange programme abroad at the University of Victoria on Vancouver Island.

To say that her experiences in Canada and London had changed Jessica would be an understatement. The bookish, hesitant girl who had left Brighton with her stuff packed into the back of her dad's Transit van had returned from her shared flat in Holborn a stylish, metropolitan type. She used Americanisms and kept herself at the vanguard of music and literature through magazines and nascent friendships with publishers or promoters, using email to stay in touch with them all (having insisted that her parents invest in a dial-up modem, on the pretence that it would be 'good for business').

Jessica sat in the large garden which surrounded the old farmhouse they had rented for the week, reading a beaten copy of *The Beach* by Alex Garland. It made her think of the trip three of her friends were planning to Thailand later that year. She was tempted to join them, although there was the prospect of an unpaid internship at Penguin Books to potentially keep her in London. Her discman played *Grace* by Jeff Buckley into her ears. She enjoyed maybe half his songs, but was trying to get into more of them on the recommendation of her boyfriend, Peter. An economics student, he was determined to make it as a singer-songwriter, and also had an unusually vociferous interest in US politics.

'Lunch in ten,' Sue called from the little wooden door that led into a dark kitchen. Jessica folded the edge of her page down, watched her sister climb out of the swimming pool and then lay back in her deckchair.

The house was a ramshackle collection of out buildings in the grounds of an equally ramshackle chateau. It was owned by an eccentric Californian who told them she had left Los Angeles for Paris in the seventies to become a *Vogue* model, but ended up as a chef instead. She now rented out the house in the summer months to get extra revenue.

Gerry had discovered it through a client, asking if they knew a house that would accommodate his family for a week, without breaking the bank. Chief among its charms was the way it was nicely segmented, giving each member of the Cadogan family their own space, as well as a communal garden and kitchen for them all to come together in the evenings. Slightly less fortunate was the lack of heating and number of mice, but he was willing to overlook these drawbacks in light of its affordability.

Jessica skipped three tracks to 'Hallelujah', her favourite song on the album. Although she would never admit that to Peter, who'd think her too obvious and probably force her to listen to the Leonard Cohen version again.

'I heard there was a hmm hmm hmm,' she sang along, her dull, monotone singing voice sounding better in her head than it did out.

Kirsty came over and laid down on the adjacent sunbed. She was still at an impressionable age – eleven – when she looked up to Jessica as a model for everything she might want to be. In return, Jessica began to introduce her to teenagerdom, through the occasional sip of wine at dinner or a reference to a boyfriend and the perils of sex. She was protective of her sister, but equally knew that she had an opportunity to ensure Kirsty arrived at the age of thirteen a little more savvy and aware than she herself had been.

Jessica smiled then closed her eyes, relaxing for a couple of minutes until the clattering noise of loose mudguards bumping over uneven terrain broke her concentration on the album. She wasn't too upset to pause the next song, which was primarily the singer caterwauling over a discordant guitar riff. *This might be one I have to pretend to like*, she thought, knowing that Peter would be ready with an over-intellectualised critique of the album the minute she saw him again. She still preferred 'Hallelujah'.

Andrew came through the gate first, pushing his bike. In the basket was half a stick of baguette, a battered oilskin bag and his t-shirt. Gerry followed soon after, carrying two fishing rods, and his red fishing tackle box, given to him as a gift a year earlier by Andrew, who had started working a Saturday job collecting glasses at a nearby pub. Gerry's basket clinked and rattled with the sound of empty beer bottles. He'd likely had three or four, Andrew maybe one.

'Catch anything?' Patrick said, looking up from the copy of yesterday's *Daily Mirror* he had bought from the little shop in town.

'Couple of perch,' Gerry said. 'Think I had a carp on the line at one point but the bugger got away. You'll come along next time?'

'Maybe.'

'Better than looking at what happened a day ago. Old news, that is.'

'I'm catching up. Anyway, I said I'll come if we go down to the Loire. Get a boat or something.'

'And what about you?' Gerry said, looking down at Jessica, who was now tapping away at her red-cased Nokia 3210.

'Fishing?' she said, as if her dad had suggested an impromptu sky dive.

'Yeah. It's lovely down there. The quiet of the lake, nice trees, singing birds. There's a big old orangery as well. I mean, it's falling apart, but someone could do it up nice and make a venue of it.'

'Thinking of pitching for some work while we're here Dad?' she said, with a smile, but without looking up from the screen and the message she was composing.

'Always working, love. You know me.'

Gerry leaned his bike up against the wall and dropped the fishing rods next to it. He sat down on the end of Patrick's sunlounger. 'You know that's costing you a bloody fortune. Sending messages back and forth to London,' he said to Jessica, in a way that suggested it might be cheaper if her boyfriend lived in a different part of the UK. 'Three quid each.'

'They're not three quid.'

'Well don't you come asking me when the bill turns up. Shouldn't be on the bloody thing anyway.'

'Well you know you could've prevented—'

'No,' Gerry said, jokingly but firmly, climbing up off the sun lounger and heading indoors.

Jessica was referring back to a row they'd had yesterday, and twice before they left, about Peter coming with them. She was about to invite him, then was told by her parents that this was strictly a family holiday – a last hurrah for all of them to go away together, before the older Cadogan children considered themselves too old to go anywhere with their parents.

It had all come to a head when they were wandering around the grounds of Chenonceau and Kirsty ran the batteries down on her sister's phone playing endless games of snake.

'Well you should've charged it, shouldn't you?' Sue said, while Gerry was off parting with fifty-odd euros for six drinks in the café.

'I shouldn't have to. Why does she need to play a game?'

'I was bored,' Kirsty said, defensively.

'Great. Well now if Peter texts I'll never know about it.'

'Jesus,' Sue said under her breath as Gerry arrived back with a tray carrying three coffees, two cokes and an iced tea.

'No bloody tea,' he said. 'Again. Bought this iced shit.'

'They don't drink it here,' Jessica said caustically. 'Not everyone does what you do.'

'Christ. What's got into you then?'

'Kirsty used—'

'P-E-T-E-R,' Sue said, sounding almost exhausted as she spelled out the name.

'Oh for God's sake. What is it now?' Gerry said.

'My phone's dead. Kirsty killed it. Now if he texts I won't know.'

'For an hour. Maybe two,' Patrick said, between drags on a newly lit cigarette.

'I wish you wouldn't,' Sue said to him.

'So do I, Mum,' he said, shutting down the debate about the smoking habit. He had unwittingly revealed it to his parents a couple of months ago, when they had all accidentally ended up in the same pub one evening.

'You can wait. Christ, what's he got to say that's so urgent?'

'Well I'll never know now, will I? And you know this could easily have been avoided if you'd have let him—'

'No. Jessica, just no. This is a family holiday. Probably our last together. If you were married to the dickhead then maybe. But you're not. So stop behaving like a sodding teenager,' Gerry said, which was Jessica's cue to storm off. And Sue's to admonish him for calling Peter a dickhead, without ever having met him.

They had reconciled later that evening, as Gerry drank Pernod and water from a mug and she sipped white wine while reading her book in the corner of the living room. Jessica knew deep down that had she actually proposed the trip to Peter, he would have declined it anyway. A week in a French country house with a family he'd never met (and all its attendant eccentricities and traditions) was not the greatest way to spend his limited holiday budget.

Peter never did text that day. Indeed neither had he the day before that or any day since they'd left Hove, with Jessica driving her parents' car, while they travelled in Gerry's newly bought camper van. The intention was to prolong their break in Europe by a week and take a scenic drive home via Brittany and Normandy.

In fact, the message she was now working out how to reply to was sent by a boy named Dan. They had met in a cocktail bar in Bloomsbury three weeks ago, where Jessica had gone fresh from a storming row with Peter about her not liking a Brazilian film. She happily gave Dan her phone number when he drunkenly asked towards the end of the evening. He was friends with her one-time university flatmate Andrea, a lazy Italian girl who smoked almost constantly and drank more coffee than could be healthy for one person.

It was clear that Dan fancied her. And this latest message was another in a series of skirted, tentative attempts to ask her out. But while he was attractive enough he lacked the bohemian, artistic spark that she felt she would need in any future partner. Even if things with Peter didn't work out, Jessica could not see herself with a trainee management consultant.

She pushed away at the buttons of her phone, the beeping as she went through the numbers and letters annoying everyone but herself.

Hi Dan. Srry taken me ages 2 get bck 2 u. In france w fam.
Cant do nxt week. Mayb 1 after? Tb x

She pressed send and immediately wondered why she had suggested he should text back. Politeness, she supposed. It would be good to have friends in London when she moved up there permanently later that summer. Most of her uni mates had gone back to their home towns and villages, dispersing after graduation like ants fleeing a smashed nest. So her circle would be reduced to Londoner Natalie, who lived with her mum in Dalston, Peter (who would surely be going out on tour with his band at some point), and Stu Anderson, who was more Patrick's friend anyway and was a year into a marketing degree at Goldsmiths. Dan would be a welcome friendly face in a city of strangers.

'Right. Lunch!' Sue called from the house. It had taken almost half an hour, rather than the ten minutes she quoted.

Patrick rushed over first, tailed by Kirsty. Jessica hung back to speak to Andrew, who had been quiet so far that week.

'How was fishing?'

'Alright. Caught a couple,' he said. 'It's more Dad's thing though, isn't it?'

'I thought you liked it.'

'I do. Yeah ... I mean, I do. But I like other things too.'

'You'd rather be off taking photos?'

'Maybe. But don't—'

'I won't,' Jessica said.

'Because it's nice for him, isn't it? Bonding and all that. If one of us didn't go he'd be there on his own.'

'You don't need to worry about Dad.'

'No, I know. I just ... with all of us growing up and that. Must be weird for them with you going off to live in London. Patrick's talking about renting a flat in the city. Soon it'll just be me and Kirst,' he said, using a nickname from his sister's childhood.

'What about you then? Thought about uni?'

'Maybe. Dad said there's always a job for me in the business.'

'He says that to everyone. You have to figure out if you're actually interested in it.'

'Come on you two,' Gerry called from the table. Jessica realised they were still hanging out by the swimming pool.

'I always thought you'd do well at uni. You'd be amazing.'

'Bit of a waste of time though isn't it?'

'Never. Go somewhere new, meet people. You could spend years working.'

'Maybe,' he said, as they sat down at the table.

Gerry put a small bottle of French lager down in front of Andrew and passed Jessica a glass of white wine. As they broke bread and shared around bowls of salad and plates of cold meat, he dealt cards.

'Right. Old Maid,' he said.

'Get in line,' Gerry called from the back of their formation of bicycles. It was the next morning, the final one before they'd have to pack up and drive back to England, and they were cycling down the straight, tree-lined main road into the nearest town. Jessica was at the front, followed by Patrick, Kirsty, Sue, Andrew and finally Gerry at the back, observing and corralling the rest of them like a domestique in the Tour de France.

La Flèche was a small but busy market town on the Loir tributary of the Sarthe. On market days the place bustled with local shoppers buying vegetables, meat, clothes and livestock. Mixed in were a few tourists, haphazardly stuttering and bluffing their way through simple orders for eight slices of ham, or asking for more vegetables than they could possibly use, relying on the honesty of the stall trader to give them what was needed.

As they arrived in the town, Jessica directed them to a side street where they could chain their bikes together. Though she didn't admit it, she knew La Flèche better than any of them, having cycled down there three times already that week to use an internet café and see if Peter had emailed her. She also liked to smoke Gauloises there while reading a Sartre novel she wasn't enjoying, on a bench overlooking the river.

'We'll stick together, yeah?' Gerry said. He spoke as though it was a question but it was really an order. He was desperate to keep the family bound as one for as long as possible during what was left of the holiday.

'Why Dad?' Patrick said. 'I fancy finding a bar. You and Mum want to get stuff for the barby. Andrew wants to take photos of fucking... geese or whatever. And those two probably want to go and look at dresses.'

'Sexist,' Jessica said.

'What?' he said, as though he'd never heard the word before, let alone been called it. 'My point is, why can't we all just do our own thing? We're not going to wander off. We're not six anymore.'

'Fine,' Gerry said, both disappointed and defensive. 'Well we'll meet back here in an hour then.'

The family dispersed. Patrick went first, in search of a bar that might have cheap French lager and maybe an English newspaper. Kirsty went with their parents, still slightly gun shy after her older sister blew up at her over the phone battery the other day. Which left just Andrew and Jessica.

'Thought I might tag along with you,' he said. 'If that's alright?'

'Sure. I'm going to try and find something for Peter. Cheese maybe. But don't tell Patrick. He'll just complain if he thinks we're driving back to England with a load of smelly French cheese in the car. Bet he won't even notice.'

Andrew smiled. This was true of their brother. His initial instinct was always to moan about something, then to actually deal with the reality of it later. Gerry used to make fun of him for it, saying he'd be perfect the trade he was going into – already imbued with the attitude of most Cadogan Family Builders' contractors.

'What about you?' she asked.

'Not bothered really. I might,' he said, holding up his camera. He had two with him. One was a digital thing he'd been given for Christmas. The other, which he held now, was a Canon that used expensive film and had a detachable flash. It was the one he'd used for his GCSE art project, developing the photos himself in the makeshift darkroom he occasionally set up in the downstairs loo at Ganton Villas.

'Go for it,' she said, as he raised the camera to his eye and took a photo of an old man. He was handing over money to a stall selling cooked chickens.

'I was thinking about what you said. Yesterday, I mean,' Andrew said. 'About uni and that.'

'Good. I hope.'

'Depends what you think of my idea.'

'What?'

'The army. I'm going to join up, I think.'

Jessica looked shocked. She had always known of his interest in the military – he had spent so much of his youth in the scout movement, almost seeing it as an apprenticeship. But she thought he might have dropped the idea of it as a career by now. Teenage Andrew seemed too sensitive and reserved for a life in the forces.

'What?' he said.

'I'm just a bit surprised, I suppose. I thought you might do university.'

'There's nothing I can study.'

'Photography?'

'It's a hobby,' he said. 'Think of what Dad would say. Mickey Mouse degree. Like when he talks about Marianne studying fashion,' he said, thinking about their cousin.

'At St Martins,' she said. Andrew didn't really get the relevance of that, but could sense the reverence in her voice.

'Yeah. Well, next year's my last at school isn't it? Plenty of time to make a decision. I suppose the point is, I'm not really good at anything else am I? I took maths A level because Mum asked me to. But I'm shit at it. And history.'

'But you're good at art.'

'Well, some of it. Not enough to make a job out of it.'

Jessica could sense him shrinking back into himself as they crossed the road to where a grey stone bridge arced over the Loir. She leaned against it. Below them the river flowed along gently, sparkles of sunlight interrupting the brown surface water, as did two or three small islands. Andrew saw a flash of blue as a kingfisher darted across the water.

'All I'm saying is that you should think about it.'

'There's nothing to think about.'

'What, so you've decided? It's the army.'

He nodded.

'The paras. I hope.'

'What if I got you a prospectus for Glasgow or somewhere? What's the worst that could happen?' she said, opening her handbag.

Jessica pulled out her cigarettes and a lighter. With a look back at the market, she turned away from Andrew and lit the cigarette.

'Look. Don't tell Mum and Dad.'

'Can I ...?' he said.

'Do you ...?'

'Sometimes. When I'm out.'

She offered him the packet and he took one, along with the lighter.

'What do you think Mum and Dad will say? When I tell them about it.'

'The army?'

Andrew nodded, as he took a drag on the cigarette.

'They won't like it. Mum will think it's dangerous. Dad will get annoyed because you're doing it because of Grandad.'

'Well I'm not. Grandad's an old snob.'

'So why are you?'

Andrew paused to think for a moment.

'Don't take this the wrong way,' he began. 'But I don't really feel like I ever fit in. At home, you know? I don't think Brighton's my town, or that I want to stay around there. The army's a life choice, isn't it? You get in, you travel. There's no worrying about careers and friends and all that shit. It's all there.'

'If you say so,' Jessica said, climbing to sit on the wall. She exhaled a lungful of cigarette smoke and brushed her hair behind her ears, before the breeze blew it back over her face again. 'You'll do what's right.'

'Stay there,' Andrew said, taking the lens off his camera. As Jessica put her cigarette to her lips, he took three photos. This, for him, was the thrill of film over digital. There was uncertainty – how things in the background could make the image entirely different to what he'd intended, or the wind and cigarette smoke might obscure or accentuate his sister's sharp features and untidy hair.

'Shit,' Jessica said, jumping down from the wall. 'Put your fag out. I've just seen them.'

Andrew ran over to the wall, and extinguished the half-smoked Gauloises, then threw the butt into the river. Jessica surreptitiously offered him a mint and they turned to face their parents and Kirsty as they approached.

'All done?' Jessica said.

'Not according to your father,' Sue said, carrying two heavy-looking bags of vegetables. 'But I'm not carrying any more than this.'

'Well it'll be your lookout if we run out of food.'

'Smells of cigarettes round here,' Sue said, looking about for whoever might be smoking.

'We're in bloody France. It always smells of cigarettes,' Gerry said. 'The sooner they ban it the better.'

'You try telling the French that,' he said, as Patrick ambled across the road. 'Look, while you've got that thing out, let's have a photo shall we? All of us.'

'I can take it,' Andrew volunteered, always happier to be behind the camera rather than in front of it.

'No. Get someone else to,' Sue said, gesturing at passing shoppers.

'Hang on,' Andrew said. 'Come over here and line up in front of this bench.'

As they did, he balanced his camera on the wall that overlooked the river.

'Do one with my digital as well,' Sue said, holding her camera towards him. 'I want to see how it comes out.'

He balanced the small, silver digital camera next to his own, checked the view on each and set the timers to ten seconds.

'Ready?' he called. And as the Cadogans organised themselves, he ran over to join them, standing on the end next to Gerry, who had his arm around Kirsty. A few second later, he heard the two clicks and went back over to retrieve the cameras.

When Andrew gave his mum the digital, she immediately set about cooing over the photo of their last holiday together. He walked away, tinkering with the camera, while Jessica caught him up.

'Are you going to tell them then? What you want to do?'

'Eventually, yeah.'

'I still think you should think about it. Uni, I mean.'

'I know,' he said. 'But I won't.'

Jessica sighed as they all reached the bikes and she started unlocking them for everyone.

'Will you give me that photo? The one of me,' she said. 'When it's developed I mean.'

'If you want. It might not be any good.'

'I'm sure it'll be brilliant. What about that one of all of us? Will you give that to Mum?'

'Don't know,' he said. 'Might keep that one. I can have it on my wall when I go.'

Andrew smiled, mounted his bike and pedalled away after his brother who'd already gone without waiting for the others, who were still organising their shopping and climbing onto their saddles. Before Jessica could go too, her mum stopped her.

'He alright?'

'Yeah. Fine I think.'

'He seems quiet to me.'

'He's good, don't worry about him. He's just a bit thoughtful at the moment.'

Jessica then climbed onto her saddle, checked behind her and pushed away into the road. She quickly caught her brothers up, settling into a rhythm as they rode back to the house and the last full day of their holiday.

Gretna

Jessica

'Hang on,' she said, finishing her tea.

Jessica went to the back of the van and began rooting around in her things until she found what she was looking for. Inside her bag, wedged at the back of her diary, was the photo Andrew had taken of her on the bridge in La Flèche. Looking at it, she was thrown back to that earlier version of herself. The cigarette in her hand, the tight-fitting red t-shirt and denim shorts. Dan didn't even know she used to smoke. She wasn't sure anyone did apart from Andrew and Peter (who now, according to Facebook, was a hedge fund manager in Amsterdam).

'Here,' Jessica said, putting the photo down in front of them. It looked like something from a magazine advert, before it was frowned on to make smoking look like an aspirational habit. 'He took this right before the family one. He framed it when it was developed and gave it to me for my birthday.'

'You keep it with you?'

'I normally have it in my bedside table. Barely ever look at it really. When I decided to come I brought it with me for some reason.

I suppose I thought he should be here in some way. If we're going to spread Dad's ashes.'

'Why don't you have it on display?'

'I don't know really. It feels like one of those photos that'll trigger a lot of questions. Who took it, where, why. Besides, I'm smoking, which—'

'Everyone knows you smoked, Jessica,' Patrick interrupted. 'Mum, Dad, us. Even Dan. You were really terrible at hiding it.'

'Dan?'

'When he first came round to meet Mum and Dad years ago. You disappeared off to the bathroom and we all saw smoke coming out of the window. Dad would've brought it up. But he knew you'd quit when you realised no one cared you were doing it.'

Jessica thought about responding to this. But her brother was absolutely right.

'You should put it on display,' Kirsty said. 'He was a good photographer. Probably could've made a career of it.'

'It's funny. He took that just after we discussed what he should do after school. He was talking about joining the army. I told him to pursue the photography at uni.'

'What might have been, eh?' Patrick said.

The three of them sipped their cups of tea and looked at the final photo in the album still on the table. It showed Gerry, Sue and Andrew standing in front of the house. Jessica remembered taking it, just before the family split – Kirsty and her parents went off to Dijon, Luxembourg and Bruges before heading home; she drove Andrew and Patrick back to Hove, then took a train into London to return to the life she was slowly building there.

Halfway through the album, Jessica had wondered why their dad had chosen this one. There didn't seem much to mark it out from other family holidays, except that it was their last together. But then, when she remembered that conversation on the bridge, it made sense.

The week after they got back, Andrew told his parents that he was going to sign up for the paratroopers when he finished his A levels. They reacted exactly as he had expected, but he'd done it nonetheless.

That holiday to France wasn't just the last family holiday they had together, it was a turning point in Andrew's life, the moment he stopped being one version of himself and became another. It could be argued that if he'd never signed up, or had decided it was better to study, none of what followed would have happened.

But that kind of thinking was hypothetical, Jessica told herself. Some things were out of our control.

'Poor Andrew,' Kirsty said, after a minute or two's contemplative silence. Jessica never quite agreed with her always taking the side of a victim. Although in this case perhaps it was justified.

'Do you ever think,' she said, but stopped. Maybe this wasn't the kind of thought she should express beyond the sanctity of her own kitchen, with Dan.

'Think what?' Patrick said.

'Never mind. Doesn't matter.'

'Clearly it does.'

Jessica thought for a moment. What she had to say could go either way. But they were here now, so why not?

'I was going to ask if you ever think that maybe he wasn't meant to stick around? I know it sounds cruel, but you have to hear me out.'

She looked at both her siblings. They seemed ready to jump down her throat, but also prepared to give her a chance to explain.

'I mean... You know there are those people who seem destined to never grow old. Like Kurt Cobain or Amy Winehouse or whoever. The burner outers. Well maybe Andrew was a bit like that. Maybe he was never going to stay with us. It just took him a while to realise it.'

'He was family,' Kirsty said.

'I do know that. And I love him, always will. But you don't

choose your family, do you? That's the saying isn't it? Maybe Andrew thought the only way to get around that was to choose not to have one at all.'

'So you're saying he hated us all along?'

'No... Kirsty... it's hard to explain. I'm saying that he got to an age when he realised he was never really part of us. So he left. I know I'm not making sense.'

'What, so he just wasn't a Cadogan?'

'Maybe,' Jessica said. 'I think that's what I mean.'

'Or it's just the two of you excusing yourselves.'

'Kirsty,' Patrick said, a note of warning in his voice.

Again, the three of them sat silently together. The only sound was the cars passing by on the motorway, and the occasional thundering truck causing the thin walls of the van to rattle and shake. Jessica noticed that Patrick's eyes were a little watery and red. Andrew was a death without a body to them. There was a finality to what he did, but never a chance to say goodbye.

'How did you tell your kids?' Kirsty asked, after a moment. 'Livvy's getting older. I'll have to tell her about him soon.'

'I waited until Max was ten to explain properly. Before that he just accepted that Uncle Andrew wasn't around anymore. Elspeth doesn't know it all yet. Just that there was an Uncle Andrew and now there isn't.'

'Same. Maggie didn't ask much about him. She never knew him so there was never anything to miss. Only Max...' he said, trailing off.

Jessica laughed to herself. The other two looked at her.

'Sorry,' she said. 'I was just thinking. It's a bit like the Father Christmas thing, isn't it? "I'll tell you but you must promise not to tell your sister and cousins".'

Patrick smiled, but the grin was swiftly wiped away when Kirsty said, 'Not that they ever see much of each other.'

'No,' Jessica said. 'Well maybe that should change, too.'

She looked at her sister and brother, both of them lost in memories of the absent member of their brood. And Jessica knew she had to bring it up again, the question she could tell they were all still asking, and say what she thought.

'Why do you think Dad sent us to Islay?'

'Not again, Jess,' Kirsty said. 'Him and Mum—'

'Yes, I know that. But . . . what if there is something more?'

'Jess—'

'Come on, Kirsty. I know you're still wondering. We all are. If Dad did discover something.'

'How though?'

'I don't know. But everything about this feels like it's leading to something.'

'I'd know if he was there,' Kirsty said firmly. 'And he's not. I told Patrick earlier, you heard me.'

'And what if you don't?'

'I do. You're clinging to something to make yourself feel better,' she said. The words were a little on the nose, Jessica thought, but her tone was kind and sympathetic at least. 'If he's there, if that's the point of all this, then you won't feel so bad about it all. But deep down you must know.'

'What?'

'Jess. We're never going to see him again. I hate to say it, but it's true.'

As she said it, Kirsty started to get up. But Patrick grabbed her arm.

'Not yet,' he said. He was staring down at the table, almost grimacing. 'I've got something to tell you both. Might as well.'

Patrick

'About Andrew,' Patrick said. As they got further into the trip, he had been aching to tell them the truth. Several times today he had almost opened up, but the moment never seemed right. He knew though that he had to say something before tomorrow, before they arrived on the beach. And so when Kirsty got up, it was now or never.

'What?' she said. 'It better not be another bloody thing about him being on this island. Because I swear—'

'It's not,' he said, cutting her off. 'It's about when he left the army. What you were talking about earlier.'

'We know what happened when he left,' Jessica said. 'He failed that medical. Asthma.'

'He didn't. It was nothing to do with that,' Patrick drew breath. It was time. 'Andrew left six months early. He was discharged after his second tour. After some assessment they did of him. He'd been told he couldn't go on another tour and he kicked off.'

'But Mum said—'

'Mum didn't know,' Patrick said, cutting Jessica off. 'Nobody knew, except me.'

'Come on, Patrick. They must've—'

'Stop,' he said. Patrick took the bottle from the box, poured himself a whisky and took a sip. 'Look. There's more.'

Kirsty and Jessica were looking at him expectantly. He had no idea how they might react; whether this, now, could mark the end of his trip.

'Andrew didn't come home after he left. He went to London. An old friend of his found my email address and told me what happened,' Patrick said, unsure of how to say what came next. 'I found him at a homeless shelter in Lambeth.'

When he looked up, Jessica and Kirsty both appeared stunned. Mouths slightly agape, waiting for him to add context.

'I'd been searching for him for a while. A bloke there helped me out.'

'He was homeless?'

Patrick nodded. 'He told me he never slept rough, was always in shelters and that. But I didn't believe him.'

'Did Dad—'

'As I said. No one knew.'

'How long?' Jessica asked. 'I mean how long had he been out there?'

'A while. Few months maybe. He always said that he was going to come home eventually. But he didn't know how to tell everyone what had happened. In the end we agreed that he could stay with me for a bit. Then we'd pretend that I'd gone to pick him up from the base and bring him home. I came up with the idea that he'd failed a medical.'

Jessica looked at the whisky bottle, which told him enough about how she had taken this news.

'So it was the second time then?' she said, after what felt like hours to Patrick. 'He'd disappeared before?'

Patrick nodded. He thought back to the days he'd spent in London ten years ago, searching for Andrew in the same places he had looked before. That time the photo didn't register with anyone. The same man who helped him in Lambeth was still there and remembered Andrew. He took Patrick's details, but he never heard from him.

After a couple of weeks it became clear that Andrew had probably bypassed the capital altogether, and had likely either gone north or across the channel into Europe.

'I went looking there again, when he left. I went back to the shelters and everything.'

'How long did you know? The first time,' Kirsty said. 'How long did you know that he had gone AWOL before you found him?'

'Not long. Weeks maybe.'

'Weeks?' she said, shocked.

'I know,' Patrick said. 'I know it sounds bad. But just look at it from my point of view. When I got that email I thought I'd find him on drugs or something. I thought I could sort him out before he saw the rest of you. Then maybe...' Patrick trailed off. He could never adequately explain why he had behaved as he did back then. Even to Suzanne, who was the only other person who had known about it until now. The only possible explanation was that he was trying to protect his parents, to stop the endless worrying that would come from knowing their son had left the army and was absent somewhere in a city of millions.

'Then maybe what?' Jessica said, softly.

'I don't know. Maybe I could've helped him I suppose. I thought for a while that I had.'

Patrick stifled tears. Every time he went over this, he found things he should have known or should've done differently. A few months after Andrew went for good, Patrick learned that discharged service people frequently struggle to hold down regular work. When he met the old friend of Andrew's who had sent him that email, Patrick realised that his brother quite possibly had PTSD after his tour in Afghanistan, where a friend of his was killed standing next to him.

All these things about Andrew Cadogan came out after he was no longer part of their lives. They piled up, convincing Patrick to never let on what he knew about that first disappearance, years before.

'I've blamed myself for so long,' Patrick said. 'I knew he had it in him. I'd seen him do it. Then when Mel,' he said, but something stopped him from continuing.

'Mel what?' Kirsty said.

'She was pregnant,' Patrick said. 'Just before the business got in trouble. She got pregnant but things were bad between them and she got rid of it. He told me in a pub once.'

'And you never—'

'I couldn't,' he said quickly. 'Andrew made me promise.'

'Andrew's gone,' Kirsty said.

'I always thought about how he'd feel if he came back. And I've broken every promise I made. Every time I told him I'd keep a secret, I meant it. I know it doesn't sound right, but it's true.'

'So why are you telling us now?' Kirsty asked.

'Because he's not going to come back,' Patrick said, tearfully.

The words seemed to hang there for an age. But then, finally, Jessica spoke.

'I understand,' she said. 'I could be angry. We both could. But I suppose neither of us know how we would've reacted, had we been the ones he spoke to.'

Jessica reached out and put her hand over Patrick's. He looked up and into Kirsty's eyes.

'Me too,' she said, and put her hand on top of his and Jessica's.

While Patrick wasn't totally sure whether either of them meant it, he was grateful for their understanding, and relieved to have told them the last things they needed to know about their brother.

Jessica

She had been planning to talk about this later in the trip. Maybe when they were on the island, or even on the way home. But given the spirit of honesty that was emerging, Jessica changed her mind.

'I've got something to say, too,' she said, quietly. Then, without waiting to be prompted, she continued. 'We could've bailed him out. Paid for therapy or whatever he needed. Sorted the business. The money was there. We even discussed it, when I got home after that awful evening at Mum and Dad's. We could have used the savings we had for doing up the house, then taken a share of the business to recoup it.'

'And Dan said no?' Patrick asked, ever keen to stick the boot in on her husband.

'No,' Jessica said, with some hesitation. 'I did.'

The words seemed to hover there for a little while. This would occasionally happen to Jessica, the sensation that something she had said might mortally offend or upset everyone in a room.

'You said no?' Kirsty said.

'I didn't think it would help. I still don't, if I'm honest. Yes, it would've bailed him out. But how would that have really solved anything?'

'He might not have left, Jessica. He might have felt supported or loved or whatever.'

'He was supported and loved, for Christ's sake. Giving someone thousands of pounds is not supporting or loving them. Helping them to change is.'

'And that wouldn't have helped him change?'

Jessica stopped for a moment. She couldn't adequately express how she felt back then. Yes, they had the money to bail her brother out and to save the business, with no ill effect on their parents. Dan, with his background as a business consultant, would have been able to straighten the commercial affairs out and steer Cadogan Family Builders through the aftershocks of the 2008 crash and recession. Andrew could have stayed on as staff, earning a wage and be given the support he needed to come to terms with whatever had happened to him when he left the military.

But doing all that didn't feel right somehow. The money had been saved to renovate their house, so they didn't have to move. Dan was becoming involved with local politics and was making noises about a run at office for the first time.

Besides, Andrew had been offered a way out of his problematic life before, and not taken it. If they had given him the money and the plan went wrong, it would have jeopardised everything. Their house would remain untouched, Dan would have a failed business in his portfolio, and Andrew could have remained just as bad as ever.

'I didn't know what would happen,' Jessica said, by way of explanation. 'Had I thought for a moment that he'd . . . do what he did. Well of course I'd have given him the money. I'd have done anything, Kirsty. Anything.'

'You know,' she said bitterly, 'I hope you see his face every time you look at that stupid extension.'

'Oh come off it, Kirsty,' Patrick said.

'No. Absolutely not. She *could* have prevented all this. Christ, had she actually thought about anything except herself and her bloody house maybe things wouldn't have gotten so bad between us. We wouldn't even be here.'

'Jesus.'

'Instead she kept the money, made Mum and Dad bail him out and then tried to sell the house to wrap it all up.'

'Don't bring that into it,' Patrick said. Jessica was surprised to hear her normally fence-sitting brother come to her defence.

'Well why the fuck not? Clearly, there's some correlation. She was the only one who wanted Dad to sell when Mum died.'

'Because there's a fucking massive mortgage on that place Kirsty!' Jessica said. 'It wasn't fair that he had to keep the business running to pay it. Working when he should've been retired.'

'He liked to work,' Kirsty snapped. 'If you ever bloody visited or spoke to him you'd have known that.'

The instinct to stand up from where she was leaning against the cooker and slap Kirsty seemed to come from nowhere. But come it did.

Jessica couldn't remember the last time she'd been in a fight.

Probably at school after some hockey match. Certainly not with her sister. The age difference between them meant that despite their rows, Jessica had comforted and advised Kirsty through her teens and early twenties. It was an almost maternal connection, until the falling out.

In the moments after she struck her, Kirsty sat at the table, shocked and holding her hand to her red raw cheek.

'Kirsty, I'm—'

'We'll drop you at Glasgow airport,' Kirsty said. 'You can get home from there. Maybe you shouldn't have come in the first place. You clearly didn't want to.'

With that, she stood, walked past her sister to the top bunk, climbed in and pulled the curtain across. A minute or two later, Jessica heard her muffled sobs and cries. With guilt coursing through her, she made to go over and offer her apologies again. She wanted to explain and rationalise why she had lashed out. But she felt a hand on her arm.

'Not now,' Patrick said quietly. 'Maybe she was—'

'Ahoy hoy!' a cheerful voice said, interrupting Patrick. It was followed by a pasty, smiling, bald head poking through the door of the camper van. 'Am I to assume you're Patrick Cadogan?'

'You are,' Patrick said, ditching the seriousness with which he was speaking to Jessica in favour of matey joviality – something Dan could never quite master when speaking with workmen. 'Come in. Or aboard. Or whatever,' he said.

'I'm Keith,' said their visitor. He was wearing bright orange overalls and big chunky black boots. He placed his clipboard under his arm to shake Patrick's hand, ignoring Jessica completely. 'I'll be helping to get The Adventurer back on its adventures,' he said, smiling. 'It's the wheel, is it?'

'Yeah. We had a blow out and I can't change it. Seems totally stuck on.'

'Aye. I had a wee look before I came to see you. Looks like all the grit and dirt and shite has fused it together,' he said, filling out some of his paperwork. 'No matter. I'll sort you out but you may be in for a bit of a wait here.'

'How long?' Jessica asked. Her mind had already drifted to thoughts of getting to the airport, finding something decent to eat and sleeping on the flight home. She always slept well on planes.

'Hour maybe. Once I've got all the shite out and changed it. Maybe a bit longer. I'd settle in if I were you,' Keith said. 'Happy memories,' he added, gesturing to the photo album that was open on the table.

Jessica checked her watch. It had just gone one in the afternoon. Plenty of time to get to the airport and on a plane. The others would still have two hundred miles to drive just to get to the ferry, if they even bothered to carry on. She couldn't see the point at this stage. The trip had proved that the Cadogan siblings were only able to be civil up to a point. But any length of time in each other's company would ultimately become fraught and end unhappily. That was just the state of their relationship now. No wonder really. Their kinship was like a marriage trying to stumble on after infidelity and betrayal. No matter how polite they could be, these things would always remain hanging over them.

Patrick signed the paperwork and set about making Keith a cup of tea.

'This yours, is it?' Keith asked Jessica, looking around the camper.

'It was our dad's.'

'Lucky man,' he said. 'Always wanted one of these.'

She thought about telling him that he could have it. But instead smiled and returned to her bunk to wait out the rest of her leg of the trip.

CHAPTER EIGHT

Somewhere outside Glasgow

Kirsty

She woke when she felt the rumble of the van starting up. After the row and the slap, Kirsty had gone to her bunk and started scrolling through Andrew's Facebook page. She must have fallen asleep as she did.

This page, more than what Jessica had done, was why she was upset. Being the youngest meant that she also had the fewest memories of her brother. Some of his biggest life moments had taken place when she was too young to either acknowledge them or store them away to look back on in years to come. And, if she was honest with herself, she had only started to think of him as a friend, rather than an annoying older brother, in her mid-teens – part of which he spent with the army. She had so little of him in her life. That's what really hurt.

It was strange. She had thought of Andrew yesterday, even before the photo album came out and reminded each of them about the ghost constantly at their sides. It was when they drove past Preston, where Andrew's one and only long-term girlfriend came from. She hadn't mentioned it at the time, but memories of Mel drifted back to her.

She was short, with a roundish face and perpetually red cheeks. Her blonde hair was cut short and she had an almost slavish commitment to wearing black jeans and band t-shirts. Andrew claimed to have met her through a mutual friend in Brighton. However, everyone was fairly sure they had met online – not least because Mel had so few friends on the South Coast, except for the girls she lived with, all doing MAs at Sussex University like her. Mel's subject was criminology and criminal justice, which she was hoping to use to work with reoffenders. Unsurprisingly, she had a morbid interest in the worst types of people and read grisly murder stories avidly.

Everyone in the family liked Mel. She and Andrew were together for two years, separating before he disappeared for no reason that anyone could understand, and which Andrew refused to talk about.

Sue had been in touch with her to ask if she'd heard anything from Andrew. But Mel knew as much as any of them. And by that point she'd left Brighton to live in Manchester, Andrew having seemed to be her only tie to the city.

Kirsty had looked Mel up on Facebook yesterday. Catchpole, the surname they all knew her by, was in brackets after her new surname, Banner. Her profile picture showed the same short hair, rosy cheeks and big smile. But now she was surrounded by a family – husband and two young boys. Below her name were the words 'You and Melanie have one mutual friend'. Kirsty didn't need to click to find out who that was.

She pulled back the curtain to look down the van. Jessica was sitting at the table, on her phone. Patrick was driving. She wondered how much longer it would be before they could drop her sister off and continue on together. Just the two of them.

'What time is it?' she called loudly, over the constant thrum of the engine.

'Almost four,' he said, not looking back at her.

'Jesus. How long were we stranded for?'

'Don't.'

'Right.'

'Well, where are we?'

'Near Glasgow,' he said.

Kirsty climbed out of her bunk. The sensation of walking through the van while it was moving was strange. She felt unsteady and uncertain.

For a moment, she thought about sitting down opposite Jessica. But that would be too awkward. Like working next to an employee you'd just sacked. Instead, she continued down the van, climbing over the gear stick and handbrake to join Patrick up front.

The view was much better from the passenger seat. She could see out across the sprawl that pre-empted Scotland's second city. The neat rows of houses, gardens and fences, interrupted by warehouses and then tower blocks which climbed out from the ground like trees in a cemetery.

'Celtic Park, that,' Patrick said, pointing at a vast, modern edifice that looked to Kirsty like a button waiting to be pushed.

'Fascinating,' she said, drily. Although she was inwardly pleased that Patrick had changed so little from the boy who got excited when he spotted a football stadium on long drives. Knowing this, their dad would often take strategic detours so they would pass within sight of Anfield, Old Trafford or one of the other churches of noise and sport that pockmarked Britain.

For all that, Kirsty was worried that Patrick driving now meant she would have to be at the wheel as they went through Loch Lomond, the Trossachs and small lakeside towns, down to the ferry terminal at Kennacraig. She was used to city driving in her little Nissan Micra – nipping about through tight roads and rarely going above twenty miles per hour. Driving a lumbering van through the dicey, winding roads of the Scottish countryside would, she was sure, be too much for her.

Then she saw a sign for the airport, and Kirsty took a sharp breath. This was it then. For the three of them at least.

Jessica

It was true that for the first hour of what was meant to be her final stretch on the trip, Jessica had considered apologising and backing down. She had delivered the slap, after all – something she hadn't done in years, although perhaps too recently for a well-respected, intelligent woman such as herself. (It had been an over-reaction to some broken crockery in a shared house. Not her finest moment.)

But the more she thought about it, the more this was the right decision. Whatever their dad's intentions, he was never going to put his family back together by forcing them into a camper van. When had a van ever made anything better?

No. The Cadogans – what remained of them – were a shattered crystal glass. The pieces were too dispersed and various for a repair job. No matter what they did, or how polite they were, there would always be something missing. It was impossible to live as they had and not end up this way. She had known it from the start of the trip and nothing had changed. There was no way back for them.

'I'll do this bit then?' Patrick had said, once the impossibly cheerful mechanic Keith had finished his work (taking a full hour longer than quoted) and wished them well on their way. The question was rhetorical. There was no way that Jessica would drive the leg to the airport even though he'd had a drink.

'Yes. I think that's . . .'

'Sure.' He hadn't wanted to say directly what they were both thinking. She could see it in his face, Patrick was rubbish at hiding his emotions.

'You can do it without me. I'm not sure I'm cut out for this sort of thing.'

With that, he headed to the driver's cab and sat down in the uncomfortable grey seat, not bothering to brush away the bits of crisps, biscuits and sandwich crusts that had collected in the stitched folds. She, meanwhile, took her place at the table, alone, while Kirsty slept or seethed in her bunk. She later ambled through, all haughty and refusing to look at Jessica, climbing in next to Patrick in an ungainly sort of way, almost snagging her slipper sock on the gear stick.

'Fifteen minutes,' Patrick said, in between musings on Scottish football stadia. If she wasn't so sick of Kirsty, she might pity her for having to spend the next few days listening to Patrick talk about that sort of rubbish. She wondered what they might do after the ashes were scattered. Part of her wanted to suggest setting fire to the camper van and pushing it into the sea, like some sort of Viking burial for recreational vehicles. But she doubted the joke would be appreciated.

'Okay,' Jessica said quietly. Now, she knew, was the time, to ensure there could be no going back. Or rather, no going any further and actually quite a lot of going back.

She opened the easyjet app on her phone and found the next flight to Luton. Unfortunately, it wouldn't leave for another four hours. Little matter, Jessica thought. Glasgow Airport would surely have a café and a bookshop and maybe even a little bar where she could take the edge off what had been a horrible couple of days. She booked one of the few remaining seats on the flight, paying almost two hundred pounds for what would be less than an hour in the skies.

Sadly, it was worth every penny.

Jessica lurched to the right, as Patrick drove the camper van left onto the slip road, taking them towards Glasgow Airport. Outside, she could see the occasional plane, flying low as it ascended, or gently descended towards the airport, bringing many of those on board home.

Jessica: All fine so far. One or two squabbles but nothing to write home about. Will tell all when you're back xx

She hit send on the message and watched as the little blue bar at the top filled and sent it to Dan. Jessica felt bad for lying. But if she told him that she was abandoning the trip, climbing off like a cyclist halfway up a mountain, he would only call and persuade her to change her mind. Better to explain it all when he was back from the holiday she should have been on. Although, Jessica was tempted to omit certain details like the slap, the drinking and the reminders of Andrew.

The part of the journey which took them just past the grey blocks of the Gorbals and into the airport seemed to pass in seconds. Jessica spent most of it wondering whether or not she'd made the right decision, every few seconds considering calling to Patrick to continue on with her in the van. But soon enough, he took the turn into the airport and she stayed silent.

'I'll park up,' Patrick said, driving towards the short stay lot, which he would doubtless struggle to get the van into.

'No,' she said quickly. 'No need. Drop off's fine.'

'You sure? I'll pay.'

'It's not about the money,' she said, as if they were talking about thousands, rather than a three quid charge for a few minutes in a multi-storey.

Patrick did as she said and followed her directions.

'Fucking bollocks,' he said, slowing down before they reached the little car park where she could get out.

'What?'

'Fucking height restriction,' he said, coming to a stop a few metres before a barrier. A car horn sounded from behind them, then three more, all of slightly different tones. An orchestra of the irritated.

'FUCK OFF,' Patrick yelled back into the van, to no one and everyone at once.

'Just let me out here,' Jessica said, climbing up from the table and grabbing her bags.

'We can't let you out here.'

'Why not? You can just get back on the road. Come on, these people are getting annoyed.'

After a moment's hesitation, Patrick pulled the van to the right, just enough to let some cars through. He shouted, 'do one,' at another passing beeping motorist, and Jessica got out of the van.

As she was hit by the smell of airplane fuel mixed with the fumes of the waiting traffic behind them, Patrick called, 'You can't get out there.'

'Why not?'

'We haven't said goodbye.'

'Well,' she said, looking for a kinder way to say what she was about to. 'Goodbye, I suppose.'

With that, Jessica hoicked her handbag over her shoulder, pulled the handle out from her suitcase and set off. In front of her, the drop off point was packed with families and friends hugging loved ones as they either left or arrived home. A girl in cropped denim shorts and a straw hat embraced a father who must've been wondering what happened to the past eighteen years, then shrieked as she saw a friend across the car park. Three lads in tight-fitting t-shirts and jeans laughed together as they climbed out of a people carrier and marched off, in search of the airport bar no doubt.

Jessica looked back to see Patrick reverse, then pull away from the barrier that had denied him entry, as well as their proper goodbye.

He offered a small, apologetic wave as he drove past. Kirsty didn't even look out.

Alone now, Jessica walked towards the terminal.

Patrick

They had been driving for fifteen minutes before he calmed down enough to speak.

'Fucking ridiculous,' he said.

'It was only traffic. God. Calm down. You were blocking their way in.'

'Not that,' he said.

'Well it was her that wanted to leave,' Kirsty said, guessing what he was talking about.

'It didn't need to happen, though, did it? You could've just said something. Apologised.'

'Apologised?' she said, incredulous at the very idea of it. 'She *hit* me, Patrick. I'm not sure if you missed that?'

'Yes. And if you'd said sorry for being a total fucking dick when you argued then she might've said sorry for that. You know what she's like. It's never her fault, is it? Never.'

'So why should I say sorry?'

Patrick didn't answer while he turned onto a new road and filtered into the fast-moving traffic that was speeding away from Glasgow, northwards.

'Because there's something bigger at play here. Dad wanted the three of us to do this together. It was the last thing he asked for. And it's not going to happen.'

'Well,' Kirsty said. But she seemed to stop herself. This was no time for point scoring and debate. There was no right and wrong.

Just three people in a bit of a mess. Rowing about it more wouldn't solve anything.

'I know,' she said, as they drove onto the Erskine Bridge.

Patrick looked out of the window as the steel cables which held the bridge together flickered past and distorted the view of the Clyde below, the banks and trees that lined it, and the city away in the distance. Like watching a scene emerge through a zoetrope.

'We'll get it done, though,' she said.

CHAPTER NINE

Inveraray, Scotland

Kirsty

It was just gone six when they stopped for the final changeover of the day. They were outside a petrol station in Inveraray, on the edge of Loch Fyne. While Patrick had gone in to buy something for them to eat later, and more wine, Kirsty crossed the road to stretch her legs. There was a small shingle beach that led down to the glassy water.

Earlier on, the weather had cleared to make room for a beautiful pink and orange sunset which seemed to bounce off of every lake surface and mountain side. The colours almost didn't seem real; like an enhanced photograph. It had faded into darkness, and with so little light pollution in this part of Scotland, it was hard to make out the landscape. Instead, she looked out on shadows and silhouettes across the water, and at the reflected glow of the moon, which began halfway across the lake and streamed back to where she stood.

'Lovely evening,' said a strange voice from behind her. Kirsty turned to see a woman of about sixty, accompanied by a slightly overweight Jack Russell who walked by her side without a lead.

'It is.'

'Visiting?'

'Passing through,' she said, thinking back to the drive through the Trossachs, during which she had sat in the front seat, listening to Patrick's interminable radio sports programmes and his occasional remarks about the dramatic scenery. Kirsty meanwhile had said very little since they left Jessica back at Glasgow Airport. 'We're driving to Islay,' she added, not wanting to seem rude to this woman who had stopped out of human kindness.

'Whisky drinkers, are you?'

'Something like that,' Kirsty said, looking back over the road to where Patrick was now filling the van with petrol.

'Say no more,' the woman said, clearly thinking that she and her brother were a married couple, rather than a pair of bickering siblings on an ever increasingly doomed mission.

The woman's dog began to walk away, sniffing pebbles and stones, wet with the lapping water of the lake. 'I think that's me,' she said, walking after the dog. Kirsty noticed then that it was wearing a neon hoop around its neck, so it could be seen when night crawled in. Although it looked like it had caught a radioactive frisbee.

'See ya,' Kirsty said, only afterwards recognising the unlikeliness of seeing whoever that was again.

Alone, she looked up into the clear sky. There was a distant light, blinking and moving steadily across the velvet canopy of night. She couldn't work out which direction the plane might be heading, based on her position on the ground. But it put her in mind of Jessica, who would be up there herself now. Probably still tapping away at her phone, desperate to land so that she could be in range of 4G signal.

Her mind leaped forward to the next time she might see her sister. Though when that would be, she had no idea. With the old family home gutted and up for sale, there was nothing tethering her to Brighton now, so a visit was unlikely. Kirsty, meanwhile, was even less likely to visit Jessica in the little town she had mistaken as a proxy for the entire world and everyone in it.

Most likely, it would be at another funeral. They would become that family who only saw one another when someone has died, making awkward conversation over vol au vants and cold chicken goujons. Perhaps they'd talk cheerfully to their nieces and nephews who looked nervous about being yammered at by grown-ups they barely recognised and whose tone would be over-familiar. Saying things like, 'you've grown, haven't you?' because Max might be a foot taller than when she last saw him, without realising that growth doesn't seem so sharp and unexpected if you're present while it's happening.

Patrick

He looked at his sister, standing there across the road, gazing out over the water as though it might yield some sort of answer for whatever she was contemplating. Kirsty was like that. The type who'd look to nature when pondering the things life was doing to her. Rather than looking inwards, where the truth might actually be.

Patrick had the phone to his ear, listening to the ring and hoping she'd pick up. He'd tried Chloe a minute ago too, standing around the side of the petrol station where they kept the gas cannisters and net bags of firewood. But it had gone straight to voicemail.

This time he got the same message again

'Welcome to the voicemail answering service. The person you are trying to call is unavailable.'

'Fuck sake.'

Kirsty had been talking to some woman with a dog. God knows why she was distracting strangers, Patrick thought, climbing back into the van. He chucked the pizzas he'd bought into the little fridge, where they joined half a bag of salad left over from last night and Jessica's coffee, stored in a nice paper bag.

He felt his phone buzz in his pocket.

'Hello?'

'You rang.'

'Yeah,' he said, sitting down on the steps that led down to the van's door, where Kirsty wouldn't be able to see him. 'Sorry, I . . .'

'No. It's fine. I was getting the kids' dinner ready,' Chloe said. Patrick checked his watch. It was about now that Maggie would be eating with Stu and Sarah too, before they put her to bed in a couple of hours. He made a mental note to Facetime her as soon as he could. 'How's it going? You sound a bit . . .' she said, trailing off.

'I am, I suppose,' Patrick said, steadying his nerves. 'Look, would you think badly of me if I jacked this in and came home?'

Chloe took a second. In the meantime he heard a scream in the background and either a plate, knife or fork clatter against the ground.

'No,' she said, at last. 'But . . . I don't know, Patrick. What's happened?'

'Jess is gone. She had a row with Kirsty. Now it's just the two of us and I'm wondering if it's really worth it. We're still nowhere near the ferry. If we called it a day now we'd be back by tomorrow morning.'

'And that's what you want to do is it?' she said. There was no judgment or sense of coercion to her voice. He supposed they weren't yet familiar enough with each other for that. The thing was that Patrick didn't really have anyone else he could call in a moment like this. At least no one who wouldn't have their own thoughts on how the Cadogan family should settle its differences.

'I don't know, I really don't. All I do know is that this isn't what Dad wanted. The two of us carrying on because we have to. Like a pair of fucking martyrs.'

'Well what did he want?'

'For us to reconnect. You know, become a family again. But it's not going to happen. There's so much water under the fucking bridge there's no bridge left.'

'And he said that did he? In the letter?'

'No. Well,' Patrick said. 'Not as such.'

'Look. Far be it from me to correct all your shit. But you told me your dad asked you to scatter his ashes on a beach in Islay, right?'

'Right.'

'So there you go.'

Patrick thought about this for a bit. It was true that they'd each read something different into the letter that accompanied the whisky, the photo albums and the keys to the van. Whether it was about Andrew's current whereabouts, a great sibling reconciliation, or his way of compelling his remaining children to find joy in the things he loved – good whisky, travelling around in a camper van, life out on the road. If he'd included a set of fishing rods that last one might have been the true reason.

But there was also the possibility that his letter meant none of that. Instead, it was exactly what it said: put aside your differences and scatter my remains where I was happiest. Patrick was just shocked that the place wasn't where he'd spent so many years, and the beach where his wife was last found. Or even somewhere close to where he'd grown up, back in Hertfordshire.

'Still there?' Chloe asked.

'Sort of.'

'Look. Don't come home, Patrick. You'll regret it more if you do than if you carry on.'

'I know you're right.'

'But . . .' she prompted.

'I'm sitting here on the steps of the van so Kirsty can't see me. We've got however many fucking hours left before we get there. And I really don't know how we're going to get through it.'

'You will. Just talk to her. I barely know your sister, but from what you've told me if anyone wants to put the mess that is your

206

family back together it's her,' she said. 'You don't mind me calling it a mess, do you?'

'Nah,' he said, thinking that mess might be too kind a term if anything.

'Well then. Ball's in your court, isn't it? And besides, if you jack it in, I'll refuse to see you for another week.'

Patrick laughed. 'And if I stay?' he said.

'Five days. Got the kids. I don't think they're ready to know about you yet.'

He laughed again, then he and Chloe said their goodbyes and Patrick got up from the steps, carrying the beers he'd also just bought from the supermarket. Kirsty was still over the road, watching the stars and the lake and breathing in the fresh air that was so abnormal to them.

With his dad in the back of his mind, and his remains still in the back of the van, he crossed over.

Kirsty

'Got pizza. Unless you're catching some oysters or something,' Patrick said, appearing next to her. 'We should get a move on. No chance of making the ferry but we need to find a place to stay.'

'Lovely isn't it?' she said, hardly listening to him.

'Stunning, Kirst. But we're already well behind.'

'So what's the rush?' she said. 'Let's sit here a minute. There's a nice little spot near the port. Found it online.'

Kirsty sat down on the damp stones and looked out across Loch Fyne. Patrick stayed standing for a moment, then joined her, handing her a cold can of Old Speckled Hen from the bag he was carrying. He seemed reluctant. But she was adamant that there was no sense in haring towards the port for no reason.

They opened their beers and took a swig. Kirsty couldn't get on with this sort of mud and sticks ale. But in the absence of anything she might have preferred, it would have to do.

'You remembered I'm a veggie didn't you?' she said.

'Yes,' Patrick said, in a way that suggested he might soon be whipping slices of pepperoni off one of the pizzas.

'Do you think Dad expected this? That it would go wrong somehow.'

'To be honest, no. He probably thought this would be one time we didn't fuck things up by arguing.'

Although she didn't want to, Kirsty agreed. This was another let down for Gerry Cadogan, who died thinking things might have just happened how he had requested.

'Should've known better, though, shouldn't he? You stick the three of us in a van for a few days and it's bound to end in a punch up.'

'Don't.'

'It's true.'

'I know it's true. That doesn't make it nice to hear,' Kirsty said, taking a long drag from her can. 'I was thinking about her a minute ago. Alone on that plane.'

'She'll have a book with her.'

'Patrick.'

'What?'

'I just think it's so sad. She should be here. The three of us should do this together. You only get one chance to . . . you know.'

'Scatter?'

'Exactly.'

'So what? I mean, we've come this far,' he said.

'I don't mean we shouldn't do it. We have to. But maybe we should, well, save some. A bit I mean. For Jessica.'

'Well that's totally mad. But fine, if you want.'

'Maybe,' she said.

Patrick threw his head back and drained his can.

'Finished?' he asked Kirsty.

'No,' she said, handing him the rest of hers. It was half full. 'You finish it, I hate the stuff.'

'Lovely.'

Patrick made to get up, in that lumbering sort of way grown men often do after they'd been made to sit on the floor. But Kirsty grabbed his hoodie and told him to 'hang on.'

'What?'

'One more thing before we get back in the van.'

'What?' he said again, looking up. The loch reflected the moon, but the hills across the water were no longer visible.

'Do you think this was always going to happen? That we'd fall out.'

Patrick sighed, as though the question annoyed him because she had already been told the answer a hundred times.

'Look, Jessica—'

'I don't mean on the trip. I mean in general. You look back at those photos and it feels like a different family. You always hear about these fall outs over money or whatever. But I never thought it would be us.'

Patrick took a swig from her beer and said, 'Me neither. I suppose these things just happen don't they. Before you know it everything is fucked. Maybe if one of us had apologised right after that night, with the house talk and stuff.'

'I always wonder if it would've been different. Without Andrew. Without Mum.'

'There's no point thinking that way, is there? Andrew went. Mum died,' he said. 'Things are how they are. Maybe it'll be different in the future. But I doubt it somehow.'

'Ever the optimist.'

'You really want to know what I think?'

'Maybe,' she said, hesitantly.

'I think it probably was inevitable. Friendships fall apart all the time. The only thing that keeps families together is a sense of fucking duty,' he said. 'Dad always said he wanted us to be like mates. Well, I suppose that's what happened in the end.'

'Delightful.'

'All I'm saying is that if it wasn't Andrew, and it wasn't Mum, it would've been something else. We grew up.'

'And apart.'

Patrick made to stand again. This time she let him get up.

'These things happen,' he said, holding a hand out to Kirsty. She took it and pulled his arm as he dragged her up off the stony beach. 'Doesn't mean we can't get on now though, does it?'

He walked across the road, back to the van, which sat waiting for them, almost proud under a single streetlight. Kirsty followed him on and climbed into the driver's seat. It was freezing cold and she was already worried about the night ahead of them. Flimsy walls and no insulation meant it was hard not to forget they were only one step away from camping.

'Away driver,' Patrick said, as she turned the key and the van rumbled heavily into life. She turned on the headlamps and they shone through the small town that bordered the water. Above was black night, deckled with stars, and interrupted by a full moon.

The van lurched off, bumping down the kerb and onto the road. Patrick turned the radio up and opened another beer.

Patrick

A nice little spot near the port, it turned out, was the car park. Kirsty had driven past the two campsites she found online, rejecting one on the basis that it was too far away from Kennacraig, and the second because it was sparsely populated and looked too much like the scene of a murder drama.

'Well why would there be people here?' Patrick had asked, grumpily. It was late, he was hungry, and it had been a very long day, both on the road and off it. 'It's the middle of October in rural Scotland. I didn't expect a load of fucking tourists. It's fine, just park up.'

But Kirsty had ignored him and carried on regardless for another few miles, until she turned off the road, through a set of chipped, yellow and black metal barriers and onto a sterile plain of asphalt, empty except for two trucks.

Patrick was the first to get off. There were no signs of life in the portacabins where they would buy tickets the following morning. Nor at the jetty where the boat would dock to let people off and on. A few seagulls crowded around an overflowing bin, the gentle wind ruffling their white feathers. Other than that, the place was grey and quiet.

He walked over to the water's edge and looked down at Loch Tarbert gently lapping against the rocks. It was a still, clear evening. He breathed deeply, enjoying the fresh air filling his lungs. It felt totally different to Dublin, London or even Brighton, where there was always the hint of smog and the mass of human life.

Occasionally he wondered if he could live somewhere like this. In his head it would be a simple, remote life. Just him and Maggie, cut off except for their immediate community. Although he was equally sure that he would soon find that kind of life frustrating and lonely, and that the intimacy of a small community would become intense and suffocating.

He tossed a stone into the water as Kirsty called out, 'First one going in.' The oven on the van was only big enough for one pizza at a time.

'Lovely,' he called back, then took a swig from what was his third (and a half) can of Old Speckled Hen since they'd left the banks of

211

Loch Fyne. He hoped the van had enough electricity to last the night with the lights on and the oven going, but decided not to mention to his sister the possibility that it might not.

Sitting down on the little kerb that bordered the car park, Patrick took out his phone and opened the photos app. He scrolled back a few months to one of him, Suzanne and Maggie. It was a selfie, taken during a summer break to Cork, on the Old Head of Kinsale. The three of them were smiling, as Suzanne's and Maggie's long hair blew in the wind and massed together. Behind them, the Atlantic Ocean was just about visible. He remembered it as being rough that day, the sea crashing against the rocks below them with a ferocity that was fascinating and terrifying.

Later that evening, they'd gone back to the small cottage they were renting, overlooking the Wild Atlantic Way. He made them pasta, Maggie went to bed and he and Suzanne had had sex on the living room couch – a rare enough thing in itself.

It amazed him now to think that someone he thought he knew so well could be leading a double existence. Even then, when they looked happy, Park was in her life and in their bed (as it turned out). No matter how much he laughed it off yesterday and how much he liked Chloe, Patrick was still very much immersed in the pain his wife had inflicted on him. And he was still utterly at a loss about what he might do to support him and his daughter when real life resumed at the end of this trip.

He checked his phone. There were messages from Stu and Sarah (one clearly written by Maggie). But nothing from Chloe. He decided to change that.

Patrick: Still going. Stopped at the port. Wouldn't mind having you around tonight xx

Chloe: Good! Xx

Chloe: PS 'wouldn't mind?' Xx

Patrick: Fine. Would really like xx

Chloe: Better xx

He smiled and was about to text again when Kirsty called, 'Ready,' across the car park. Patrick locked his phone and ambled back towards the van. Its lights made it stand out in the otherwise dark port – a shining beacon against a backdrop of pure nothing.

She had laid out two plates and two glasses for wine, as well as the bottle of whisky, which sat in the corner of the table with two tumblers. A third was noticeable by its absence.

Kirsty was tossing a bag of salad in olive oil.

'Where'd you get that?' he said, pointing to the tin bottle that looked as though it'd come right out of a display in an Italian restaurant.

'Jessica left it.'

'Jessica brought her own olive oil?'

'Remember who you're talking about,' she said. 'Anyway, it's delicious. Peppery.'

She placed the salad down on the table, where Patrick was now sitting.

'You okay?' she said, as she turned back to get the first pizza and put the second in.

'Fine,' he said, forcing a weak smile. 'Do I not look okay?'

'No. I mean, yes ... Or no. Whichever means you do.'

'Right,' Patrick said. It would be no surprise to him if Kirsty were to say that he looked a fright. Today had contained a month's worth of emotions and recriminations. From the constant remembrances of Andrew, the fight and finally the painful reminder of a life he had had until so recently. Or at least the life he thought he'd had.

After they'd eaten, Kirsty cleared a space on the formica table – pushing aside plates with cold, dried out slices of supermarket pizza – and placed the third photo album there. This one was black, with the same chipped and worn gold edging the first had.

'What about Jessica?'

'What about—' Kirsty began, then caught herself before she finished what would undoubtedly be a caustic remark. 'If we've got to finish what we started, that means this too,' she said, gesturing to the album, then filling the tumblers with whisky.

'No,' he said, firmly. 'Not without her.'

'So what, we'll never look at it?'

'Maybe, one day we might.'

'Bloody hell, Patrick,' she said, annoyed. He knew this Kirsty. It was the one who felt that her proximity to their parents gave her greater claim to them. Maybe this was what Chloe meant by talking to her. Perhaps Patrick could get past this hard done by front to the sister behind.

'Dad chose those albums for a reason. Whatever else he wanted from this, he wanted us to talk about them together. So you either look through it alone, or we wait for her.'

'So never look through it then?' Kirsty said, draining her glass and refilling it. She was calm as she spoke. There were no raised voices here, but the tension was evident. Probably to the both of them.

They were briefly interrupted by the headlights of another truck arriving at the port. As it swung around to park, it illuminated the insides of the van, making a display of the untidy kitchen waiting to be washed up, as well as the floor – muddy with a few days' worth of footsteps tramping in and out across the lino.

'Maybe,' Patrick said.

'And what if we never see her like this again? If it's only bloody funerals and weddings when the three of us are together?'

'I've got a question,' he said ignoring her. Although she didn't say anything back, he took her silence as a nod to proceed. 'Why didn't you get annoyed with me? Earlier I mean. When we were talking about him.'

'Because . . .' she began. 'Because *she* could've prevented it, couldn't she? It was only money. And she could have, Patrick, she admitted it.'

'But so could I? If I'd told everyone what happened first time. Maybe he'd have got some sort of treatment. Or Dad wouldn't have let him run the business, knowing that he might be unstable.'

'I understand why you kept it to yourself. You were protecting Mum and Dad. Jessica was protecting herself.'

'That's bollocks,' he snapped. 'Sorry, Kirsty. But that's total bollocks. I know why I did it.'

'Why then?'

'Caution. As fucking ever. I know everyone thinks it. I never say anything until it's too late. Well there it is again.'

'Fine. So maybe I should be annoyed at you too then?'

'Maybe,' Patrick said, angrily, as Kirsty finished her second drink, got up from the table and stormed off as far as it was possible to storm in a small camper van. Then she got into bed.

He, meanwhile, picked up the whisky bottle, and poured himself another measure.

PART 3

PART 3

CHAPTER TEN

Kennacraig, Scotland

Kirsty

Having woken up before her brother, Kirsty stepped quietly into the main body of the van. The windows were misted up and the floor was freezing cold. She had slept badly, disturbed by the wind, which rattled the little window next to her, as well as the occasional groans and loud snoring from Patrick, who she was certain had gone to bed drunk. For a moment she allowed herself to feel sympathetic towards Suzanne for having slept next to that every night.

Yesterday had been difficult, but cathartic in a way. Patrick had shocked them. But, for her at least, more about their brother was beginning to make sense. If only Jessica hadn't flounced off, she thought, as she gently placed the kettle on the hob.

As she waited for it to boil, Kirsty quietly unclipped the little latch that held the cupboards above the table closed, and took down the box containing her dad's ashes. She smiled at them, as though what was inside was still in front of her in human form. Today was the day. Regardless of Jessica or Patrick suspecting they would arrive on Islay to some great surprise involving Andrew, this was about scattering these remains on the beach and saying goodbye in the way that he'd wanted.

'You're to play The Faces,' she remembered him saying, barely two weeks before his death when he told her about arrangements for his funeral and afterwards. 'You know the one.'

And she had. 'Ooh La La'. It was his favourite, played at every major birthday and family party. It was the song he was carried in to at his funeral (he insisted on being sent to cremation with 'Snooker Loopy' by Chas & Dave, not because he liked it, more that he thought it'd be funny). Patrick later drunkenly sang it at the bar with a few of Gerry's oldest friends, those who themselves hadn't yet paid for years of smoking, pints and hard work with an early death.

Patrick's bear-like snores told her that he was still asleep. So Kirsty opened the Spotify app on her phone and, at the top of the screen, saw the playlist 'Dad'. She'd downloaded the songs from his funeral, just in case there wasn't enough reception on the island to play his favourite again at the pivotal moment.

She opened the door of the van and stepped out onto the car park. It was a bright, sunny morning. Reflected rays decorated the still water, with a small boat speeding across it towards one of the salmon fisheries. Her breath made little clouds against the backdrop of green and brown hills that looked almost bald with the lack of trees atop them. Kirsty had no idea what the places she was looking at were called, which was quite reassuring in a way.

A few more cars and trucks were parked around them, having arrived during the night. One was bright, light blue and branded Bruichladdich – a whisky she remembered from her dad's collection in the living room cabinet, most of which had now gone to Patrick or one or two of his friends.

'Why whisky?' she'd asked her dad a few months ago, when he was bemoaning the cancer that had made it impossible for him to drink it anymore. He knew she wouldn't be satisfied with the simple answer that it tasted nice.

'I suppose because it's unique. Every bottle's different, even when they go through the same process. Different barrels, different water.

There's never two the same. And you have to give it time and a bit of trust. That one over there,' he'd said, pointing to a burgundy and white box that had been in his cabinet for well over three years. 'That was distilled fifteen years before it went into the bottle. Just sitting in a warehouse for all those years. No one knew what was happening inside the barrel. The bloke who made it could've died before it was finished. Then as soon as it goes into a bottle that's it, it'll never change again. Frozen in history the minute the cork goes in.'

'It's like time travel.'

'A bit,' he laughed. 'I suppose it is. You're tasting exactly what happened to the whisky the moment it came out of that barrel. If the sea air blew in or some daft sod coughed in it, it'll be there. That's why it's so interesting.'

In the distance over the water Kirsty saw what she assumed was their ferry coming towards them. It moved slowly, the corner it took around a vacant outcrop of land describing a big arc in the water.

There was still half an hour before the 8:15 departure to Port Askaig on Islay. But this felt like a moment nonetheless. The vessel that would carry them to their destination, more than six hundred miles from where they'd begun this journey in Brighton.

She went back into the van. Still pondering what her dad had told her about whisky, she opened the box and took the Port Ellen out. Why this one, she thought? As a noise from above made her jump.

Patrick

'Bit early,' he said, jokingly, looking down from his bunk at Kirsty holding the bottle of whisky.

'Jesus fuck, Patrick. You almost gave me a bloody heart attack.'

'Well don't drop it. We'll need a dram for later.'

She placed the whisky back in the fishing box, closed it and pushed it under the table.

'What're you doing anyway? No cheating with the photos,' he said, trying to sound jovial, intent on putting last night's argument to rest by simply not talking about it. Like a couple who wake up knowing they're both in the wrong.

'I wasn't,' she said. 'I was just...'

'Just what?'

'Nothing. Something occurred to me earlier. But it's nothing,' she said, sounding a little defensive. 'That bump's gone down.'

'Good,' he said, still sore about it happening in the first place.

'We better get ready. The ferry's across the water. Will be here soon.'

Kirsty retreated to her bunk and pulled the curtain across to shut him out.

He yawned. He was tired but a restless energy had kept him up for hours after they had turned in and he'd barely slept. Perhaps it was relief at finally getting his secrets about Andrew off his chest yesterday, despite everything else that happened. Though equally it might've been the messages he'd exchanged with Chloe at around midnight when he was in bed a little bit drunk.

He read her most recent message again.

Chloe: Good luck today. To both of you (but especially you). Proud of you for sticking it out xx

Patrick: Sorry. Fell asleep. Thanks. Will be hard, but hopefully a bit of a release. Almost looking forward to it. Is that strange? xx

Chloe: Not at all. Everyone deals with it in their own way xx

Patrick was composing another message – something meaningless to say good morning that only a new-ish couple would bother with – when he was shaken from his reverie by the blast of a horn signalling the arrival of the ferry. Then a knock came on the door of the van.

'Hang on,' he called down, noticing that Kirsty was still in her bunk, shuffling around trying to get dressed in the small space.

'Can you?' she called.

'Doing it.'

Still wearing jogging bottoms and an AC/DC t-shirt, Patrick climbed awkwardly into the cab of the van and opened the window. A young man with uneven stubble and a tatty woollen beanie hat was there, chewing gum and holding a pad and pen.

'You's bought a ticket?'

'Not yet,' Patrick said, mildly dazzled by the morning sunlight hitting him full in the face. He couldn't imagine how rough and stupefied he looked.

'Thirty then.'

'Right, hang on,' he said, grabbing his wallet from the glove compartment. 'Card okay?'

The man nodded, scribbled something down on the pad and handed a piece of paper to Patrick.

'In your window,' he said, taking Patrick's credit card and tapping it against the card machine he had strapped to his waist like a gun in a holster. 'There. Boarding now. Away ye go,' he said.

As he walked off, Patrick was sure he heard the man say 'fucking English'.

'Right,' Patrick called through the van. 'Buckle up, we're going.'

He started the van to shouts of 'no' and 'hang on', which he ignored and drove forwards, onto the ferry. They were now on the last leg of their journey.

CHAPTER ELEVEN

Port Askaig, Islay

Patrick

The crossing took around two hours. First they sailed through Loch Tarbert and across open water, from where Patrick could see remote beaches and headlands, but little human life. Then up the Sound of Islay to the small port where they disembarked.

He spent most of the journey on deck, away from the groups of people he assumed were going whisky tasting, as his parents once had, and the truckers travelling across to Islay for work. He sat on a damp metal chair, surrounded by lifeboats and industrial-looking equipment, enjoying the cold, salty ocean spray as it whipped up off the blue-green water.

While Patrick was looking out for whales he had been told lived or travelled through this part of Scotland, Kirsty spent most of the crossing in the women's toilet being sick, or in the café, bent double with her head between her knees. The combination of the gentle bounce over the water and what she called a 'slight hangover' proved enough to ruin her day before it had even started.

So it was that when they arrived, instead of getting straight on the road to the south of the island and Port Ellen beach, she and Patrick found themselves sitting on a little harbour wall in Port Askaig. As they looked out to Jura, Kirsty took deep, steadying breaths, one after the other.

'It was that bloody whisky,' she said.

'One dram.'

'Two.'

'Well you topped yourself up. You can't blame me.'

Kirsty didn't answer this, instead sucking in another great lungful of Scottish air, as though its freshness contained some elixir which would magically rid her of the hangover.

'Dad once told me that good whisky doesn't really cause hangovers.'

'Yeah. There's a chance he might've been talking shit, there.'

'Christ,' she said, as if she was about to vomit again, although managed to catch herself.

They sat together for a few moments longer, gazing out over the water as the breeze picked up and rushed through the trees which surrounded the small port. Across the Sound, Jura's small seaside cliffs rose up, leading onto its green shores and rocky hills. Patrick watched the occasional ripple caused by a fish or frog and felt one or two drops of water hit his face. These might have been rain, or just drops blown off the leaves around them.

'What's the plan, then?' he asked.

'I don't know really,' Kirsty said. 'I've never done this sort of thing before.'

'What about Mum?'

'That was a bit different, wasn't it? There were more of us.'

'Suppose,' Patrick said, remembering Hove beach, when they said their final goodbye to Sue Cadogan. That time Gerry and Jessica had both been there too. Now, only two thirds of the family were left, the rest with their various excuses for absence.

Their dad had given them each a handful of his wife's ashes, saying things like, 'don't drop 'em', or 'that's her legs' as he divided them out. Anything to file away the sharp edges of grief he'd been living with every day since becoming a widower. On the count of three, they had thrown the ashes into the air and scattered some on the beach. Then they returned home, where they cooked sausages and drank cider to her memory. Less than a month later they were back in Hove, for that fateful night in the kitchen which tore the family apart.

Despite the fact they were all adults, the presence of a parent gave the whole thing a sense of authority, which today was lacking now only the kids were in charge.

'We could do the same thing again, I suppose?' Kirsty offered. 'Share them out. The ashes I mean. Or we could hold the urn together and do it.'

'Maybe,' Patrick said, picturing the awkwardness of the pair of them holding the urn and emptying it onto the beach, waiting as the bits and pieces that got stuck in the corners filtered out. 'It feels like there should be a bit more ceremony to it, doesn't there? Like someone should say something.'

'What? Are you volunteering?'

Patrick laughed. His dad had always been the speechmaker of the family. The one at ease with his own voice and the presence to tap a wine glass and send a party into silence so that he could 'just say a few things'. His speeches invariably took far longer than anyone in the audience was prepared to give him.

'You've got the song, haven't you?' he asked Kirsty.

'Ready to go,' she said, holding up her phone, which awakened it to the lock screen showing a selfie of Kirsty and her daughter – the niece Patrick barely knew. 'I don't know. It just feels like we should do more than dump his ashes in the sea and bugger off home again.'

'Maybe. We'll think of something,' he said. 'Feeling better now?'

When Kirsty looked up Patrick noticed that her face was pale, but decided it was better not to mention it.

'Not really,' she said, climbing up off the grass and leading him back to the van.

Kirsty

The drive down from Port Askaig to Port Ellen covered nearly all of the small island. As they travelled, the van bumped down the small, quiet road to Bridgend, then along the uneven but eerily straight single-track road to the small town. There was little but fields either side of them, interrupted by the occasional farm house or tractor. And the only sounds were the noisy thrum of the van's engine, along with Patrick's occasional observations about peat bogs. He told her how these were dug up to add the smokiness to the island's whisky. Kirsty didn't really care about that, but at the same time knew he was only relaying this dull information to distract himself from what they were on their way to do.

Eventually, they came upon the small town. A strip of grey bungalow houses down one side of the road, and a short dry stone wall the other, gave way to a large, ugly industrial building.

'Is that?' she asked, wondering if it was where the whisky they had been sent up here with was made.

'No. That's the maltings. They do the—'

'It's okay,' she said, cutting Patrick off before he could launch into a description of what went on in the factory. They passed it, driving on into a large bay, where the northernmost channel of the Irish Sea lapped up against the beach of Port Ellen.

The bay was wide and U-shaped, surrounded by a grass row that led onto a narrow, sandy beach. Sporadically positioned benches looked out onto the water, all of them empty. The sea was two shades of blue – light in the shallows, then growing darker the deeper it got further out. The beach itself was mostly empty too, except for a couple and their dog on the other side of the bay, where a row of cottages looked out onto the water.

Patrick pulled up on the side of the quiet road, turned off the van and pulled up the handbrake.

'Well. Here we are then,' she said. 'We better get—'

'Do you fancy a drink first?' Patrick said. 'I can see a pub down there. Just something to take the edge off, y'know? Raise a toast to Dad before we ...'

Had she been asked as recently as half an hour ago, Kirsty would've said a drink was perhaps the last thing she wanted. But now that they were here, on this beach and finally ready to scatter Gerry Cadogan's ashes, she was willing to do almost anything to delay it.

'Something soft, perhaps.'

'Of course,' he said, as they put on their coats and stepped out onto the path which led down to the beach. Kirsty carried the black and gold box with their father's remains in it.

It was windy out, with strong gusts whipping up the dry sand and blowing through the thick, spiny sea grass that separated the road from the beach. Kirsty worried how this might affect the scattering, suddenly troubled by the image of a gust blowing her dad's remains back into her face and disappearing into her greasy, unwashed hair.

Patrick led them down the coastal road, into what was billed as a town centre but was really just a Co-Op, a small hotel and a pub called the Ardview Inn. He opened the door for the two of them and went to get some drinks while she found a table, returning a moment later with two pints of Guinness and two whiskies in tulip-shaped glasses.

'Oh bloody hell Patrick,' Kirsty pleaded. 'I wanted a sparkling water. I've got to drive later. So have you.'

'We've got hours yet. The boat back's not till half six.'

She checked her watch. It was only now coming up to midday.

'I feel dreadful, I can't,' she said, looking down at the pint.

'Well today's not about you, is it? It's what he would've wanted.'

'Patrick,' she said. 'You're like a sodding teenager sometimes.'

'Come on. One more for the road, for the old man.'

Kirsty thought about disagreeing, but he was probably right. Had their dad been here, the first thing he would've done was go to the pub.

'I don't even like bloody Guinness.'

'He did,' Patrick said, with a mischievous smile. 'You know you say that a lot? Bloody I mean. You hardly ever swear. But when you do it's always bloody. Just like—'

'Don't say it,' she said.

'To him then,' Patrick said, with a cheeky smile.

As he tapped his glass on the urn, then raised it to the sky for the toast, Kirsty noticed raindrops begin to patter against the window of the pub. It had been dreadful when they scattered their mother's ashes as well. Rainy and windy and cold.

If they couldn't be buried together at least their parents would be given a similar goodbye, she thought.

Then, still looking out of the window, a familiar shape appeared. It went past quickly, but Kirsty knew exactly who it was. A face she would recognise anywhere.

'What?' Patrick said, alarmed.

'It can't be.'

'*What?*' he said again, more urgent this time.

CHAPTER TWELVE

Jessica

'You haven't done it yet, have you?' she said, having flung open the door like a ragged winter's traveller arriving at an inn.

It was a poky, low-ceilinged pub, with white walls and aged wooden furniture. The only decorations were whisky themed, except for a jukebox beneath one of the windows. Not her sort of place at all really. But then she doubted there would be much choice on this sodden little island.

'Jess?' Kirsty said. She seemed stunned and annoyed and almost pleased all at once. Jessica was unsurprised. Her sister always had the capacity to mean more than one thing at the same time. There was a sub-plot to almost everything she said.

'Is he still in the box? Dad I mean.'

Jessica threw her handbag down on the chair at the end of their table. A nearby group of drinkers, all wearing baseball caps with a distillery's logo, stopped their notetaking about whatever tasting experience they'd just been on, and turned to watch the soap opera unfolding.

'Yes, of course he is. What are you ... I mean. Where—'

'I changed my mind.'

'You'd bought a ticket,' Patrick said.

'Yes, well. As I said, I changed my mind. Some things are too important to miss.'

Jessica looked down at her feet as she spoke. This white lie about a sudden epiphany was easier than admitting she had arrived at the security gates and opened the zipped part of her handbag where she kept her passport to find only an empty Fruit Pastilles wrapper, and a business card for an attractive man who had once visited her shop with the aim of selling her a new telephone system.

Of course, she had immediately looked up trains and how else she might find her way back home. The expense wasn't the important thing, really. Dan would understand, once she explained the whole debacle to him.

But then she saw something at the arrivals gate: a young girl, maybe no older than fifteen years old, tearfully embracing her father.

Jessica found herself thinking back to her own younger years. The times when she had said goodbye to her dad, or shared a moment with him. Those rare occasions when it was just the two of them – the father and his firstborn girl. And instead of seeing things from her own perspective, she finally saw them from his. The point of view of this man who had raised his children and one by one watched them drift away from him, each to a greater or lesser extent.

She saw Gerry Cadogan taking her for her first day at school, where she cried and begged to come home, and (as he told her decades later) how he'd cried in the car and wished she could come home too. Then she saw him next to her in the driver's seat of his Cadogan Family Builders Ford Transit van – filthy with crisp packets, empty boxes of Lambert & Butler, and crunchy, sun-damaged copies of the *Daily Mirror* – driving her and her worldly possessions to London for university. She saw him outside the doors of the church where he had once pretended to get married for the sake of his officious and snobby parents-in-law, about to accompany his eldest daughter down the aisle for her own wedding. And she saw him holding her children in the hours after they were born.

Gerry Cadogan had never asked for much back from Kirsty, Patrick, Andrew and herself. His demands as a parent had been few, except for love and understanding. Now, he was asking for something. And together they had come close to doing it, until the squabbling and recriminations that so broke his heart years ago rose up again.

Without her, there would be only two of his children there to carry out his final request – half the number he'd had. And as soon as she saw that young girl in the airport, and remembered the life she'd shared with her own father, Jessica knew she couldn't do it to him. She didn't believe in any sort of afterlife and couldn't countenance the nonsensical suggestion that he was 'looking down on us', as some distant relatives had vacantly suggested at his wake. Nonetheless, there was a vague presence; a less than corporeal version of her father, but a version. Jessica couldn't bear to be the cause of that most devastating of parental feelings: disappointment.

It was then she realised that if she was going to take another long journey, it should be to finish what she started. Not to run further from it.

'Why are you in a pub, anyway?' she said.

'We thought it would be a good way to send him off. One for the road and all that.'

'Very on brand. And you brought him along, I see,' she said, gesturing at the urn and wondering what the other drinkers must be thinking.

'Sit down,' Patrick said, hurriedly getting up from his seat. 'I'll get you one.'

'No whisky,' she said, adding, 'Patrick. I said no whisky,' when she saw the barman pouring a measure into one of the funny-shaped glasses he and Kirsty were drinking from.

'Here you go, then,' he said, arriving back at the table.

'Guinness and whisky,' she said. 'Lovely.'

'That's a good one, give it a chance,' he said. 'You might develop a taste for it.'

'Doubt it.'

'You never know. With a bit of time and effort.'

'Why on earth would I expend time and effort trying to develop a taste for something so bad for me? It's madness.'

Jessica took a seat at the head of the table, with Kirsty and Patrick facing each other. It was still raining outside, getting a little harder now. She dreaded to think what this might do to the ashes spreading ceremony. Gradually, she became aware that the two of them were looking at her.

'What?'

'You're not going to tell us what happened, then?' Patrick said.

'What's to tell? I changed my mind and came here,' she said, keen not to expand on what happened at the airport. Either the Fruit Pastilles packet or the sudden epiphany.

'Other than what made you change your mind. And how the hell you got from Glasgow Airport to this pub.'

'Bus,' she said, bluntly. 'There's one from Glasgow right to the ferry terminal. It was a bugger because I just missed the ferry you were on. Spent two sodding hours in that little hut before the next boat came.'

Patrick and Kirsty sipped at their drinks, neither saying anything.

'What?' Jessica prompted.

'Nothing,' Patrick said.

'No, come on. What?'

'Honestly, Jess. I'm just stunned that you took a bus. I genuinely thought you might've chartered a plane or something. Where's your luggage anyway?'

'In the van. You didn't lock it, by the way.'

'Patrick!' Kirsty said, scoldingly. It was the first time she'd spoken since announcing Jessica's name when she appeared in the pub.

Sensing that something needed resolving, Patrick said he was going to the loo and left them at the table. Either that, or he was desperate to avoid whatever unspoken conflict was playing out between the two of them.

For a few seconds, Kirsty didn't even look at Jessica. They could have been two entirely separate people sharing a table in a busy pub – more content to ignore one another and stare at their phones than strike up any sort of meaningful conversation.

'I'll speak then, shall I?' Jessica offered, which Kirsty met with a glare that suggested she'd spat on her shoes. But she still said nothing. 'Look, I'm sorry, okay? I don't know where it came from. And I haven't hit anyone in *years*.'

'It must've really meant something then.'

'Kirsty. Please.'

Kirsty turned in her seat to face Jessica.

'It's not just the slap, is it?' she said. To Jessica's surprise, Kirsty didn't sound angry, but more frustrated or upset. 'It's everything.'

'Everything? You want me to apologise for everything?'

'No—'

'What, everything I am? Everything I've done?'

'No. Jessica, listen for Christ's sakes.'

Kirsty seemed to draw breath, as though she was about to do a sky dive or a bungee jump, rather than make peace with a relative.

'You know I've always had this thing, haven't I? About Mum and Dad. How I stayed around and you both left. I suppose you could call it a chip on my shoulder.'

I suppose you could, Jessica thought but didn't say.

'But it's there anyway. This idea that I did more. I helped more.'

'Because you did. There's no way of getting around it, Kirsty. And we're grateful you were around and decided to live nearby. God knows, if you hadn't.'

'They would've been fine. Gotten along, but I never let myself accept that. Maybe I wanted to be needed.'

Maybe you did, Jessica thought to herself.

'You must've thought about moving somewhere else, though. After uni or something. A few more years in London? Abroad?'

'I did.'

'So why didn't you?'

'I don't know really, just never got round to it. Then Livvy happened and . . . Well. You know the rest.'

Jessica nodded, but didn't quite believe what Kirsty said. Privately, she had always thought her sister stayed in Brighton because she felt it would be too cruel on their parents to have none of their children nearby. Again, there was Andrew, hovering over them. Jessica and Patrick had grown up and become their own people by the time he left. Kirsty was still forming herself, and it was entirely possible that the loss of their brother had had far more impact on her decision making than it did for the other two. From the fact that she left Durham University to study closer to home, to falling pregnant with a boyfriend who never seemed right for her. She had tried to make it work, so she could build a family life less than a stone's throw from where she herself had grown up.

'There's nothing wrong with the life you decided to live.'

'But that's the problem, I don't know if I ever did decide. You left, didn't you? And Patrick. And then Andrew really left. But I stayed, with Mum and Dad, I mean. I was always nearby, always dependable. I never found my place in the world.'

Jessica laughed. 'What do you think I have?' she said. 'Or Patrick has? Christ Kirsty, he's sleeping on Stuart's couch.'

'You're pretty settled.'

'Fine, I'm settled. But it's luck, not judgment. We've stayed where we live because of Dan's fucking career aspirations. Not because I love it. I'm a follower, I suppose. When I met Dan I was in London. So was he. When he wanted to move out to start a family I said yes. I have my shop and my friends. But really, if we had to pack it all up and go somewhere else I probably would. Patrick's the same. He'd have gone wherever Suzanne told him to. I'm always surprised he didn't end up in America at some point.'

'Poor Patrick,' Kirsty said, apparently distracted by the thought of her brother and what he would be returning to after this trip. 'Bringing up that little girl all by himself, while she goes off on this digital nomad bollocks.'

'I thought you knew a couple of them, in your hip Brighton scene,' Jessica said, absolutely hating the way she sounded, and knowing it made her appear ten years older and ten times more conservative than she actually was.

'I do, they're twats,' Kirsty said. 'Anyway, you're doing yourself down. You're not a follower if you're happy. And you can have your time.'

'Maybe,' Jessica said. She took a moment before continuing. What she was about to say didn't come naturally to her. Any sort of genuine outlay of feelings always required something of a run up and usually two or three glasses of red wine to loosen her tongue, as well as the emotional straitjacket she kept on most of the time.

'You alright?' Kirsty said, leaving Jessica wondering if her discomfort was that obvious.

'Yes . . . well no, I mean,' she said, taking a sip from the Guinness. The rich, metallic taste reminded her of when she went through a period of drinking Guinness and black at the same time as being very into Irish writers (and an Irish boy) at university. 'Look, Kirsty. I want to say sorry again. And . . . well this may sound ridiculous, given . . . everything. But I want to ask if we can't just get along? Because – don't talk,' she said, seeing that her sister was about to respond and break her flow. There would be no way she'd get going again if that happened. 'Because for all the politics and all that. Well, this, the trip I mean, it's actually been helpful. Good for me, even. I've enjoyed spending time with you. Being . . .' she said. 'Being us again.'

Jessica took another sip of her drink, if only to stop herself from talking more. Kirsty didn't say anything for a minute. Instead, she reached out and placed a hand on top of Jessica's and gave it a little squeeze. Just like Dad used to do when she was upset or stressed or otherwise in a less than perfect mood.

'Me too,' she said, finally. 'And I'm sorry, too. We should've made up before you... well...'

'No. It's fine.'

'Still,' she said, as Patrick returned to the table.

'Ah. Good,' he said, sitting down and draining what looked to be at least a quarter of his beer. 'No more scrapping.'

'It wasn't scrapping,' Kirsty said.

'Bollocks. It was scrapping.'

'Whatever it was,' Jessica interrupted. 'We're past it now,' she said, with a smile that Kirsty mirrored.

'We were just saying that the trip's been helpful,' Kirsty said. 'Fun, even.'

'Fun?' Patrick said, sounding a little surprised. 'What was your favourite part? The blazing row, the tyre blow out or the fucking awful memories?'

'Patrick,' Kirsty said.

'Sorry. Joke.'

'We mean,' Jessica began, 'that it's been good to spend some time together.' She still couldn't bring herself to say what she really thought; that she wanted to consider these two as friends again, wanted them as part of her life. 'Besides, my favourite part, clearly, was finding out that you can be caught shagging about through your FitBit.'

'Hilarious,' Patrick said with a smile, as Kirsty and Jessica laughed.

'I am sorry though. I know we laughed, about how it happened. But it is awful.'

Kirsty now put her hand on her brother's and Jessica added hers to the top.

'Honest, it's fine. I've made my peace with it.'

'And the girl?' Kirsty said. 'What was her name again? Carol?'

'Chloe.'

'Yeah, her. Are you...?'

'Dunno. Bit early maybe, isn't it?'

'Not if you like her, Patrick.'

'True enough,' he said with a smile.

A few more whisky connoisseurs (noticeable by their branded baseball caps) ambled into the pub and found a table near them. Meanwhile, the Cadogan children stopped talking and returned to their drinks.

Jessica noticed there was something different about the silence between them now, compared to what it had been a month, or even as recently as a week, ago. Then it had been tense; thick with the things unsaid and scores yet to be settled. Now, it felt more comfortable. Like the quiet that falls between old friends who might have nothing to say to each other, but are nonetheless happy in each other's company.

If this was how it would now be between them, perhaps the plan had worked. The time on the road and visits to the past had forced them to talk and be honest and connect. Maybe the blood had been let and they were back to some approximation of the happy family which ceased to exist all those years ago.

As they finished their pints and sipped their whiskies, the rain stopped. There was no clearing in the clouds to let the sun through, and no God rays beaming down onto the lapping waters of the bay. But this was likely as good as it was going to get. Still grey, still moody, still threatening.

'How are we going to do this then?' Jessica asked.

'We were just thinking,' Patrick said. 'Before you got here, I mean. Kirsty's got the song lined up. Then I suppose we all just take some?' he said, hesitantly.

'I'd like to say something. If that's okay? I feel like someone should. For Dad.'

'That'd be nice,' Kirsty said, as the three of them pushed back their chairs, and she picked up the urn. Jessica followed the two of them through the pub, hanging back a bit to wipe away a tear that had formed in the corner of her eye and was threatening to spill out. She was pleased to be back.

Kirsty

As they stepped out of the pub and onto the beach, Kirsty felt a few raindrops touch her face and roll down her cheeks. Despite the sky clearing a little, the weather was still iffy. She held the urn tightly as they crossed the road to the beach, walking across the little bit of grass and onto the wet sand, which compacted and cracked beneath their feet.

'Where do you think?' Jessica asked, looking at the wide bay. They had no idea where exactly their dad would want his remains scattered. He'd mentioned nothing about a place with a good view, or a spot that held particular significance for him.

'A bit nearer the water maybe. We can put some on the beach and some in the sea,' Kirsty said. She stumbled over the word *put*, but couldn't really think of a better one.

They walked on for a couple of minutes. Gradually the sand became wetter and less firm and they left footprints as they went. Three sets of them, precisely half the number their complete family would've created.

Above them, the sky darkened even more. The rain got a little worse and the wind picked up. Patrick pulled his coat up around his neck and strode into it, determined to get to the water's edge.

Just then, something occurred to Kirsty.

'Shit.'

'What?' Jessica said, turning to face her where she'd come to a stop.

'The whisky.'

Jessica looked up at the sky and her face was almost pained.

'We have to, Jess. You know that. Dad—'

'Fine,' Jessica said and Patrick gave the keys to Kirsty.

She started a brisk walk back to the camper, which sat like a monument on the side of the road, old and covered in mud and grime. Jessica called for her to hurry, and she broke into a run.

Once on board, Kirsty grabbed three plastic cups, and opened the fishing box where the whisky was kept. As she pulled it out, she noticed something written on its box.

BOTTLED IN 1983.

She had been remembering earlier that morning what her dad told her about the bottling, the barrels and everything in between. How every bottle was unique; frozen in time, place and history the moment the cork went in.

This particular whisky had gone through that process thirty-five years ago, right here in Port Ellen, at the distillery only a decent stone's throw from where her brother and sister were now standing. And no matter what had happened to it since, where it had gone, or who had owned it, that moment was still captured by the contents within.

She held the bottle Gerry Cadogan had given them, one frozen in time in 1983. Either a few months before, or a few months after, Andrew Cadogan was born in Brighton, six hundred miles south.

Kirsty rushed off the van and ran across the beach to where her sister and brother were huddled together like penguins, sheltering from the cold, wind and rain that was falling again.

'Well then?' Patrick said, gesturing at the cups she was holding. 'Hurry up. It's fucking freezing out here.'

'In a minute,' she said, over the noise of the wind. 'There's something I have to tell you. About Andrew.'

'Andrew?' Jessica said.

Kirsty nodded and said, 'He's here. Sort of.'

But no one heard the sort of. Instead, right after she said 'he's here' they began barking questions at her, asking where and how she knew and when she found out.

'No! Stop,' she said. 'Just bloody listen, will you? I said sort of.'

'Fucking hell, Kirsty.'

'He's this whisky,' she said, and saw the perplexed look on both their faces. 'I mean, look at the date on the bottle.'

'Nineteen eighty three,' Patrick said.

'The year he was born. A couple of months ago I asked Dad why he liked whisky so much. He said it was something to do with how it became frozen in time when it was bottled. It never changed until it was opened again. And this one,' she said, holding it up, 'was bottled here, right when Andrew was born.'

The pair of them looked at her blankly.

'Fuck. He's not *here*,' she said, pointing down at the sand. 'He probably never has been. He's here, this is how Dad sent him with us. I was thinking about it this morning. That's why he told us to come to Islay, of all places.'

Kirsty pointed to the bottle. She almost wanted to hold it aloft, like the monkey at the beginning of *The Lion King*. Instead, she just stood there, while the two of them watched her, the rain soaking them through.

'Jesus. I suppose he thought it would be profound.' Jessica said, looking down at the urn. 'Him, us, and some . . . *version* of Andrew here.'

'You don't think it is?' Kirsty asked.

'In a way, I suppose,' she said reluctantly. 'If Dad thinks the closest thing we've got to a brother is a sodding bottle then so be it.'

'It must've been why he bought it. A reminder or something.'

'Sentimental,' Jessica said. But it didn't sound like a criticism.

They all stared at the bottle until Patrick said, 'Well open the thing then.'

Kirsty did the honours as they walked to the water's edge. She was about to pour some into the cups when Patrick grabbed the neck of the bottle from her and took a large swig.

The sea had become choppy. Two groynes stuck out from the water, forming a guard of honour into the ocean. Over to the right the malting house plumed smoke into the air, while in front of them a small fishing boat bobbed around where it was tethered to a dock. The cold Irish Sea was gradually wearing away at this outcrop of shore. Kelp mingled with stones and old bits of plasticky blue twine that had washed up on the sand.

'Ready then?' Jessica said. Patrick handed the whisky over to Kirsty, who took a swig, then gave it to her sister. The bottle was nearly empty now. Maybe one sip each left (two for Patrick).

Jessica took the lid from the urn and proffered it to Kirsty and Patrick. They each took a handful of greyish-brown ashes from the plastic bag that had been unceremoniously stuffed into it. The urn was little more than a decorative box, which could just as easily have housed jewellery as it did a parent. Then Jessica took one herself.

'Well we got here, Dad,' she said, and Kirsty realised she was beginning the 'few words' she was going to say. She decided not to play the song, at least for now. Let her sister have the moment. 'There were times when it looked like we might not. And a couple when it looked like *I* might not,' she said, with a look at the two of them that seemed almost apologetic. 'But we did. And it was a good idea . . . what you did or planned or whatever.

'Because we have talked. We have been honest. And we have reconnected. So, I suppose what I'm saying is well done. You were a good parent, right up to the last, and then a bit beyond that. I know it wasn't always easy, Dad. There were some hard times. Awful times, really. But we've never doubted you and your love. We miss you.'

Patrick and Kirsty, both with tears in their eyes echoed her last sentiment. Then Jessica said, 'Three. Two. One,' and together, they tossed the ashes towards the sea.

Some caught the wind and rain and some blew back at them, covering Kirsty's jeans with a fine layer of grey grit. The rest settled on the wet sand.

The three of them went back for a second handful, and Patrick stepped out so the bottoms of his boots were in the water as he scattered Gerry's remains on the surface. They floated there for a moment before being consumed by the sea.

Patrick and Kirsty reached in again, for the final lot.

'Wait,' Jessica said. 'Let's take some home. We'll scatter them on the beach there, like Mum.'

Neither Patrick nor Kirsty said anything to this. Their silence was agreement enough. Then Patrick grabbed the whisky bottle, emptied the little that remained in his mouth and took a small amount of their dad's remains.

'What—' Kirsty began, but she soon saw.

Patrick balled up his hand and gently poured the ashes into the neck of the bottle which had begun its life in this small Scottish town, back in 1983. Then he filled it with water from the bay, making a cocktail of ashes and ocean, replaced the cork and kissed the label.

Kirsty thought she heard him say 'sorry', though she couldn't be sure.

He held the bottle by its neck, ready to throw it into the sea. Just then, she heard a dog bark and turned around.

There, just far enough away that she couldn't make out his features, a man was walking a golden retriever. He wore dark-blue jeans, wellington boots, a jacket and baseball cap, stopping every so often to pick up a tennis ball and throw it a little further on down the beach for his dog to collect.

For half a second, she thought it could be him. Andrew. He was about the right age and build. She thought about stopping Patrick, who had arched his arm back. But as the stranger came closer, she realised he was just that. A stranger. Not Andrew. Not her brother. Not her father's son.

With a grunt, Patrick threw the bottle out into the sea. It travelled maybe thirty metres before dropping in with a small splash. It was too far away to make out whether it would float, drift back towards the shore, or sink to the bottom of Port Ellen bay.

'Right,' Patrick said, turning towards them. 'Shall we?'

'Yes,' Kirsty said, and the three of them walked back across the beach to the camper van. There was one photo album still left to explore.

Kirsty had looked inside it already. Lifting the cover that morning, while Patrick was still asleep, she immediately recognised the first photo on the opening page. It was of a family that had grown with new life, and contracted with unexplained absence.

The winter after he went.

Christmas and New Year 2009 – Ganton Villas, Hove

Gerry stood behind the camera he'd mounted on a chair, which was itself stacked on top of a table, and looked through the viewfinder.

'Dan. Forward a bit,' he said, flapping his hand to emphasise the point. 'Jessica, you stand at the front and hold little Maxi out. See if he gives us a smile. Man of the moment.'

He said it with a cheerful, loving glance at his grandson. Another, slightly wary one followed at his youngest daughter, Kirsty. Despite being twenty, she sometimes had an air of jealously about her with all the attention Max got. Presumably, she thought, at her own expense. She didn't seem to react, however, knowing that tonight of all nights was not the time.

'Sue,' he called. 'Sue!'

'I heard you the first time.'

'Well why didn't you answer me then?'

'What is it?' she said, refusing to rise to it.

'How'd you do the timer on this bloody thing? Need a degree in rocket—'

'Little button with the clock on it, Dad,' Patrick said.

'Well how am I supposed to know that?'

'It's a little button with a clock on it.'

'Cheeky git,' Gerry said, pressing the button. The number 10 appeared on screen and he rushed back to the rest of the family, hoping the edifice beneath the camera wouldn't topple in his absence. 'Right. Positions.'

'Everyone say sausages.'

'Sausages,' everyone said, echoing Sue like a congregation repeating Amen after the vicar. Approximately two second later, just long enough for their faces to have relaxed back into half smiles, the flash went and the image was captured.

The Cadogans and their various partners cheered. Dan and Jessica closed ranks around their infant son, while Patrick took Suzanne's hand and led her towards the kitchen so they could refresh their drinks. And Kirsty sat down on the sofa to compose another text message to Luis, the Brazilian boy she was dating from university. He was spending that night at a friend's party in Stockwell.

The decision to spend New Year's Eve together was actually more of a mandate, passed down by Gerry and Sue. Christmas was too tricky and political – Jessica and Dan had a strict alternate years policy with their sets of parents, and it was his turn (the addition of a grandchild had only made them more stringent about not changing it). Patrick and Suzanne had booked tickets to New York, to stay with her family there until the thirtieth of December. Only Kirsty would be around.

'Your dad and I think,' Sue had begun, when she phoned each of them, back in October. She had said the same thing each time, as though she was in a call centre and reading from a script. 'That we should see in the New Year together. If we can't do Christmas, I mean. This year has been awful for all of us. So it's important we start the next as close as we can be.'

Patrick knew he couldn't refuse. Suzanne had her heart set on seeing in 2010 on Primrose Hill, watching the fireworks over the Thames across the city. It was something she'd never done before. But exceptional circumstances, and all that.

Jessica and Dan had no plans anyway. Parenthood made New Year's celebrations little more than a bad reason to stay up beyond ten o'clock.

Only Kirsty was really sore about it, desperate to be in Stockwell with Luis and his mates. She also worried about what he would drink and take, and then what he might do under the influence of it all.

With the photo taken, Jessica and Dan went to put Max to bed. Patrick accompanied Suzanne outside for a cigarette. Gerry and Sue began to set up a buffet in the kitchen. Which left Kirsty alone with the large Christmas tree that dominated the end of the room, blocking the window that looked out onto the garden.

She went over to the television cabinet, on top of which sat photos of them all. Her mum ensured equal representation – two each, no exceptions. Kirsty pulled her black hoodie around her body and zipped it up, flaking off a little more of its Strokes logo in the process.

There they all were, arranged in some order only her mother knew.

The two of Jessica showed her on graduation and her wedding day. Patrick's were him and Gerry at Watford's Championship Play Off Final, where they beat Leeds three–nil, and the other leaning against his van. It was on the day he'd bought it and set up his own home improvements business, distinct from the family one. Kirsty's were of her holding up her A level certificates and on stage, playing the bass in the dreadful punk band she'd given up when she went to university.

And there were two more photographs. Of the man gone from their lives, but not yet absent from the gallery of honour.

The first showed her big brother, Andrew, in his military uniform, taken on the day he completed his training in Catterick. Gerry and Sue had travelled up there to see him. The second was taken of him last year with his girlfriend, Mel. The relationship that had broken down shortly before he walked out of their lives earlier in the year.

Kirsty picked up the photo and quietly, though not quite to herself, said, 'Miss you, mate,' and replaced it, feeling the nervous, uncontrollable swelling which meant she was about to cry over his absence, again.

It was mostly Gerry holding the camera that evening, taking photos as his family played games and ate together. The sense of enforced fun that pervaded the whole thing reminded Jessica of a team build-ing away day endured by office workers the world over. She was perpetually on the edge of making some excuse about being tired because of Max and going to bed early. Or even pretending to fall asleep on the couch (something she'd done at several dinner parties with Dan's friends when she wanted to leave early). But the greater good of it all kept her there, if not quite gamely joining in.

At around half eleven things went through a brief lull, while Sue melted some Dairy Milk for a chocolate fondue she was going to bring out to mark the turn of the year. And Gerry went to his study to pick out a whisky for those 'who wish to partake at midnight,' he'd said, looking only at Patrick and Dan.

Jessica noticed Suzanne go outside for a cigarette again, but Patrick didn't join her. It was freezing out there, and raining a little.

'How'd you think it's going?' she asked her brother, sitting down next to him on the big couch that faced the television (the other two one seaters were slightly at an angle – bad for watching).

'Other than exhausting?'

'I know. But do you think they're okay?'

'To be honest, I think that as long as we're here they're okay. It's tomorrow I'm worried about.'

'It brings it all into focus, doesn't it?'

'What?'

'New Year's. It makes you assess things. Then you think about how you're going to start the next one. The things you have, the things you don't have. It can be a philosophical time.'

'Yeah,' Patrick said. 'Plus they'll be hungover. Makes it all worse, doesn't it?'

'Hmm,' Jessica said, at once impressed and depressed at her brother's ability to boil things down to a more basic, route one truth.

'Look, I wasn't going to mention it tonight, but—'

'What?' Jessica said. 'She's not pregnant is she?'

'No. Jesus . . . No,' he repeated, almost as if he was confirming it to himself. 'No. I didn't want to mention it tonight, but I might as well. Suzanne's been offered a new job. A promotion really.'

'That's great. God knows we can do with good news.'

'Yeah, well that's the thing. It's not really. The job's in Ireland. Dublin.'

'Oh.'

'I know the timing's not ideal—'

'So she's taken it then.'

'No. Well, not quite. We're still ... y'know.'

'Patrick. If you're already talking about the timing not being ideal, then she's taken it.'

'Not officially. But the money's amazing. The tech sector's expanding massively over there. And it's not as if my job keeps me here. People are still going to want their walls painted in Ireland, aren't they?'

Jessica sipped at her rum and coke, sticking her little finger into the glass to fish out a breadcrumb that had dropped into it. She ran her hand down the red jumper she was wearing to check there were no crumbs on that either.

'Well say something.'

'What do you want me to say? Clearly, you're going to do this. Even though the timing literally could not be worse. Barely six months after one child disappears, another leaves the area.'

'Right. Well you can turn that in. You left the area ten fucking years ago and haven't come back. Suzanne moved to London from sodding America. Then here. She's just asking me to—'

'You know very well why we live near London. Dan's an only child and it's nice for his parents to see Max. Besides, I'm opening up my own business, we've built a life there. You *were* building one here until—'

'What are you two bickering about?' Kirsty said. Neither of them had noticed her come into the room and sit on the arm of the sofa. She was drinking from a can of pear cider.

'Patrick's moving to Ireland,' Jessica said.

'Jess.'

'Well you are.'

'Patrick,' Kirsty said, annoyed. 'This couldn't wait, like, six months?'

'It's a promotion for Suzanne,' he said.

'Right. So she's in Beaconsfield—' Kirsty gestured towards Jessica.

'Berkhamsted,' Jessica corrected her.

'Whatever. I'm in Durham for the next six months. And you're off to Dublin. Leaving the two of them alone. Right when they shouldn't be.'

'You'll come back,' Patrick said to Kirsty. 'Christ, we'll come back at some point. It's temporary.'

'Until it isn't,' Jessica said.

'And what? I'm just meant to stick around here then, am I?' Kirsty said. 'Like their bloody keeper.'

Patrick was getting fed up now. He drained the remainder of his beer and put the glass down on the table with a little more force than was necessary.

'Look. Mum always said we shouldn't feel we have to stay around here for them.'

'And things change, Patrick. Life changes.' Jessica said.

'Well why don't you move back here then?'

'Because relocating my entire life is harder than keeping yours here for the next few months. That's all I'm saying.'

'I wish I'd never said anything,' Patrick said.

'And I'm glad you did. Otherwise we might never have known until the day before you moved.'

'She is right, Patrick,' Kirsty said. 'You always wait until the last minute before you say anything. No matter how important it is.'

It was at times like this Patrick wished he could tell them he did actually have it in him to be proactive. That he wasn't always passive and hesitant. Otherwise, in all likelihood Andrew would've disappeared far sooner than he did, and possibly with worse consequences.

'Look. I'll think about it, alright? Just let's not row about it tonight,' he said. Then taking their mutual silence as agreement he raised his empty glass and said, 'truce.' His sisters tapped theirs against his and repeated 'truce'. Patrick got up off the couch to get another drink when the lounge door opened and Gerry and Sue came in, carrying the camera and a bowl full of Twiglets respectively.

'Here they all are,' Gerry said, raising the camera. 'Now stay there you two. Patrick you go and sit back down.'

He did as his dad instructed and Gerry took at least six photos of the three of them together.

'We've got one just like this from ten years ago, remember?' he said to Sue. 'Except they were sat on that bloody awful pink sofa we had. Monstrosity, it was,' he said with a laugh. 'Up there,' he said, pointing to the corner of the room, where a small collection of brass or silver-rimmed photo frames sat on top of the seldom-used piano. 'Give us it. Let's have a look.'

Kirsty, who was nearest, grabbed the picture and looked at it. Clearly, it was taken much more than ten years ago. The passing years had compressed and bunched together in her father's mind, obscuring time and memory. She was still a baby, for one thing, sat on Jessica's lap and holding a clump of her sister's long brown hair in her chubby little hand.

As soon as she looked at it, Kirsty wanted to put the picture back, not to hand it over to her dad. But he grabbed it and held it out in front of Sue and himself. Immediately, the jolly smiles faded from their faces. Sue stifled a sob and hurriedly left the room, followed by Gerry who was saying, 'I didn't know, love. I didn't remember.'

Before he left, he'd dropped the frame on the floor. Jessica picked it up and sat back on the couch, with Kirsty and Patrick on either side of her.

A large crack in the glass now stretched horizontally from one side of the frame to the other. Even so, it was not hard to see why it had got to their mother.

The focus of the image was not baby Kirsty on her big sister's lap, who was staring down at her. Or Patrick, slumped in the corner wearing a purple and green Watford away kit, not even looking at the camera.

No, it was Andrew, sat in the middle of the couch, mouth agape and teeth visible, arms up at either side of him. Playful and exuberant alongside his staid siblings. Posing, while the others ignored the camera, he was the reason the picture had been taken. The others were just in shot.

It was not the photo of the three of them together which Gerry had hoped to echo decades later. This was one he would never be able to recreate.

'Shit,' Patrick said. He could hear his mum crying. Deep, breathy, violent sobs like he'd never known before, not even when her own mother died. These were the sharp cries of tragic, unexpected loss, rather than the sadness of people passing with time.

Just then, the clock in the hall chimed. It was midnight.

No one said happy new year.

CHAPTER THIRTEEN

Port Ellen, Islay, Scotland

Kirsty

They were all in tears by the time she turned the page of the album which revealed the photo of the three of them on the couch, taken shortly after they'd bickered about Patrick's move to Ireland. He went, of course. That was never really in doubt. Once Suzanne had decided on something there was little he or anyone else could do to change her mind.

The memory of that New Year's Eve was ever lasting. 2010 was meant to be the year they adjusted to life without Andrew. Instead, it brought further sadness and heartbreak. A year of their dad thinking up ways to find his son, and of their mum pleading with him to stop, convinced he would come back of his own accord.

'He'll know when's right.'

As it was, almost everything in 2010 was a prompt for a memory of Andrew. Sue's return to work as a receptionist at the local gym reminded them of the remortgage that was necessary because Andrew had almost bankrupted the family business. Patrick's bi-weekly trips home from Dublin only happened because he felt guilty and wanted to be around. People were always more attentive in the aftermath of something dreadful. It usually took a year or two for them to drift away again.

Later in the year, Jessica announced she was pregnant again. Kirsty couldn't escape the thought that she had convinced Dan the best way to mend her broken family was to patch it together with a new person. A quite literal bundle of joy. Though she never mentioned it.

'You okay?' Kirsty asked Jessica and Patrick.

'Fine,' he said. Jessica just nodded. 'Wish we had more of that Scotch,' he added.

'I didn't know he'd had them developed.'

'I'd forgotten he'd taken them.'

'It was Max's first Christmas with them,' Jessica said. 'The camera was barely out of their hands.'

'Of course,' Kirsty said.

'Are there any more?' Jessica said, taking the photo album from her sister and turning the page in the hope, or perhaps dread, that there'd be more snapshots of their collective past.

But there were no photos. Instead, taped to the next spread, was an envelope. It was beaten and discoloured and creased. On the front was a German postage stamp, slightly obscured by an air mail franking sign in blue ink. It was dated August 2019, just over a month before their dad died. The address on the front was written by an untidy hand Kirsty didn't recognise.

Gerry Cadogan
6 Ganton Villas
Hove, BN6 7JP
ENGLAND

Above the address, Gerry himself had scrawled *OPEN THIS* in his own unsteady handwriting.

'Shall I?' Kirsty suggested, and the others nodded.

She pulled the envelope away from the photo album and lifted the flap on the back, the old glue offering little resistance, then took out what was inside and laid it on the table.

It was a pile of maybe three or four pieces of scrap paper, on top of which was a note written on lined A5 paper, in the same hand as the address on the front of the envelope.

I thought you should know. I am the only other person who knows about you.
   I am very sorry.
   Judith

With her heart in her throat, Kirsty moved the note aside to reveal a short newspaper article, no more than two hundred words in one column. At the top of it was a photo of Andrew Cadogan, captioned *Der Verstorbene, Matthew Starling*.

'Matthew Starling?' Patrick said. He sounded a little surprised, a little confused. Maybe even a little hopeful.

'Nice name,' Kirsty said. It brought to mind the murmurations she watched swarm and sway over the sea in Brighton during winter evenings. The thousands of birds moving as one. No one excluded, no one left behind. It was unlikely that Andrew had thought of that when he picked his new name, whenever that was. But the poetic nature of it wasn't lost on her.

'What does it—' Jessica began.

'Hang on,' Kirsty said, as she scanned the article. It was written in German and there was no translation. Though it wasn't necessary. Kirsty knew a bit from her GCSEs. Enough to make out the most salient, terrible facts in any case.

She swallowed, forcing down the dread that was coming up, and spoke.

'He died,' she said, unable to look up from the scrap of newsprint and into the faces of her siblings. 'Last June, I think. I don't know what this says. But it seems to have been a car accident.'

'Fuck,' Patrick said. He snatched the piece of paper away from his sister and looked at it, as though the words might magically reorganise themselves into English. Kirsty knew he had barely ever been to a German lesson at school, with the teacher having joked about his preference for hanging out near the chip shop smoking instead.

'You can't—'

'Who's this?' Patrick said, cutting Kirsty off. 'Anna. Anna Starling.'

Kirsty took the paper back from him and read as much as she could again. Individual words came back to her, though phrases were less forthcoming. Nevertheless, she knew the one that explained this unknown name.

'His daughter,' she said quietly. 'Andrew had a daughter. I think it's saying that he's survived by his daughter Anna and wife Judith. Anna's four.'

'The same age as . . .' Patrick said, but he trailed off.

The realisation that he had a niece the same age as his own daughter was clearly too much to bear. The knowledge they might be friends as well as cousins; that in another, close, possible world there could be two more Cadogans to cushion the blow of loss they had experienced when their parents departed. 'Fucking hell,' he said. 'Andrew.'

Kirsty replaced the article and the letter in the envelope from Judith.

Outside, the rain hammered persistently and rhythmically against the thin walls of the camper van. It felt like it was getting darker, although that was most likely just the dark grey skies which spanned overhead. The beach that was now home to their dad's ashes looked dirty and uninviting. Discarded Coke cans and washed-up plastic bottles mingled with nets and clumps of vivid green seaweed. It was almost as if she hadn't seen it all before.

'Jessica,' Kirsty said. 'You've not said anything.'

'He knew, then,' she said, after a second or two. 'Dad knew all about this kid and his wife. He knew his name, and that he was dead.'

'Well, only for a bit.'

'And he didn't say. Instead he—'

'What difference would it've made?' Patrick said. 'If he'd told you about Andrew two weeks before he died, what would you have done?'

'I . . . well,' Jessica said. But it was apparent she didn't know what she would've done. None of them did. 'He made us think . . .'

'No he didn't,' Kirsty said. 'Whatever you thought about where he might be was on you. Dad wanted us to come on this trip so we'd be nicer. He knew that if he told us about Andrew before we did all this we'd have argued about it and blamed each other.'

It was an assumption, Kirsty knew that. There was no knowing why Gerry Cadogan had put the news of their distant and now dead brother at the end of the albums he wanted them to look through. No knowing what he wanted out of this except for his three remaining children to be close again.

'Some reward,' Jessica said. There was no bitterness in her voice, instead a note of sadness, a little regret.

'Probably all we deserve,' Patrick said.

Kirsty left the table to get the fishing tackle box.

It was now empty. The whisky was finished. The photo albums explored. The ashes scattered. She picked up the heavy books of old memories and dropped them inside, along with the box for the whisky, and the envelope containing the article about Andrew and the note from Judith.

She wondered if they might ever meet this woman and her daughter, their niece. Unlikely, she supposed. They were not Andrew Cadogan's family, they were Matthew Starling's. They shared his friends, his life and his history, whatever version of it he chose to tell them. They were their own family, a unit quite separate from the people in Hove with whom he had shared blood but little else.

The note was a kindness, rather than a connection. A gesture towards a man who had spent his life trying to keep his family together and happy, and had failed.

Kirsty closed the box and locked it, then placed it back under the table for their journey home. She looked down at Patrick and Jessica. Both were blank, staring at their hands clasped on the formica table, as if considering their next moves in a chess match.

'Right,' she said. 'I think I need a drink after all that. Pub?'

PART 4

CHAPTER FOURTEEN

Berkhamsted, Hertfordshire

Jessica

'Right,' she called. 'Everybody ready?'

'Almost,' Dan called back.

Jessica could hear the ruffle of coats and shoes falling out of the rack in the understairs cupboard. All of which suggested that neither her husband nor her children were in fact ready. Instead of being all set to leave, right on eleven, the three of them had frittered away more time faffing with phones and games and whatever the hell else they were doing.

'I said we're leaving at eleven. It's already ten past.'

'I'll make it up on the drive,' Dan called back.

'No shortcuts. And no speeding,' she said, gun shy of motorway accidents ever since she was at the wheel of the camper van when the tyre burst. Even though that incident at Gretna, and the time it gave the three of them, turned out to be exactly what they had needed.

Jessica checked her phone. There was a message there from the Airbnb host in Brighton, offering a guided tour around the neighbourhood when they arrived later that day. She considered replying to say that, having grown up down the road, there would be no need. But the fact was that Jessica had spent so little time on the south coast in the past few years that a tour of the much-changed city might be helpful.

With the bustling and fussing still going on – Dan always took far longer than she did getting the kids ready – Jessica went into the living room and picked up the photo that had just recently been added to the corner bookshelves.

It was of Patrick, Kirsty and herself, rain soaked and windswept, against the backdrop of Port Ellen beach. They were on their way to the pub when a man with a dog passed them and Kirsty had asked him to take a photo.

'For posterity,' she had explained, when Jessica and Patrick looked at her in bemusement. They failed to understand why she would want these minutes after discovering their long-lost brother was dead enshrined in digital print. 'We should remember today.'

They were exhausted and emotional. Patrick and Kirsty forced smiles. Jessica herself wore a sort of half-grin that was a show for the camera rather than a representation of how she was feeling.

When they were in the pub later on and nursing pints of Guinness, Patrick had made the suggestion which led to the trip Jessica and her family were now about to take.

'I was thinking. We should spend New Year's Eve together again. Now that we know everything. I hate saying it, but it's probably what Dad would've wanted.'

Jessica knew immediately that he was right. The questions which had caused the rifts between the three of them were now answered. The disagreements that had emerged following Andrew's disappearance were resolved. There was no reason for them not to be friends again. And it made sense to end this year and begin the next in this way.

'Right. Ten seconds,' Jessica called into the house. At which Dan and the kids came tumbling into the hallway in a mess of coats and bags and scarves and hats. Max and Elspeth were first out of the door, running down to the car. While Dan set the burglar alarm and checked the lights in the living room for the ten thousandth time.

'Ready?' he said, kissing Jessica on the lips. He had been more affectionate recently, kinder as well. It was as if the trip north had let a little blood from their relationship too and relieved some pressure.

'I am.'

Around two hours later, Jessica was driving down roads intimately familiar from her childhood, pointing out landmarks to the kids. They were so young the last time they came here it was unlikely they remembered much of it.

'That's the church your nan and grandad had their wedding photo outside of,' she said, when they passed St Philip's.

'But not where they got married?' Max said. Jessica had shown the two of them some old photos shortly after she returned from Islay. And for the first time told them the truth about her family, including all the uglier bits.

'Nope. That was a registry office. I think it's flats now.'

'Everything's flats now,' Dan said grumpily.

'We got married there, though,' she added, cheerful to counter Dan. 'Your dad and me.'

Minutes later, she turned a corner onto a road she was recently so sure she'd never see again. Ganton Villas. Jessica drove slowly down towards the old white house and pulled up outside. She looked at the stairs leading up to the front door, and the big windows which allowed passers by and neighbours a view into each floor (something she was keenly aware of as a teenager with a second-floor room facing onto the street).

'Right. Here we are then,' she said, taking care to control the timbre in her voice. She had not been expecting to, but Jessica felt overwhelmed and emotional at being back. As if the house had been saved along with her family.

She led the four of them up the path, each carrying bags, and rapped three times with the kitsch, lion's mouth door knocker her dad had bought solely to wind up her mum.

It was Kirsty who answered. She was wearing blue denim dungarees and a rainbow-striped jumper that reminded Jessica of the cake she'd had made for Elspeth's last birthday.

Ganton Villas – Hove, Sussex

Kirsty

'Ah! You're here,' she said, slightly taken aback, given the hour. 'Right on time.'

'Don't sound so surprised.'

'Come on in,' she said, ignoring her sister's comment. And how strange it was to be inviting Jessica into a home that still felt like hers too. 'Patrick's just... well...' Kirsty didn't know what to say, what with the kids being here. There were many nice things about living with her brother. Hearing precisely what he was up to in the morning when his girlfriend stayed over was not one of them. It rather threw her back to their adolescence, when all sorts of blind eyes were turned to typical teenage behaviour. 'He's here somewhere,' she said.

Jessica, Dan, Max and Elspeth followed her through to the kitchen. She put the kettle on and threw tea bags into three mugs.

'You two?' she said, to Max and Elspeth. Neither of them looked particularly thrilled to be here, at their grandparents' old house, for New Year's Eve. But what else would they realistically be doing? she wondered. 'We've got some squash, I think. Or water.'

Kirsty made the drinks and joined them at the table. This too felt slightly odd. The kitchen was the only room she and Patrick hadn't really touched since they moved into Ganton Villas, shortly after returning from Islay. The crockery belonged to them, and there were one or two pictures on the walls. But it was still ostensibly their dad's room, the one place in the house from which his fingerprints had not yet been fully removed.

'What's it like then? Being back home,' Jessica said.

'Nice. I think it'll take a while to make it feel like ours though. Instead of Mum and Dad's.'

The decision to live at Ganton Villas had been made in the van on the journey home.

At first, they had tried to drive from the Hebrides back to Sussex in one go. But it became apparent somewhere around Manchester that they would need to stop overnight, and so checked into a service station hotel near Warrington.

Jessica was showering, rinsing the days spent sleeping in the van off. Kirsty and Patrick were left alone together in the vast, half-empty restaurant space, surrounded on all sides by fast-food outlets.

'Where are we dropping you off, then?' Kirsty had asked, while the two of them picked at Burger King chips.

'Somewhere near London I suppose. I told Stu I'd be back to-morrow evening.'

'Okay,' she said, taking a slurp of chocolate milkshake. 'And then what?'

'What do you mean?'

'What happens then? If you live in England again you can't very well stay on Stu's couch, can you?'

Patrick didn't say anything to this. Kirsty wondered if she'd been too cruel, too blunt, in her stark reminder of his status as a single parent, with no job and nowhere to live.

'I know,' he said, taking a swig from a can of Marks & Spencer own-brand lager.

'You can probably find somewhere in London. On the outskirts maybe,' she offered, knowing that prices in the city would preclude him from living anywhere either nice or big.

'I don't want to live in London. I'm thinking that we should move back.'

'Brighton back? Or Hove back?' she said, noticing that Patrick was looking thoughtful. 'What?'

'Hove. Look, I was thinking earlier. What about Mum and Dad's?'

'Well there've been viewings, but no one's made an offer yet. I don't think you should rely on the money from that to get somewhere. Besides, Hove's very—'

'No. I mean living there. Me and Maggie.'

The notion had shocked her. Kirsty had assumed the house would be sold and they would split the money three ways. Ganton Villas was far too big for Patrick and Maggie on their own.

'You can't be serious, Patrick. You mean you want to move back?'

'Maybe,' he said, quickly adding, 'I'd put some money into it, though. I know you and Jess are . . . well . . .'

'Right.'

'Or,' he offered, sounding slightly hesitant. 'You could move in, too. With Livvy.'

'What? Live with you?'

'Think about it. You've got that flat. And it's fine, but it's draughty and the neighbours are bellends. You could sell up, so could I, and we could buy it together.'

'Yes. But we'd be, like, living together.'

'And what's so bad about that?'

As soon as he said it, Kirsty knew that there would be nothing bad about that. The house was big enough for them to have their own space when they needed it. And it was certainly better than the two of them living in little flats or rentals around Brighton.

'Is this because of the woman? The one you've been texting Chloe.'

'No,' he said, with a smile that told Kirsty it was almost certainly a bit because of her. 'I suppose I think it's time to come home.'

Patrick moved in two days after they arrived back and took the old family home off the market. He found a school for Maggie in Hove. Then together, they transferred ownership of the house and used the proceeds of the sale of their old homes to give Jessica her share.

Over the next couple of months Patrick decorated and renovated each room, in a strange but fitting echo of what their dad had done decades ago, when he convinced Sue Cadogan to move into a wreck that had a lot of potential. It gradually became a hybrid of their parents' and their own home. All Cadogan, either way.

'He'll be down in a minute,' Kirsty said, when she heard the creak of the floorboards that signalled Patrick was moving about upstairs. She had just finished showing Jessica around the ground floor. The redone lounge, now painted dark blue on two walls and filled with furniture which suggested Patrick had something of an interior designer's eye. And their dad's old office, which was now a little snug with its own TV and sofa for when there were disagreements about what to watch (usually these were between Patrick, who wanted to watch football, and everyone else).

'No rush,' Jessica said. 'It's nice to come back here. I didn't think I ever would.'

'Me neither. He's done well with it, hasn't he?'

'He has. It feels like a home. But a different one, if you know what I mean?'

Kirsty smiled. She looked out into the garden where Maggie, Livvy and Elspeth were playing together, making slushy snowballs from the dusting they'd had a couple of days ago. Max sat in the living room playing on some handheld video game it was nigh on impossible to separate him from.

The garden was the one area of the house that was still noticeably Gerry Cadogan's work. The flower arrangements, lawn, pond and furniture. Even as frozen, dried out and dead as it was now, with the hydrangeas brown stalks rather than plush pink blooms, the lavender a husk of its summertime self, and the bulbs dormant for another couple of months.

She and Patrick had agreed to leave it as his. They would tend and care for it, but it would remain their dad's.

'You're happy here then?' Jessica asked. 'Living with Patrick's not too much of a pain?'

'Not at all. I like it. Easier than the van, anyway,' Kirsty said.

She heard the squeaky door open upstairs and muffled voices.

Patrick

'You'll be fine,' he said. He looked back and she was still applying lipstick. It was the nude colour she wore most days, except when they were going out to dinner or to a bar when she would wear something brighter – red or purple. She pulled her hair back, held it in a ponytail and looked in the mirror. Then sighed and dropped it back again.

'Patrick, the last time I met your sister I was the barmaid at your dad's funeral.'

'And?'

'And that's a bit weird, isn't it? One minute you're serving her

268

vodka tonics and saying sorry for your loss. The next it's all happy families. And from everything you've said about what she was like.'

'I know. But she's changed,' he said. 'A bit anyway. She's ... well, more easy going.'

'But still not actually easy going?'

Patrick thought for a minute, wondering if he could ever imagine a version of his sister – even when she was at her very best – who would just let things slide.

'Exactly,' Chloe said. She brushed her fringe and smiled into the mirror, paying particular attention to her teeth.

'I don't know why you're so nervous.'

'It's a big thing, isn't it? Spending New Year's with people. With your family. And we're late going down so they're all going to think we were ... that.'

'Well. They're not—'

'Don't,' she said.

Chloe sat down on the bed and pulled her shoes on. Patrick looked over. They'd had a lazy morning in, the remnants of which were still around the room in the shape of tea cups, plates covered in toast crumbs and daubs of marmalade, socks and underwear chucked half under the bed. Sections of the newspaper which Patrick had run out in the freezing cold to buy earlier were now creased and discarded on their bedside tables.

Yesterday was the first night they'd had together for almost a week. Chloe had spent Christmas at her parents' house in Bath and stayed down there for a bit while her kids had some time with their dad. Patrick had been back at Stu and Sarah's, on the couch again but much happier than he had been during his first stint with them some months ago.

It felt strange to live like this. There were echoes of old teenage and early twenties relationships in how they stayed round each other's houses, eventually gaining enough confidence to leave a toothbrush next to the sink; or in how they both got nervous meeting new sets of friends and family. That they had both been married before accentuated this, with neither of them ever having expected to be going through the early-stage excitement and uncertainty of a new relationship again.

For all that though, it felt good. Patrick was comfortable with Chloe. And he was learning to accept that she was comfortable with him. Their kids got on well enough, and their ex partners got a little defensive when they found out the people they had let down had moved on. It was all as it should be.

'How do I look then?' she said, standing in front of him wearing a grey lambswool jumper, black jeans and red Converse.

'Awful.'

'*Patrick.*'

'You look lovely. You always do. Now come on.'

Chloe followed him out of the bedroom and down the stairs to the hallway.

Patrick had painted it cream shortly after he and Maggie moved in, and had assembled a picture wall of their family. His eye was always drawn to two photos – the one of his sisters and him on the beach in Islay, and the one of the four of them on the sofa at Christmas years ago, Andrew the centre of attention.

His brother had rarely been far from Patrick's thoughts since they got back from the trip. For a couple of weeks he had even considered contacting Judith and trying to establish some sort of relationship between the two entirely separate families, linked tangentially by one man. But before he did so much as a Facebook search, Patrick reminded himself that Andrew left for a reason, and while they all had their own interpretation of what that was, it was important to respect it. Judith hadn't reached out, she had shared some news. That's all she wanted and none of them had a right to take it any further than that.

'At last,' Jessica said as he passed by the photo wall and into the kitchen. He cringed a little, knowing that Chloe was already feeling shy about meeting her.

'Shut up,' he said mockingly, hugging his sister and shaking his brother-in-law's hand. 'Good journey?'

'Fine. But I don't want to talk about that,' Jessica said, pushing past him and making for Chloe with her arms outstretched. 'This must be—'

'Chloe,' Patrick said. 'Chloe, Jessica.'

The two of them embraced as if they'd known one another for years. Or at least Jessica did. For her part Chloe looked a little nervous. Jessica, he knew, could do that to people.

'So lovely to see you,' Jessica said.

'And you. Again.'

'You know, when I first saw the two of you . . . talking,' she said, skirting around the topic of the funeral being the last time the pair of them were in the same room, 'I thought he was flirting with the barmaid. Had a right go at him.'

'Well he was I suppose,' Chloe said and Jessica laughed more than the joke warranted. Was this how she was trying to make a good impression now? Patrick wondered.

'Anyway,' he intervened. 'What's the plan?'

'Well I thought maybe we could have a walk first,' Kirsty said. 'Pick a nice spot. Then go back after dinner and do it then. At midnight.'

'Sounds good,' Jessica said, taking a sip of her tea. 'Fitting.'

So it was that when they had finished the dinner Patrick cooked, eaten dessert and drunk close to a bottle of wine each, Kirsty, Jessica, Dan, Chloe and himself put on their coats and met in the hallway of their old family home. Patrick took it upon himself to carry the fishing tackle box, having retrieved it from the camper van that morning, where it had stayed since the autumn.

'It's going to be freezing, isn't it?' Jessica said.

'Said minus two,' Kirsty said.

'Christ. Well let's just be quick about it shall we?'

Patrick led the little party of five out, down the steps, onto the street, and towards the stucco mansion blocks at the end of their road, beyond which was the Kings Esplanade. On the way they passed the camper van, parked there and gathering dirt and dust again. Patrick couldn't bring himself to sell it just yet.

A little ramp led them down on to the stony beach, where they had spent so many days as kids. Patrick walked fast (it was colder than even he expected), holding his iPhone torch in front of him to track his path across the stones. The rest of them followed, muttering about how freezing it was.

'About here?' he called out, through the noise of the rushing wind and lapping sea. Earlier on when they had gone out with the kids they had picked a spot in front of the beach huts, where there was an old concrete wall they used to kick a ball against.

'Anywhere,' Jessica called out. 'Just hurry!'

'Hey. This is supposed to be profound.'

'It's too cold to be profound.'

Patrick dropped the fishing tackle box down onto the stones and opened it up. First he pulled out a bottle of whisky and five cups, passing them round and pouring a small dram into each. Next he took out the urn that contained the last remains of Gerry Cadogan, as well as the one which had sat on the top of their fireplace for years, containing the last of his wife, and their mum, Sue. He held both boxes open for his sisters to take a handful of ashes, then the three of them walked down to the sea, until their shoes were just about in the water.

'Ready?' he called back to Chloe, who pressed play on the song he had cued up on a portable speaker. And as the first strains of the guitar riff to 'Ooh La La' played out, Patrick called, 'three, two, one.'

Together, Patrick, Jessica and Kirsty Cadogan threw their hands into the air.

ACKNOWLEDGEMENTS

There are a few people I'd like to thank for their part in bringing this book to readers, or for their help in my career as a writer.

First up is the team at Orion, particularly Alex Layt and Britt Sankey, for all their hard work in getting books out there and into the hands of readers and reviewers. As well as the editors who've shaped this book from its early drafts – firstly Ben Willis, and secondly Lucy Frederick. And my agent, Charlie Campbell, for all his advice, guidance and good humour (and the odd drink here and there).

I've been fortunate in my young career as an author to have received some quite incredible support from friends and from people in the media, who've done wonderful things to share my work. I'd like to thank Steev Glover, Keeba Roy and Matt and his staff at Waterstones in Berkhamsted for just this. Nina Pottell at *Prima* magazine, whose incredibly kind words about my first novel will stay with me forever. And anyone who bought a book, left a review, recommended it to a friend – thanks, it means a great deal.

As is the case for many authors, writing books is far from my full time gig. So I'd like to #shoutout my friends and colleagues (past and present) at Octopus Group for being behind my creative ambitions outside the world of content marketing. And the people who gave my writing a nudge when it needed it, or who lent a kind word. In particular Craig Taylor who first published me in *Five Dials* magazine and helped me to think I should try a leg at this books lark.

Finally, I want to thank my family, who thankfully bear little resemblance to the one in this book. My son, Rufus, who is far too young to read this, but I'm sure is nonetheless delighted to be mentioned. And, mostly, my wife Alice, whose endless love and support I couldn't do without.

Thank you all.

CREDITS

Jamie Fewery and Orion Fiction would like to thank everyone at Orion who worked on the publication of *The Way Back* in the UK.

Editorial
Lucy Frederick
Ben Willis

Copy editor
Claire Baldwin

Proof reader
Kate Shearman

Audio
Paul Stark
Amber Bates

Contracts
Anne Goddard
Paul Bulos
Jake Alderson

Design
Debbie Holmes

Joanna Ridley
Nick May

Editorial Management
Charlie Panayiotou
Jane Hughes
Alice Davis

Finance
Jasdip Nandra
Afeera Ahmed
Elizabeth Beaumont
Sue Baker

Marketing
Brittany Sankey

Publicity
Alex Layt

Production
Ruth Sharvell

Sales

Jen Wilson
Esther Waters
Victoria Laws
Rachael Hum
Ellie Kyrke-Smith
Frances Doyle
Georgina Cutler

Operations

Jo Jacobs
Sharon Willis
Lisa Pryde
Lucy Brem

A ten-year love story in twenty-four hours:
Our Life In A Day

**The rules are simple: choose the most significant moments
from your relationship – one for each hour in the day.**

You'd probably pick when you first met, right?

And the instant you knew for sure it was love?

Maybe even the time you watched the sunrise
after your first night together?

But what about the car journey on the holiday where
everything started to go wrong? Or your first proper fight?

Or that time you lied about where you'd been?

It's a once in a lifetime chance to learn the truth.

But if you had to be completely honest with
the one you love, would you still play?

**For Esme and Tom, the game is about to begin.
But once they start, there's no going back...**

'A beautifully told story of real love and real life. I loved it'
Miranda Dickinson